$10,000 reward for information
leading to the arrest
of parties responsible for the
attack on Alice Esterhaus

A half smile quirked the corners of editor Walker Shearin's mouth. Had to hand it to the boy—he knew how to stir things up. 'Course, he was no boy now. Late thirties, Walker estimated. Rough years, all of them. His face had shown wear and tear when he placed the ad.

Walker tossed the form into the In box for Shirl to process. Then he walked to the big picture window overlooking Ridge Lane. Calm and quiet, as usual. People in Hope Springs weren't in much of a hurry. People in Hope Springs didn't ruffle easily.

The tall man in jeans and windbreaker walking head down along the sidewalk didn't seem to catch anybody's interest now. But, Walker thought, that unconcern wouldn't last long. His trial had torn the town apart twenty years ago. And it would be interesting to see who got the most stirred up by Will Travers's return.

Dear Reader,

I love small Southern towns, as you might have guessed if you've read some of my earlier books. I've found a new town I hope you'll like as much as I do.

About two years ago my husband and I visited Hot Springs, Virginia. The town and a grand spa resort grew up around the hot springs. It was gracious and quaint and one of those places where your soul feels peaceful right away.

A Father's Vow is the second of a series of books about the people of a similar town—Hope Springs, Virginia, a town whose motto is You'll Need No Other Medicine But Hope. But when Will Travers returns to Hope Springs after running from his problems for almost twenty years, he finds that not everyone in Hope Springs is ready to forgive and forget the crime he was accused of.

I hope you'll stick by Will as he tries to overcome his past with the help of the young nurse who once testified against him. And I hope you'll enjoy Hope Springs so much you'll come back for book number three next spring.

Happy reading!

Peg Sutherland

A FATHER'S VOW
Peg Sutherland

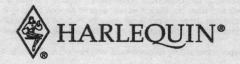

HARLEQUIN®

TORONTO • NEW YORK • LONDON
AMSTERDAM • PARIS • SYDNEY • HAMBURG
STOCKHOLM • ATHENS • TOKYO • MILAN • MADRID
PRAGUE • WARSAW • BUDAPEST • AUCKLAND

ISBN 0-373-70807-6

A FATHER'S VOW

This book is dedicated with much love and gratitude to the English teacher who first inspired me with the words, "Have you ever thought of being a writer?"
Mrs. Evelyn Relfe, you touched my life with your love of the language, your laughter and your dedication to challenging children to live up to the best in themselves.
May children always find their own Mrs. Relfe.

CHAPTER ONE

NOTHING HAD CHANGED.

Except Will Travers.

As he drove along the main drag in Hope Springs, Virginia, for the first time in almost twenty years, Will knew he wasn't the same cocky, eager young man who'd once walked these streets. And he never would be again.

You'll Need No Other Medicine But Hope.

The slogan on the town's welcome sign, which he'd passed in his pickup truck only moments before, came back to him with bitter irony. Hope. One of many things in short supply in his life.

Will glanced across the cab of his truck at his young passenger. Eight-year-old Kyle had been impatient all the way from Washington, D.C., fidgeting in his seat, checking the clock on the dashboard to see how much time remained in the trip Will had told him would take most of the day. Kyle had even refused to stop for burgers and milk shakes or the petting zoo touted on billboards along the highway.

"I wanna get home," Kyle had said, staring out the window, his young voice unyielding. "Hurry up, okay?"

Home. Nine months in D.C. hadn't made the

apartment the boy had shared with Will—the man he refused to call Dad—home. Hope Springs was home. That stung, although it was natural enough. After all, Kyle had spent most of his eight years in Hope Springs with his mother, his aunt and his cousins. Will was a stranger to him. And that wouldn't have changed if Kyle's mother—Will's ex-wife—were still alive. If not for an early-morning accident on a snowy mountain road, Kyle would have remained happily at home in Hope Springs.

Will could only wish the little town really would welcome the boy back home, for he knew they wouldn't welcome the man.

Nevertheless Will had driven straight through. And now that they were here, Kyle was no longer fidgeting. He was no longer peering impatiently out the window. He was slumped in the passenger seat, his eyes on a level with the bottom edge of the rolled-up window.

"What's wrong?" Will asked.

Kyle adjusted his cap. He always wore the bill in back, the popular look in D.C. Now he reversed it, slipping the bill lower over his face.

"Kyle?"

"Nothin', okay?"

Will believed he hadn't adopted that impatient tone with *his* mother until he'd been at least thirteen. Kids grew up faster today. Kyle had mastered the arrogant inflections of adolescence within two weeks of moving in with Will after Ginger died. Nothing had changed it—not bribery, not spoiling him and not getting tough with him, which had come hard with a grieving boy.

"You don't look very happy to be here after being so all-fired eager to come back," Will said.

Kyle ignored him. The silent treatment was Kyle's favorite method of dealing with his father.

Will smothered a sigh and kept driving. His first impressions of his hometown hypnotized him. An American flag still fluttered in front of the library, as it had every clear day during his childhood. The bookstore, the candy store, the old hardware store all looked the same. In fact, the brick buildings had changed little since they were constructed along Ridge Lane in the 1920s. The main street of town curved and rolled, gently following the terrain, hugging the side of the wooded hill that rose toward the main landmark, Heritage Manor. The town had grown up more than a century earlier around the gracious old resort and spa, its progress ebbing and flowing with changes in society and the economy. Buildings harking back to the previous century were still scattered among the other businesses. The Victorian house next to the library had been spruced up, though. Three cradles sat in a row on the broad porch, with an enormous Siamese cat serving as sentry.

Triplets in Hope Springs? Will wondered if the mother was someone he knew. Some woman he'd been to high school with, maybe getting nervous as the biological clock ticked, trying fertility drugs and ending up hitting a grand slam.

Will turned his imagination off. It was an old habit of his, the way he entertained himself. He invented lives for the people he saw and then didn't feel quite as lonely. And it was better—safer—than getting close to real people, finding out who they really were, what their real stories were. Because eventually real people also wanted to know *his* real story.

And that was always when the friendships cooled—people asking questions over a beer after work. Where was he from? How had he made it to Washington, D.C.? Wife? Kids? Family? And Will always backed off, shut them out, refused to get close. Weaving tales about strangers was easier than negotiating the land mines in his own past.

He turned off Ridge Lane onto Loblolly, made the second left between the high school and a day-care center onto Birch Street. He held his breath. The cries and giggles of the children from the day-care grew more distant. Then an old house set back from the street came into view. It looked shabbier and smaller than he remembered. The white clapboard was dingy, in need of painting. The door of the screened porch hung slightly askew. Shrubs grew up over the windows.

Where the hell was Paul? he wondered. He hoped his younger brother hadn't let the place fall into this kind of disrepair before their mother died.

"Why're we here?" Kyle sat up in his seat, suddenly interested as Will pulled the pickup into the rutted gravel drive. "This isn't Aunt Becky's."

"We're not going to Becky's." Will killed the engine and gave the hand brake a yank. He'd guessed from his mother's letters that she barely knew his son. But it galled him to realize Kyle didn't even know where she'd lived. "This was Grandma Travers's place. Now it's ours."

"No!" Kyle kicked the dash with the expensive sneakers that represented one of Will's attempts at bribery. "I'm not gonna live here. This isn't home. I wanna go *home*."

Will felt his temper rising on a wave of wounded feelings, but he shoved it down and out of the way. Anger wasn't the answer. It wasn't Kyle's fault Ginger had died. It wasn't Kyle's fault Ginger—and no doubt her sister, Becky, too—had raised him to think of the father he never saw as some kind of lowlife. It wasn't Kyle's fault he hated Will.

That didn't make it hurt any less. That hadn't made it any easier to live with the boy's sullenness these past nine months.

Will opened the truck door and got out. "*This* is home. You got your way and we're back in Hope Springs, and that's as close as it's going to get to the way things used to be." He saw the boy's lower lip start to tremble and ached to take him into his arms and comfort him. But he wasn't up for the rejection he knew would follow that gesture. "Come on, son. Let's unload."

For once, at least, Kyle didn't tell him not to call him son.

Unloading the back of the truck didn't take long,

even with a foot-dragging eight-year-old as helper. None of the furniture in Will's D.C. apartment had been worth hanging on to, so they'd loaded up clothes and little else. Will had hoped the house where he'd grown up might still be full of his mother's furniture, her dishes, her pots and pans.

He wasn't disappointed about that. What he hadn't expected, however, was that the house would also be full of dust and cobwebs and signs that squirrels had made themselves at home. There was no sign that his brother had even been in the house since their mother died two years earlier. Will ground his teeth together to keep from swearing. Melvin Guthry, the old attorney who had contacted him two years ago about the inheritance—which had consisted of the old house, back taxes and little else—had assured him that Paul still lived in Hope Springs. Will had assumed his brother would look after things.

He'd obviously been wrong.

"It's all dirty," Kyle said petulantly. "We can't live here."

Will stuck his head in the kitchen pantry. "Brooms, mops, cleanser. I think we can manage."

"I wanna go to Aunt Becky's."

Will ignored his son's whine.

Kyle looked in the refrigerator. "No food."

Will handed him a spray bottle and the bucket of rags and sponges that were right where Nadine Travers had always kept them, in the back of the pantry. "Start on the refrigerator, then."

"Me?"

"You."

While Kyle grumbled and ran water into the bucket, Will roamed the house. The old-fashioned fleur-de-lis wallpaper in the living room was the same, as were the television and the old upright piano Nadine Travers had never played again after Webster Travers died. The furniture was covered by dingy sheets, but the outlines looked familiar—the old camelback sofa, a recliner, the big swivel rocker where his mother seldom sat for more than ten minutes without thinking of one more chore that needed tending.

Will shook off the nostalgia. He'd leave the sheets in place until the worst of the dust was gone.

He continued to the bedrooms. His mother's clothes still hung in her closet. They were dreary, gray with dust, reminding him of the way Nadine Travers's face had also gone gray after Will's problems. Worse, even, than after Will's father had died. The weight of her grief had seemed to collect on her face, dragging down the flesh and leeching it of color and life.

Fifty-seven. That was how old she'd been when she died. Too young to be old and broken from so much misery.

"Damn!"

Will shoved the closet shut and went on to the next room. In the room he had shared with his brother, all signs of his existence had been obliterated. He moved past it quickly. In the cramped bathroom with its old claw-footed tub, he caught a glimpse of pink crocheted covers fitted over the box of tissues and the extra roll of toilet paper. Water dripped into the tub from the leaky faucet, wearing away the porcelain and leaving a rusty spot beside the drain.

Will wished he could think of someone to ask for reassurance that he'd done the right thing, bringing his son back here. He needed somebody to tell him everything would work out all right.

But there was nobody. There had been nobody for too long. He should be used to it by now.

BY BEDTIME, THE TWO of them had lifted the worst of the grime in the two bedrooms and the kitchen. They went for takeout at a place called the Tex-a-Tavern. Will hoped no one would notice or remember him. The clientele in the dimly lit restaurant had the look of tourists—khakis and polo shirts, walking shoes and visors. He escaped unrecognized with their tacos and soft drinks.

They ate in silence, went to bed in silence and had breakfast in silence the next morning. The silence ended only when Will explained to Kyle that he would be enrolling in school that morning.

"Why?"

"Because you're eight years old. Eight-year-olds go to school."

"I just got here. I should have a week off. Or two."

When Kyle had arrived in Washington, D.C., still

raw from his mother's death, Will had kept his son home for a week before enrolling him in school. His plan had been to comfort his son, to give him time to get accustomed to his new surroundings. He'd also hoped to get to know the boy, whose mother had taken him away when he was seventeen months old. He hadn't seen Kyle since, because Ginger had refused to let him visit on Will's turf. She'd also done the one thing guaranteed to keep Will at a distance—she had returned to Hope Springs.

The first week of his reunion with Kyle hadn't panned out. Kyle would accept no comfort, remained wary, rejected his father's attempts to get to know him. Will had assumed all of that would change with time, but he'd been wrong. Kyle was stubborn and unbending.

A Travers all the way.

At least in the months they'd been together, Kyle had learned that arguing with his father was pointless. When it became clear the first morning in Hope Springs that enrolling in school was not up for debate, he trudged along behind his father, the silence between them restored.

Will didn't like the startled looks from the women behind the desk in the office at the elementary school. He didn't like the nudge one of them gave the other as she pointed out his name on the paperwork he'd filled out for Kyle. He didn't like the way they pursed their lips and avoided his eyes.

Yep, nothing had changed in Hope Springs, Virginia.

When the process was finished and Kyle was sitting in a roomful of third graders, Will walked out the front door of the old school and looked around.

What now?

The ancient oak still grew in the middle of the intersection of President's Drive and Old Oak Street. What few cars came through the intersection circled it carefully, bumping over the roots that buckled the pavement. The tree had been there longer than the brick school or the stone church or the municipal parking lot on the corners. It had been there longer than anyone still alive in Hope Springs, and the town had long since decided it was wrong to do anything but work around something that enduring.

Will had always thought that was a virtue, until he realized that other attitudes in the small town could be just as enduring.

He knew what he had to do. He knew what he'd come back to do. There was no other way to bring up his boy here, no other way to make peace with his past.

He had to prove them all wrong.

He marched up President's Drive the two blocks to Ridge Lane, the town's main drag. The familiarity of everything struck him again. The real-estate office was different and the old diner had changed hands, it appeared. Things looked somewhat more prosperous, but it was only the people who looked substantially different. He didn't recognize a single soul, which he supposed was no surprise. Twenty years

changed people much more than it changed buildings and landscapes.

That didn't stop him from feeling certain that
everyone he passed recognized *him,* though. He
imagined distrust and suspicion in the eyes of everyone he saw. Did they remember the trial that had
ruined his life?

If they don't now, they will soon enough.

WALKER SHEARIN DIDN'T sell many full-page ads
for the *Hope Springs Courier,* the twice-weekly
newspaper where he'd been editor for six and a half
years. Most of the ads in the *Courier* were small,
except for the double-page spread Hurd's Hardware
did for its once-a-year spring sale and the half page
the IGA did every week to let folks know that
ground beef and chicken drumsticks were on special.

So Walker looked down at the ad-reservation
form, then up at the broad back retreating through
the *Courier's* front door.

Of course it wasn't every day that a man the
whole town had unofficially convicted of murder
walked into the *Courier,* either. Walker amended his
thoughts. The whole town, with the exception of juror number nine, that is.

Walker, who had been right out of school when
he'd covered the trial for the *Courier* twenty years
ago, had a theory about that trial. He believed that
somebody on the jury knew who really had committed the crime Will Travers had been charged
with. And that was why someone on that jury had

been persistent enough to convince the other eleven jurors to acquit in a case the whole town had believed was open-and-shut.

Nobody had been interested in his theory then, particularly Hadley Wakefield, the longtime editor. Walker wondered if anybody would be interested today.

He looked down at the ad. After this appeared in Wednesday's paper, Walker predicted that plenty of people were going to be interested in the case again.

$10,000 Reward for Information
Leading to the Arrest
of Parties Responsible for the Attack
on Alice Esterhaus

The corners of Walker's mouth quirked in a half smile. Had to hand it to the boy—he knew how to stir things up. 'Course, he was no boy now. Late thirties, Walker estimated. Rough years, all of them. His face showed wear and tear.

Walker tossed the form into the In box for Shirl to process when she came in. Then he walked to the big picture window overlooking Ridge Lane. Calm and quiet as usual. People waved, stopped to chat on their way to whatever their days held. People in Hope Springs weren't in much of a hurry. People in Hope Springs didn't ruffle easily.

The tall man in jeans and a windbreaker walking head down along the sidewalk didn't seem to catch anybody's interest now. But, Walker thought, that unconcern wouldn't last long. The trial had torn the town apart twenty years ago. And it would be interesting to see who got the most stirred up by Will Travers's return home.

PAUL TRAVERS DIDN'T usually buy the *Hope Springs Courier*. He wasn't interested in the local gossip or the specials at the supermarket. He might live five miles out of town on the highway toward the Blue Ridge Parkway, he might cash his paycheck at the local bank, but otherwise he kept his distance.

He didn't buy this Wednesday's edition, either, but a folded copy lay on the otherwise cleared desk in his classroom at the Blue Ridge Academy for Girls. Paul frowned. He didn't like people intruding on his space. He picked up the folded paper, wondering what had been so important that somebody at the academy wanted to make sure he saw it. The people there usually left him alone to teach his science classes and go home.

The paper had been opened to a full-page ad with plenty of white space and very few words.

But the words struck a blow to Paul's icy control. Will was back.

There could be no other explanation. No one else would dredge up this old scandal and rub everyone's nose in it again. Just Will.

Paul resisted the urge to wad up the paper and fling it into the wastebasket beneath his desk. He also resisted the urge to shove his fist through the blackboard behind him.

He folded the paper so the ad didn't show and put it into the trash can. He swallowed the bitterness in his mouth, but it seemed to gather in his throat. Breathing was difficult. The jury might have acquitted Will, but Paul had long since convicted his brother. And not just of the attack on the schoolteacher. Just as surely as if he'd held a gun to her head, Will had killed their own mother. Nadine Travers's broken heart had never healed after her firstborn son left town in disgrace.

Apparently that wasn't enough destruction for Will Travers to leave in his wake.

The bell rang. Paul heard the clatter of feet and the muted shrillness of the girls' voices from the dining room, where breakfast had just ended. He drew a deep breath. He would forget about Will. He'd put him out of his mind for twenty years. He could do it for as long as he needed to.

LARRY TEMPLETON SAW the ad after his wife pointed it out over their morning coffee. He'd been reading the Richmond paper as he usually did before walking across the Blue Ridge Academy campus to his office. Nancy always perused the *Courier* when it came out to see who was celebrating a golden wedding anniversary and who had filed for divorce in the past week. Nancy wasn't from Hope Springs, but she tried hard to keep up and fit in—an effort Larry applauded.

"Good heavens! What in the world is this?"

He didn't look up from the stock listings. "Hmm?"

"Who's Alice Esterhaus?"

That captured his attention. He hadn't heard the name in years. But like everyone who'd been around Hope Springs all their lives, Larry remembered. "What about her?"

"It says here that someone attacked her. And somebody's offering a reward."

Larry laid the Richmond paper down carefully although he wanted to snatch the *Courier* away from Nancy. "What are you talking about?"

She turned the paper toward him and he saw the ad. His breakfast heaved in his stomach. Will Travers. That was all it could be. A fine mist of perspiration broke out on Larry Templeton's upper lip.

JUROR NUMBER NINE began to tremble when she saw the ad. For twenty years this had been her nightmare. For twenty years she had lived with the guilt.

She stared at the single stone in her mother's ring, the stone that marked the birth of her only child.

She told herself she'd done the right thing. She'd held out, pounding home the words "reasonable doubt," even though none of the other jurors had seen a glimmer of "reasonable doubt" when the deliberations had begun. She'd turned the jury around and endured the frowns and cold shoulders of the other eleven each time she saw them on the street for years afterward.

She'd done the right thing, she'd said over and over. That was the only way she'd been able to live with herself.

But she knew better. She hadn't done the right thing. She'd taken the coward's way out.

LIBBY JEFFRIES STARTED her Wednesday morning the way she did every morning. She showered and put on one of her crisp white uniforms—a uniform wasn't really necessary under the circumstances, but she liked the formality of it. It gave her the feeling that everything was in its proper place in the world, that everything was under control. Then she made coffee in the roomy old kitchen, brought in the *Courier* from the front porch, put it on the tray with the coffee and morning medications and took the tray down the hall.

She nudged the door open with her hip and smiled at the shriveled-looking woman in the bed. "Good morning, Mrs. Esterhaus. It's going to be a beautiful day."

Mrs. Esterhaus smiled. The doctors said those smiles didn't mean much, but they meant the world to Libby.

Libby opened the blinds so the autumn sunshine could pour into the room, then gave Mrs. Esterhaus the morning doses of all her daily medications. Finally she sat down in the straight-backed rocker beside the hospital bed that had replaced the massive mahogany four-poster years ago and began to read the paper to Mrs. Esterhaus.

It was the least she could do. Libby had never forgotten all the times Mrs. Esterhaus had read to her before Libby had been able to read for herself.

She read the story on the front page about the sprucing-up going on at Heritage Manor. She read the story about the influx of visitors expected in the next month as the autumn colors reached their peak. She read the story about Ginny Bryant winning the contest in the Richmond paper for her sweet-potato pie.

"The recipe will be on page four beside the ad for the IGA," Libby said. "Maybe I ought to try it. What do you think, Mrs. Esterhaus?"

Mrs. Esterhaus didn't answer. But Libby liked including her in the conversation, even though the doctors continued to say that Mrs. Esterhaus didn't understand anything that went on around her. She had limited movement, but her expressions weren't limited. And Libby took that as a sign that something was going on in Mrs. E.'s heart, even if she couldn't find a way to express it beyond a smile or a frown.

Libby also took it as a sign that one day Mrs. E. would break out of her silence, although the doctors held out little hope for that after all these years.

Having finished page one, she opened the paper. That was when the ad, which took up all of page three, caught her eye. She gasped, her hand flying to her mouth. She glanced at Mrs. Esterhaus, anxiety curling around her heart. Mrs. Esterhaus seemed to be enjoying the play of the sunshine on her peach-colored blanket. She hadn't noticed Libby's reaction.

Libby tried to find her voice. She tried to take in the stories on page two, opposite the ad. But the words on that page were reduced to meaningless squiggles. She might have been as confused as Mrs. Esterhaus for all the sense any of it made.

The truth was, Libby could remember only one thing. She remembered being eight years old, sitting in a courtroom, looking out over a sea of faces. But she'd been able to see only one face—the face of Will Travers. Libby had never forgotten that day, or the look in Will's steely gray eyes.

Even at eight, Libby had been certain about what he'd been trying to tell her. That, given a chance, Will would do to Libby Jeffries exactly what he had tried to do to Mrs. Esterhaus.

And now, it seemed, he was back.

CHAPTER TWO

OF ALL THE THINGS Will had to do the morning his ad appeared in the *Courier,* only one felt urgent to him. First he had to get his son off to school, and he knew he should see about finding a job, about getting a phone hooked up.

But what he needed most was to see Mrs. Esterhaus.

"Finish your cereal." He realized he sounded brusque, but he couldn't seem to muster another tone of voice when he talked to Kyle. Brusqueness was the only substitute he could find for the catch he got in his throat whenever he wanted to say something he knew the boy wouldn't welcome. Things like *I know you miss your mother* or *I know you don't believe it yet, but I do love you,* both of which he'd said repeatedly in those first few months.

Both of which had been ignored repeatedly.

Kyle shoved a spoon around in his bowl, fishing for another slice of banana and slopping milk over the rim in the process. The flakes were already a soggy mess. "I'm not hungry."

Will checked his son's schoolbag to make sure everything he would need for the day was tucked inside. Pencils and notebooks and a lunch that would have to do without the homemade cookies a mother might have seen to. He was contemplating the inadequacies of being a mere father when Kyle surprised him with a question.

"Do you have to drive me today?"

"You want to walk?"

Kyle shrugged. "Maybe... Or...I might have a stomachache today."

Will felt his gut tighten. How many bellyaches had Kyle had during the months he'd attended school in D.C.? Too many to count. Kyle had hated the huge public school in the nation's capital, could talk of nothing but how swell it would be to return to Hope Springs. But now that they were here, it seemed that Kyle still wasn't satisfied, that whatever he'd had in mind hadn't materialized. Exasperated and defeated by the whims of an eight-year-old, Will tightened the strap and set aside the schoolbag, then looked at his son, who refused to look at him.

"What's wrong, son?"

Kyle grimaced as he always did when Will called him son.

"You wanted to come back. We're back. But you're still not happy. You've gotta tell me what's wrong."

Kyle pushed away from the table. "I better brush my teeth."

That was a first—voluntary toothbrushing. Will caught Kyle by the arm as he passed and pulled him to a stop. "Not so fast. I thought we agreed back in Washington that it doesn't help not to talk about what's wrong. That we can't fix anything if we don't talk.''

Kyle nodded, his eyes focused on his feet. Will felt the edge of his exasperation sharpening.

''You did want to come back, didn't you?''

Another nod. Hair flopped in his eyes. Warring with Will's frustration was a need to touch the boy, to brush back the silky hair. He refrained, held in check by the certainty of rejection.

''Then what's wrong?''

''You didn't have to come, too. I could've stayed with Aunt Becky.''

Seared by the blunt words, Will released his son's arm. ''Go brush.''

Kyle bolted, his athletic shoes clumping noisily on the bare wood floor. Will sat with his hands between his knees, his head down. Of course. Kyle hadn't wanted to return to Hope Springs; he'd wanted to return to the life he'd known there. He'd wanted his mother back. And according to an eight-year-old's logic, that meant coming back to Hope Springs. Will sighed. What a mess. What a hopeless mess. Maybe it would be better to do exactly what Kyle wanted—leave him with his aunt.

No, he couldn't leave the boy—even if it some-times seemed the right thing to do for Kyle's sake—because right now, this boy was all he had, his only hope for finally having some semblance of a life. Will had lived in hell for too long. Kyle's presence would force him to find some way out.

He would make this nightmare go away once and

for all. He had to. Kyle's mother had been right. He had to clear his name.

How many times had Ginger told him that, pleaded with him to do that, during the twelve years they'd been married? And every time he'd shut her out. The same way he shut out everybody else.

"Please, Will," she'd said the night they'd brought their newborn son home from the hospital. "Let's go home."

"We are home," he'd said, automatically stiffening.

She'd clutched Kyle a little more tightly to her chest. "Hope Springs is home. This town is just…a place to live. A place to hide."

Her words had angered him. As much as she loved him, as much as he loved her, she clearly didn't understand what it had been like for him. She clearly couldn't imagine the pain and humiliation of having the whole town believe him guilty of assaulting Mrs. Esterhaus. He still acutely remembered walking around Hope Springs in the week following the trial and accepting that the jury's finding of reasonable doubt wasn't going to change a single mind.

Will Travers had almost killed his high-school English teacher. That was what everybody had believed, and nothing was going to shake their belief. Will couldn't even blame them. Things had stacked up against him pretty convincingly. And no matter what the jury had voted, Will had found himself shunned by people who had watched him grow up, people who had known his mother all her life.

To hell with it. That had been Will's attitude. Let them hang on to their certainty.

He'd watched his wife breathe a kiss onto the downy fuzz on his son's head and had tried to think of some way to make it all go away. He'd thought leaving Hope Springs would accomplish that. It hadn't. The memories had followed him; he'd carried the bitterness with him. "You've been talking to your sister again," he'd said to Ginger.

"I miss my family. And I'm not planning to live without them for the rest of my life. I'm not planning to raise my baby without his family, his cousins, his grandparents. Think about it, Will." Then she'd turned and walked into the nursery.

He had thought about it. He'd thought about losing the one person who had stood by him in his disgrace. Ginger's parents and most of the town had been horrified by her decision to marry him. "Poor girl," they'd all said. But he and Ginger had been happy. In love. At first, living in Washington had been an adventure. With Ginger beside him, Will hadn't felt like such an outcast. He'd worked in construction, then landscaping, and she'd gone on to school for her degree in special education. They'd been married for twelve years before Kyle was born, twelve years marred only by Ginger's persistent dream. She wanted to go home to Hope Springs.

"They've forgotten by now," she'd said a million times.

"They'll never forget," Will had responded a million and one times.

After Kyle's birth, Ginger became ever more restless and ever more determined to take her son home. She grew angry, and eventually bitter. When she finally returned to Hope Springs, she'd asked Will to stay away.

"Your past has ruined our lives," she'd said the day she left. "I won't let it ruin Kyle's."

Will had figured she was right.

Then Ginger had died and the boy had come to live with him. Kyle had hated the city. He'd hated his new school. Soon it had become apparent that he hated his dad. And the reason, when it had finally come out, was that Will's absence hadn't protected his son, after all. People in Hope Springs still talked; Kyle still heard the stories.

Will used to catch Kyle in the middle of the night, sitting up in bed, staring at the pool of light created by the streetlight outside his bedroom window. It went on night after night, week after week. Will's attempts to talk to the boy had all been futile—until the night of his disastrous birthday party two months ago.

Kyle had refused to invite any of the kids from his new school or the neighborhood to share his birthday cake. He'd barely eaten any of the cake himself and had shown no enthusiasm for the gifts Will had wrapped with such hope and excitement— not even the toy computer the clerk had assured Will was the hottest ticket with kids Kyle's age. Kyle hadn't wanted to go to a movie or a video arcade. And when Will had seen his son staring out the window for the umpteenth time, he'd sat on the bed and refused to move until Kyle had told him what was wrong.

The boy's words had been hostile, a sharp attack that he'd followed up with an equally sharp look.

"You tried to kill an old lady, didn't you?"

The words had produced an inner shudder. The last time Will had heard the accusation was when he'd finally felt safe enough to confide in a friend on the landscaping crew he supervised. His friend had expressed support and understanding, but in the weeks that had followed, his friend had withdrawn, then gossiped. Word had gotten out; his crew had grown hostile. He'd been right all along. His secret was too ugly to share. Will had walked out on the friend and the job. But he couldn't walk out on his son.

"No, Kyle, I didn't."

Kyle had grunted.

"It was all a mistake. The jury said I didn't do it."

Kyle had pulled his knees tightly against his chest and edged closer to the wall.

"Who told you this?"

"Different people."

"Who?"

"Kids." Eight-year-olds weren't supposed to sound bitter, but that's exactly how Kyle had sounded to Will.

"What kids?"

"At school."

"Here?"

"At home."

The sick feeling in Will's gut turned to rage.

"And Aunt Becky. She said I could call her anytime. If I felt scared."

If Will had it in him to kill, he would have gladly throttled his ex-wife's sister at that point. "Have you ever been afraid of me?"

"No."

Kyle hadn't hesitated. Will was grateful for that.

"You never have to be. I've never hurt anybody. I'd never hurt you."

Kyle had almost looked at him then, but seemed to catch himself in time.

"If you don't believe anything else, I hope you'll believe that I'd never hurt you."

But in the days that had followed, it had become clear to Will that Kyle didn't believe any of it. He'd obviously been unable to escape his father's notoriety in Hope Springs. But even that was better, apparently, than being dragged away from the only home he'd ever known to live with his infamous father.

Who could blame a kid for hating a father who only brought him shame and misery?

So Will was back in Hope Springs, determined to clear his name. He didn't have a clue where he'd get ten thousand dollars if anyone came to him with information. But he'd cross that bridge when he came to it, sell his truck if he had to. Because one way or another, he was going to be free of this old accusation. Not for his own sake, but for his son's.

And the best place to start was with Mrs. Esterhaus.

He wasn't a detective and he didn't have any idea how to go about finding out who might really have hurt the old woman. But he had the idea that if he could convince Mrs. Esterhaus he hadn't done it, that would somehow get the ball rolling.

He let Kyle walk to school, although he tagged along a few blocks behind the boy just to make sure he ended up where he belonged. His gaze lingered on Kyle as the boy walked into the schoolyard. He was so small, his shoulders so narrow, his jeans hanging on nonexistent hips, cuffed three rolls deep so they wouldn't drag on the ground. Kyle stopped at the door to stuff his cap into his schoolbag, letting loose the mop of flyaway blond hair that sometimes showed a hint of the copper color he'd inherited from his mom. Along with Ginger's freckles and her turned-up nose. Only his eyes—those cold, dark eyes—had come from his father.

An eight-year-old shouldn't have cold eyes. Will knew that.

He turned away when Kyle disappeared into the school.

Walker Shearin, the editor of the *Courier,* had told Will when he placed the ad that Mrs. Esterhaus still lived in the same house on Old Oak Street. Will headed in that direction, his heart beginning to thump with apprehension.

He hadn't been allowed to see Mrs. Esterhaus after the attack. They said she didn't have any memory of the attack. But maybe that had changed. Maybe she remembered now but hadn't realized it was important to tell people what she knew because he'd been acquitted. Maybe...

He walked down the quiet, tree-canopied streets of Hope Springs and coached himself not to get his hopes up.

Whatever the outcome, he needed to see Mrs. Esterhaus. She had meant so much to him all those years ago. Before the attack, she had been the only one who'd believed in him, besides his own mom and his worshipful little brother. Mrs. E. had spent hours after school coaching him for his college entrance exams; she'd said she could help him get a scholarship.

Then someone had almost killed her.

And Will had to know whether Mrs. Esterhaus believed that he was responsible. And, regardless of what she believed, he had to see her face-to-face and tell her he would never have lifted a hand against anyone. And especially not her.

Blood pounded in his veins. He was afraid. So afraid, he missed the turn onto Old Oak Street and had to backtrack. Then he caught sight of the little yellow frame house where Mrs. Esterhaus had drilled him in the rules of English grammar, teaching him to diagram sentences and remember all the parts of speech.

"You could be a writer someday if you wanted

to," she'd said. "You have a gift. But you have to nurture that gift. Do you understand what I'm saying, William?"

And he'd nodded, wondering why this sturdy, gray-haired woman had taken under her wing the troublesome son of one of the town's have-not families.

The little house looked shabbier than it had before. The eaves needed painting and the roof needed replacing and the shrubs and ivy had grown wildly, overtaking windows and choking out everything but weeds. The lawn was dotted with bare patches. The front gate had been removed.

He walked to the porch and up the front steps. He knocked, noticing that his hand was shaking.

How big a mistake was this? he wondered.

There was no answer, but through the sheer lace curtains that covered the oval of cut glass on the front door he saw the flicker of someone dressed in white moving down the hallway. He pounded on the door.

He wouldn't leave until he'd seen her.

The flicker of white came back. The door opened, only by inches. A chain held the door in place. He saw a rigid young face.

"You need to go away."

He could tell by the animosity and nervousness in her voice that she knew who he was. He wondered if he should know her. She looked vaguely familiar, but he couldn't place her. She looked too young for them to have been in school together.

"I want to see Mrs. Esterhaus."

"You can't."

"Why not?" he demanded.

"She's...resting."

He took it all in. The young woman was in uniform. A starched white uniform.

"You're a nurse," he said.

"That's right."

A nurse. Mrs. E. still needed a nurse. He realized, from the way his spirits sank, that he'd been hoping things had turned out better than everyone had predicted. He coached himself to remain calm. "When can I see her?"

She started to push the door closed and he caught it, prohibiting her from shutting it in his face even though the chain kept him out. As the door jerked against the chain, he saw the shiny red nametag on her left breast.

Libby Jeffries, RN.

It took a moment for the name to sink in. Libby Jeffries, the eyewitness who had convinced everyone but the jury that Will Travers had tried to kill his teacher and mentor.

Will's old rage at being falsely accused boiled to the surface. Never mind that this stone-faced registered nurse had been nothing but a child when the assault and trial had occurred. She had ruined his life.

He shoved against the door again, this time with real venom. "To hell with you, Libby Jeffries. This chain won't keep me out if I make up my mind to come in.''

She flinched but held her ground, even when the door shuddered against the chain and bumped her shoulder.

''I'm sure that's true,'' she said. ''But you won't get to her as long as I'm standing.''

Her words sounded like forged steel, but he saw her trembling. Shame for his bullying and his anger washed over him. He backed away.

''I'm—''

She slammed the door, rattling the oval of glass he could smash in a heartbeat.

''—sorry.''

LIBBY LEANED AGAINST the door, every inch of her body shaking. Her heart must be pounding loud enough to attract attention on Ridge Lane. She heard his footsteps on the porch and prayed he was leaving. But it took a while for her to gather the courage to turn and look.

When she did, he was gone.

The next thought came to her with a start.

He could be at the back door. Or at one of the windows.

On trembling legs she double-checked the back door, then every window in the house, including the tiny bathroom window. Everything was locked up tight.

She should have checked as soon as she'd seen the ad. She should have...what? If Will Travers was determined to get in, there was little anyone could do to stop him. Of that she was certain.

She splashed cold water on her face at the bathroom sink, avoiding looking in the mirror. She had to keep a grip on things. She had to figure out what to do. She was responsible for more than her own well-being; she was responsible for Mrs. Esterhaus, too.

This time she wouldn't fail the old woman.

This time.

The words echoed in her head, mocking her. She dried her hands and walked down the hall, still wary, her legs still unsteady. Her thoughts threatened to go back to the last time, but Libby was adept at padlocking her memory. Glancing at the front door, she stopped at Mrs. Esterhaus's room. The old lady was dozing, arms at her sides, head cocked toward the window as if she might see or hear something interesting from the world outside her room.

Libby swallowed a ragged breath.

Twenty years ago Libby had believed Mrs. Esterhaus was ancient. From the vantage point of her eight long years on earth, Libby had studied the teacher who lived next door to her and assessed the evidence. The gray threads in her hair, which marked her as far older than either of Libby's parents. The veins and wrinkles on her square, strong hands. The drab navy skirts that covered her knees. The funny half glasses that sat on the end of her nose or dangled from a silver chain around her neck.

All those things had marked Libby's neighbor as an antiquity.

Libby now realized that Alice Esterhaus had been barely over fifty. Energetic enough to have time for a little girl who loved stories and for teenagers who didn't deserve the extra help she lavished on them.

Pursing her lips against her own bitterness, Libby turned away and walked toward the kitchen to tidy up. She gazed at the front door again, saw nothing beyond the glass and lace, apart from the fading maple out front with its apron of fallen red leaves. There was nothing outside the kitchen window except the overgrown lawn and the deteriorating glider in back. The whole place looked dreary and forlorn, and it tugged at her sense of order.

Things hadn't looked this way when she'd returned to Hope Springs right after nursing school. Libby had worked as the school nurse for a year, before Mr. E.'s cancer had sent him to bed. It had seemed the perfect idea for Libby to move in, to take care of the sickly couple. It had become both her mission in life and her refuge from life, a way to avoid the world that sometimes made her edgy and nervous. She'd cared for the pair of them for almost two years. Then, after Mr. E.'s death four years ago, his estate had hired her to stay on with Mrs. E. Libby had been grateful for the excuse to limit her interactions with a world that hadn't quite felt safe for twenty years.

Libby dropped the kitchen curtain. She should talk to the new attorney who had taken over Melvin

Guthry's practice, Sean Davenport. He managed the estate and could hire someone to get things back in order.

She brushed up crumbs and emptied the coffee-pot, her gaze straying to the window again and again. The wooden arbor over the glider listed to one side; rust on the glider springs probably meant the two-seater would no longer glide. Both glider and arbor would need paint to be presentable. More likely they would tumble first and save someone the time and expense. Even the vines creeping over the arbor were no longer the climbing roses and Confederate jasmine Mrs. Esterhaus had once prized; weeds and ivy had all but choked out the blooms.

Libby rinsed the few dishes, keeping her eyes down. She didn't like thinking about how much things had changed. Things were supposed to change in twenty years. She knew that of course. But this wasn't change so much as slow death.

She remembered sitting in that glider. It was hard to say which had bloomed more sweetly, the roses or the jasmine. Although for a young child, the most alluring smell of all had been the freshly baked cookies.

''Oh, Elisabeth Anne, I'm so glad you've stopped by,'' Mrs. E. would say, smiling and putting a gentle hand on Libby's shoulder. ''I've just taken cookies out of the oven, and I was thinking it would be a shame if someone didn't sample them while they're still warm. Could you help with that, do you think?''

Then Libby would nod shyly and follow Mrs. E.

through the back door and into the old-fashioned kitchen for a plate of cookies and a glass of milk.

"How would it be if I read to you while you sit in the glider and eat your cookies?"

They would go back into the yard then, with cookies and milk and a copy of *Little Women* or *The Secret Garden* or *Mrs. Wiggs and the Cabbage Patch*. Mrs. E.'s voice was strong and gruff, but when she read, the stories jumped right off the page and came alive in Libby's head.

Sometimes the cookies grew cold as the stories completely captured her attention.

She couldn't wait to get to school and learn to read for herself. The wait had seemed impossibly long. But Mrs. E. promised her that the day would come when Libby would be reading while Mrs. E. ate cookies. Libby used to laugh at that.

Mrs. E. had been right, of course.

The day it happened, Libby had read a chapter from *Tom Sawyer*. Haltingly and with many mispronunciations, but Mrs. E. had pretended to be enthralled. "I can't wait to hear what happens next. Do you suppose you could come by after school tomorrow and read just a little more?"

Delighted with her success, Libby had promised.

That night everything had changed.

Libby had been in her room, putting away the spelling list her father had helped her with after supper. It was late spring and the days were longer, but dusk was already falling, and soon the sky would be completely dark. Time for Libby to be in bed.

Then she'd heard the cries—faint cries wafting through her bedroom window. Cautiously she'd looked out and heard another cry, coming from the other side of the dense hedge that separated her house from Mrs. Esterhaus's. She started to turn and run downstairs for help, but something crashed in the house next door. Paralyzed with fear, Libby watched Mrs. E.'s back door slam open. Somebody ran out—a teenager in a leather jacket. He ditched something in the bushes and kept running.

In the waning light Libby had recognized the leather jacket and thought surely nothing bad could have happened. The teenager in the leather jacket came to see Mrs. E. all the time. They were friends; she supposed Mrs. E. read to him, too.

The leather jacket had belonged to Will Travers.

Libby shivered at the memory and all the ones that had followed.

It was time for Mrs. E.'s bath.

CHAPTER THREE

LIBBY HAD ALMOST talked herself out of her fear by the middle of the afternoon.

She was hanging sheets on the line in the backyard, inhaling the fresh fall air tinged with a hint of burning leaves. Autumn in Hope Springs was her favorite time, the time when even the tourists who trickled in for the fall colors seemed less frenetic in their search of a good time than the spring and summer tourists. In the autumn, Hope Springs began to grow peaceful again.

Libby craved that peace, especially today. She needed it to silence the voices in her head.

The voices of the playmates who had taunted her in childhood: *"'Fraidy cat, 'fraidy cat. Libby's just a 'fraidy cat."*

The voice of the child psychologist they'd taken her to in the months after the trial, when she hadn't been able to eat or sleep: *"You do understand, don't you, that your dreams aren't real?"*

The voice of her mother, dead almost five years now, pushing her to attend church suppers and singles' outings: *"There's not a thing in the world to be afraid of. Nobody ever died from a little shyness."*

The voice of Darren, the day he broke their engagement: *"Lib, I'm marrying you, not that old lady. If you're not ready to get out of this house and on with your life, you'd better let me know now."*

None of them really understood. None of them had ever been able to understand the fear and mistrust and guilt that consumed her, that made her so protective of herself and Mrs. Esterhaus. Others called it "fear and isolation." Libby called it "peace and routine." Life was just the way she wanted it.

Will Travers would not disturb that peace. Over and over she'd reminded herself that if Will Travers had any further notion of hurting Mrs. Esterhaus, he would have done so long before now.

And twenty years was too long to wait to get revenge against anyone. He wasn't back to cause trouble. He wouldn't be that foolish. Surely.

She pinned a flower-sprigged pillowcase to the line. She bent to retrieve a towel from her basket and heard something behind her. A footfall on dried leaves.

Alarm spiked through her. She whirled to see Will Travers standing beside the wobbly arbor. A small cry escaped her lips. She dropped the towel and the clothespin.

"Sorry," he said. "I didn't mean to startle you."

Terror welled up in her throat. She took a cautious step backward, toward the door.

"I came back because...I know I scared you this morning."

His eyes, half-hidden beneath his furrowed brow,

were as dark as a storm. The frown looked permanent, etched into his face like the mark of his guilty conscience. He was compact, it seemed to Libby, but hard. He struck her as rugged and lithe as he moved toward her, as dangerous and mesmerizing as the wildcats in the nearby mountains.

"I wasn't very nice and..."

She took another step backward, stumbling against the basket of clean linens. She tried to catch herself, but she was awkward in her fear. She toppled over the basket and hit the ground with a thump that seemed to knock the air out of her chest.

Omigosh, omigosh.

He hovered over her, his hand out. It was a broad, long-fingered, rough hand.

The hand that had beaten Mrs. Esterhaus senseless.

Scooting away, Libby scrambled to her feet, picking up the basket as she did so, holding it between them like a shield. "I told you before. Get out of here."

Her voice didn't tremble. She thought it might pass for gutsy if not exactly fearless.

He looked down at his feet, shoved those big hands into the front pockets of his jeans. "Listen, miss, I got started on the wrong foot this morning. I didn't come to cause any trouble. I have a son now, and it's because of him that I came. I know what you must think, but—"

"You're damn right you know what I think," she said, the words rushing out before she had a chance to think about the fact that she never ever swore. But he didn't know that, and maybe her language would make him think she was tougher than she was. Maybe. "I think you almost killed the nicest lady I ever knew and you got off scot-free. I'll kill you myself before you lay another hand on her. Or me. You can take that to the bank, Will Travers!"

Then she turned and ran for the back door, praying he wouldn't follow, because her legs felt like rubber, too weak for speed. She wondered how fast he might be, knowing he would be too strong for her to make good on her threat. When she reached the door she realized he was still standing beside the clothesline, beside the drift of spilled sheets and towels. He looked bewildered and unsure. Libby steeled herself against sudden compassion for him. He'd been so young then. Maybe...

"I'm calling the police," she threatened. "If you're smart, you'll leave. Right now."

"Miss Jeffries, wait. I—"

Then she slipped through the door, latched it behind her, threw the dead bolt with trembling fingers and stood with her hand at her throat for several seconds. Her pulse roared beneath her ice-cold fingertips. *Call the police. Now.* She dropped the clothes basket. *Move.* She groped across the counter for the portable phone. *And don't go soft. He's dangerous. Don't forget it.*

She dialed the emergency number and waited, blood pounding in her ears. She wouldn't be able to hear when they answered. They would ask what was wrong and she wouldn't hear a thing except her own fear racing through her veins.

When the dispatcher responded, Libby heard her, after all, and struggled to reply. "This is Libby. He was here."

"Libby Jeffries? Over at Mrs. E.'s? Who was there, honey?"

Libby's legs began to give out on her. She sank to the floor, still clutching the phone. "Will Travers."

"Who?"

She wasn't sure she could say it again. She began to move toward the cutlery drawer. If she had a knife, she wouldn't be defenseless. Fear parched her throat and mouth. "Will Travers."

"Will— Will *Travers?* Lord have mercy, honey. We'll be right there."

The dispatcher stayed on the line with her the whole time. It seemed like hours. She found out later it was only four minutes. She had a butcher knife clutched in her hand when Sheriff Al Tillman came pounding on the front door. She made it to the door in a haze of fear.

"Everything's fine now, Lib," the sheriff said, taking her right hand gently in his and prying her fingers away from the wooden handle. "You need to let go, Lib, before somebody gets hurt."

"Okay," she said, loosening her grip on the knife. "Okay. I'm calm now."

"Did he hurt you? Did he hurt Mrs. E.?"

"No! I didn't let him near her." It occurred to

her that he hadn't actually tried to get near her. He hadn't even followed her to the door.

"Okay, you sit down." The sheriff ushered her into the living room. His voice was like his skin, as dark and rich as freshly ground coffee beans. Al Tillman was tall and lean and soothing, the perfect man to have around in an emergency. People in Hope Springs always said that about him. Libby began to relax. She did as he suggested and sat, although she resisted the soft pull of the couch cushions. She sat bolt upright, fists clenched in her lap.

"Okay, Lib, let's see exactly what did happen."

He was there almost an hour, asking her questions and calming her down. When he finally got the whole story about the two visits from Will Travers, he wasn't happy, but he didn't seem worried, either.

"Now, I want you to listen to me, Libby," Sheriff Tillman said before he left. "I've talked to Ginger Travers's sister. That's Becky Marr. You know Becky, don't you? Now, Becky said they never heard a word about any trouble out of Will, even in all those years when he and Ginger were still married."

"But they got divorced," Libby said, as if that might prove something.

"That they did. But Ginger never said a word about him raising a hand to her. Or to the boy."

"Still—"

He interrupted her and she looked down, away from the dark eyes that beseeched her to be calm.

Her gaze skittered to the gun holstered at his waist. Her heart leaped again.

"Lib, we all know what he did. But it was a long time ago. And teenage boys, well... All I'm saying is, maybe there's nothing to worry about."

A gun. That's what she needed. Was it as heavy as it looked? Could she actually manage to point it at someone?

"Don't even think about it, Lib."

She looked up. He'd caught her eyeing his gun.

"A gun is not going to make things one iota better. I can promise you that."

"But, Sheriff Tillman—"

"Let's give him the benefit of the doubt, why don't we. Assume he isn't here to cause trouble. But that's not to say we're not going to keep a close eye on him."

"Why can't you do something? Make him leave town?"

He studied the rim of the hat that matched his khaki uniform, then shoved it over his short, springy gray curls. "I can't do that. I've got a fine line to walk here. He's a free man, you know. Never was convicted of a thing."

Libby looked away as he said it. The words felt like a slap, an accusation.

"Now, Lib, that's not your fault. I don't want you thinking that. There's not a soul in town blaming you for that."

Maybe not. Or maybe so. When the sheriff left, Libby pondered that as she hadn't for years. Maybe everybody else in Hope Springs had let it go. Certainly nobody ever acted as if they held Libby Jeffries responsible for Will Travers being a free man.

But at least one person blamed Libby, held her solely responsible for the travesty of justice.

Libby blamed herself.

She fixed an afternoon snack, the way she did every day, and carried it in to Mrs. Esterhaus. Then she would massage the withered muscles in the old woman's legs and read to her until she drifted off to sleep again. She would fix dinner later, feed Mrs. E. and turn on the television for the news that sometimes seemed to capture Mrs. E.'s attention. She would administer Mrs. E.'s medications, and tuck her in for the night and go upstairs to the room she'd fixed up for herself.

Thinking ahead to the rest of her carefully structured day calmed her further.

She especially looked forward to curling up in her room. Her bedroom, directly over Mrs. E.'s, was the first place she'd felt completely safe since her childhood had spun out of control. It was homey, with lots of pink-and-cream chintz pillows on both the overstuffed swivel rocker at the window and the sleigh bed with its down comforter. The dresser, the chest of drawers, the little rolltop writing desk were all covered with knickknacks she'd brought from home, most of them things that had been her mother's—china figurines and the collection of teacups that had belonged to Charlotte Jeffries. A shelf of books, mostly children's classics she sometimes doubted she'd ever have the chance to read to a child. A crystal vase full of shells she'd collected the summer she and Darren went to Virginia Beach, right before he left town.

She even enjoyed watching from her window as the rest of the town went about its business—walking to church, heading for open house at the elementary school or a high-school football game. Watching Faith O'Dare and her new husband pushing the baby carriage, little Patrick sitting up and shaking his tiny fists and grinning at everyone who passed. It was hard to believe that he almost hadn't made it when he came into the world a year ago. Catching a glimpse of old Mr. Guthry spooning with the new attorney's mother, who had moved into the Harrilson place. Sometimes Clem passed and waved to her. Clementine Weeks was the town mechanic and an unlikely friend for a woman like Libby, but Clem couldn't be convinced of that and kept making friendly overtures.

She loved them all, but it was so much easier to keep them at a distance. Since losing her mother and her fiancé—since losing her childhood—she'd been content with living out her life from the safety of her upstairs bedroom window. That's as close as she got to most people. Even her best friend, Meg, only scratched the surface in getting close to Libby.

Mrs. Esterhaus was her excuse of course. An invalid needed so much attention, time and energy— that was what she always said when anyone tried to draw her out. Nobody knew enough to argue with that except Meg. Everyone else said Libby was a saint to take care of Mrs. E. the way she did.

Meg would simply give her that cynical look and say, "It's time you got a life," or, "Nobody expects you to give up your own life for an old woman who's never going to get any better."

But Libby expected it. Libby blamed herself. And she could think of only one way to make it up to Mrs. Esterhaus.

"I have your favorite this afternoon, Mrs. E.," she said now, smiling gently at the old woman who had become her mission, her purpose in life. "Butterscotch pudding. With extra whipped cream. Sound good?"

Mrs. E. gave her a smile. Libby knew better than anyone that Mrs. E.'s brain had been so damaged she could never talk again. But Libby always talked to her, anyway. Coaxed a smile out of her several times a day and told herself that a soothing voice and a gentle touch could somehow penetrate what the doctors said could no longer be reached.

Libby saw herself as more than Mrs. E.'s live-in nurse. She was the woman's companion and protector and family. In turn, the old woman was Libby's friend and confidante.

"I know you probably don't want to hear this," Libby said as she spooned up some pudding for Mrs. E. "But it's weighing heavy on my mind this afternoon."

Mrs. E. swallowed and looked at Libby expectantly.

"I know." Libby smiled. "You're a good listener. You've helped me more than you know just by listening to all my silly little problems."

Only Mrs. Esterhaus knew how betrayed and abandoned Libby had felt when her widowed father had started dating Vera Templeton. She would have been ashamed to tell anyone else, even if there had been someone else to tell, because she knew her feelings were childish and selfish. Just talking about them had helped her cope. Just as saying everything out loud had helped her deal with her grief when Darren had moved to Phoenix.

Mrs. Esterhaus knew everything about Libby— even how friendless she sometimes felt in a town where she'd known every soul since she was a child.

"I just feel like it's all coming back to haunt me, Mrs. E.," she said. "And I don't know how to... what to... I'm so confused."

Libby hadn't been confused at first, all those years ago. When the sheriff—old Ozzie Wiedermann, in those days—had come to the Jeffries home after they'd found Mrs. E., Libby had been sure of every detail. No matter how many times he'd asked her, she'd told him about hearing Mrs. E.'s cries and seeing the man run out of the house and throw something into the bushes. And sure enough, they'd found Mrs. E.'s fireplace poker in the bushes, right where Libby had directed them. She'd told them about the leather jacket, too, and about all the times she'd seen the boy in that same leather jacket coming and going at Mrs. E.'s.

Nobody in Hope Springs had been surprised. They all knew who the leather jacket belonged to—didn't that young hooligan Will Travers wear it everywhere, day and night, winter and summer? And hadn't he broken his poor mother's heart a dozen times getting into scrapes after his father had died? Hadn't everyone warned Mrs. Esterhaus that the boy was trouble, a waste of her time?

Nobody was surprised and everybody was glad there had been a witness, even if that witness was an eight-year-old girl. Everyone agreed the little Libby Jeffries was sensible and reliable.

They hadn't known that Libby would let them down.

There was no physical evidence, except for Will's fingerprints all over Mrs. Esterhaus's house; which was to be expected, since she tutored him there several afternoons a week. They never even found the leather jacket, which Will swore he had lost a few days before the attack. Probably covered with blood, Ozzie Wiedermann said, so the boy had been smart enough to dispose of it.

But with Libby on the stand, everybody had said, they wouldn't need physical evidence. An eyewitness was better than fingerprints and blood samples and all that scientific mumbo-jumbo. Ozzie had said that time and again as the trial progressed.

Then it was time for Libby to testify.

She'd been having nightmares. She hadn't told a soul, because she knew they were all counting on her. But she'd been waking up drenched in sweat every night, too afraid even to cry out and certain she didn't deserve to cry for help, anyway, since she hadn't been brave enough to help when her friend Mrs. E. had needed her.

Every night she'd dreamed the same dream, where she was running down the stairs and through the back hedge and into Mrs. E's kitchen. Mrs. E. was already on the floor and that boy whose picture was in the paper all the time now was standing over her. He turned to Libby and said, "You're too late." And he was frowning just the way he was frowning in the high-school-yearbook picture they'd put in the paper, looking so fierce and angry that Libby's heart almost broke through her rib cage. In her dream Libby chased the boy off and tried to wake up Mrs. Esterhaus. The teacher turned to her once and said, "You're too late," then closed her eyes and turned into a big head of cauliflower right in front of Libby's eyes.

She'd had the nightmare for the first time after she overheard her dad tell her mom that Mrs. Esterhaus might never come out of her coma. And if she did, he said, she would be a vegetable.

Libby didn't know exactly what that meant, but her mom had started to cry and said, "Poor Mr. Esterhaus. However will he manage?"

So by the time Libby walked up to the witness stand in the courthouse, she didn't feel as confident as she had when she first told Ozzie Wiedermann about seeing the man in the leather jacket. Her insides felt like cold oatmeal—thick and lumpy and heavy. And she was afraid that the scream she'd been holding inside every night for a week might finally break out right there in front of everybody.

The courtroom was huge and dark and cold. She started to shiver. Everyone was looking at her and talking behind their hands, and the judge banged on his desk with his hammer once when the man Ozzie Wiedermann told her to trust asked her a question. While the lawyers and the judge were whispering and glaring at each other, Libby had time to look around the courtroom and notice exactly how many people had their eyes on her.

Then she saw him. Will Travers.

They'd told her not to look at him, but she couldn't help it. He was staring at her, and his dark eyes grabbed her like a magnet. He was frowning and angry and his fists were clenched on the table in front of him.

When the lawyer came back and asked her the next question, Libby couldn't take her eyes off Will. Even when the lawyer finally seemed to understand what was happening and stepped between them, Libby could still see Will Travers's eyes boring into her.

She knew what they were saying to her, even when she couldn't see them anymore.

He would kill her, the way he'd meant to kill Mrs. E.

Her throat closed up. She knew the lawyer was asking her questions, but she couldn't seem to hear them. She could only hear the voice in her dream.

"You're too late." When she tried to say something, she could only stutter.

They had finally let her go home.

The next day the jury had let Will Travers go home, too.

A million times in the years that had followed, Libby told herself she had failed Mrs. Esterhaus and everyone else in Hope Springs. And now, having Will Travers come home to flaunt the injustice in the face of every law-abiding person in town, well, it was almost more than Libby could bear.

Mrs. Esterhaus's little dessert bowl was scraped clean when Libby looked back at her.

"I'm glad you liked it," she said, pushing aside the heaviness of old memories. Most of the time these days, she didn't dwell in the past. She managed to stay in the moment, paying attention to the good she could accomplish for Mrs. E. "I thought we'd have tomato soup for dinner. How would that be? It's cool enough for soup already, don't you think?"

Mrs. E. looked perturbed, it seemed to Libby.

"I know," she said. "You're right. I am worried about something. I... Maybe I shouldn't mention this to you. But...he's back, Mrs. E. Will Travers. He's back in Hope Springs."

Mrs. Esterhaus clutched at the sheet that was folded neatly at her chest.

"I know," Libby said, touching the knotted knobby hand. "But there's nothing to worry about. Nobody's going to let him get close to you."

And, although everybody said Mrs. Esterhaus
didn't understand anything that was going on around
her, Libby knew the old woman well enough to see
that she was agitated by the news. Mrs. E. began to
thrash her fists, tangling the sheets. Her face grew
tight and her lips moved.

Libby brushed her palm reassuringly over the old
woman's arm. "Oh, dear. Please don't worry about
that, Mrs. E. You'll never see Will Travers again. I
promise."

It was a long time before Mrs. Esterhaus's agitation wore itself out. And even when she napped,
she whimpered in her sleep. Libby was sorry she'd
said anything. Even a mind with no clear memory
could obviously retain something of terror and be-
trayal.

Libby sat beside Mrs. Esterhaus's bed as the light
faded, wishing there were some way she could make
Will Travers pay for what he had done.

CHAPTER FOUR

WILL FIGURED he'd just made matters worse with his second visit to Mrs. Esterhaus.

The story of his life.

He had another hour or so before school was out, so he decided to tackle the next unpleasant task on his list. He would visit his brother.

The local phone directory had no listing for Paul, so he asked at the gas station where he refueled his pickup. He didn't recognize the paunchy man who made change for him, although he guessed they were about the same age. When he asked about Paul, the man gave him a wary look.

"You Paul's brother? Will?" Every bit of speculation hidden beneath the loaded question was revealed in the man's mistrustful expression.

"That's right." Will shoved his change into his jeans and waited.

The man stared at him, sizing him up. "I reckon if Paul wanted you knowing where he lived, he'd tell you himself."

Anger rose in Will's throat. The attendant was right of course. Paul wanted nothing to do with his brother. He'd made that clear when their mother died—through Melvin Guthry, the attorney who'd handled the estate and who, incidentally, had defended Will.

Will bit back his testiness. "We've been out of touch."

"Yeah." The man hitched up his jeans and leaned across the counter. His wariness had been replaced with concern. "Listen, pal, I figure what happened twenty years ago is ancient history. Let sleeping dogs lie, that's what I say. Maybe others feel the same, I don't know. But if you come along and start kicking that sleeping dog, he's likely to rear up and take a chunk outta your hide. Know what I mean?"

Will nodded. He turned to go, but stopped at the door and turned back. "He's my brother."

The man pursed his lips, then reached for two soft drinks in the nearby cooler. He passed one to Will. "It's a little ways out of town," he said as he twisted the cap on his bottle. "I don't think he's crazy about company."

Will followed the directions the man gave him. Paul lived in a cabin on one of those steep gravel roads that spilled off the edge of the wooded mountainside. The driveway was marked only by a mailbox covered in ivy, a rural box number stenciled on the side. The ruts were deep and bone-wrenching. The clearing where the cabin nestled had also been allowed to grow up in vines and a tangle of weeds.

Not crazy about company, the service-station attendant had said.

One wall of the cabin had been built into a huge granite stone that jutted out over the cliff. A stone fireplace marked the other end of the cabin. The clapboard looked sturdy, the wood having weathered to a silvery gray that blended with the granite. A pickup truck a lot like the one Will drove had been backed up to the woods. A short flight of stone steps led up to the only door.

He heard the cabin door slam as he got out of his pickup. Sighing, he approached and pounded on the door.

He knocked again, then rattled the door when there was no answer after a reasonable length of time. He peered around the corner, saw that the cabin clung to the edge of the cliff.

"I'm not leaving till I see you!" he called out.

Then he sat on the bottom step, glancing at his watch, gauging how much time he had before Kyle came home from school. Enough time, maybe, to convince Paul he meant business.

He hadn't realized until now that he'd harbored some shred of hope that things might have changed. Or could be changed, now that they were both older, now that they could take a few minutes to sit down and talk everything through. You couldn't explain things to a fifteen-year-old, which Paul had been at the time of the trial. At fifteen, kids went off half-cocked, wouldn't listen, couldn't be reasoned with. Not much different from eight-year-olds, it struck him. But Paul was grown now. He'd been to college. Will knew that from his mother's letters. Paul wasn't an unreasonable hothead anymore.

At least he'd hoped that was the case. Apparently

Paul was no more interested in the truth than he'd
been all those years ago.

*"I hate you. I hate your guts. You've ruined ev-
erything."*

Those words had echoed in Will's mind for years.
Will had figured he could handle being mistrusted
and despised by everyone in Hope Springs. But
hearing it from Paul, from his own brother...

That's when he'd known he had to leave.

Will was agitated, but the longer he sat there on
the cold, hard stepping-stones at his brother's cabin,
the calmer he grew. He'd forgotten, after all those
years in the city, that the mountains could do that
to him. He watched a pair of red squirrels in a game
of chase, startling a chipmunk, who skittered across
the moss-covered rock that formed the ledge where
the cabin perched. Birds called to one another, and
somewhere not too far away water trickled over
rocks.

Maybe Paul had the right idea.

The sound of the door opening startled him when
it finally came. He didn't turn.

"Nice place," he said.

"You're not welcome here."

The last time he'd heard his little brother's voice,
Paul had been a teenager. Nothing of that boy remained in the deep rasp of the voice behind him.

"I figured."

When Paul didn't reply, Will stood and turned to
face his brother. Seeing him almost did him in.

The angry fifteen-year-old he had carried in his

memory vanished, replaced by a glaring man with a neatly trimmed chestnut-colored beard. He wore round wire-rimmed glasses and a corduroy shirt with the sleeves rolled up, revealing well-turned forearms. One more thing had been lost to Will that he could never recover—his younger brother.

Emotion caught in his throat.

He swallowed hard, forced himself to concentrate on the hard look of unwelcome in Paul's eyes. He wouldn't, couldn't, think about the boys they'd been, how close they'd been. How Paul had worshiped him the way little brothers often worshiped big brothers.

"We have to talk about the house," he said, instead of dragging out the little speech he'd worked up in the back of his mind on the way out here.

"There's nothing to talk about. I told Melvin Guthry I wanted nothing to do with that house if it meant sharing it with you."

"We could sell it. Split the money."

"I don't give a damn what you do."

There wasn't any anger in Paul's voice, just a quiet rock-solid determination, plus the polish and self-confidence his education had given him. Paul didn't intend to bend.

"What good does this do?" Will asked. "Hanging on to old stuff like this?"

Paul stared at him in silence for a long time. "It keeps you from bringing any more poison into my life. That's what good it does."

Will wanted to say it then, the way he always

wanted to say it when the shadow of the old accusation hovered over him. *I didn't do it. I swear I didn't do it.* But he refrained. He'd said it time and again twenty years ago. For all the good it had done him.

"It's over, Paul."

"If you believed that, you would never have left. If you believed that, you'd have come back a long time ago."

Will couldn't argue with that.

"The jury said—"

"The hell with what the jury said!" Paul's voice boomed across the ravine. "What the jury said didn't mean a damn thing. It didn't give that old woman her voice or her mind back. And it didn't save my mother from a long, slow death."

Will grew cold and still inside. "What's that supposed to mean?"

"You know damn well what it means."

"No. You'd better say whatever's eating you."

"Okay. I'll say it." Paul took a step closer; he looked tightly wound, his body tense, his expression cold. "You killed my mother just as surely as you all but killed Alice Esterhaus. You just didn't have the mercy to do it quickly. You did it with guilt and shame and misery. She was fifty-seven when she died and she'd been a broken old woman for years. That was your doing."

The words pierced Will's protective shield, words he'd forbidden himself from thinking for far too long. He'd known, of course, the burden his mother had carried because of his problems. But he'd told himself it wasn't his fault; he'd done nothing wrong. It was the town, the people who had accused him, who had hurt his mother.

"Self-righteousness doesn't look good on you, little brother."

The punch Paul threw was unexpected, and Will couldn't jump fast enough to miss it completely. Paul's fist glanced off his jaw. Hurt like hell, too. Denying the reflexive urge to rub the spot, he backed out of range of his brother's reach. The last time Paul had hit him they'd been nine and twelve. Will couldn't even remember what the argument had been about. Something stupid, he supposed, like whose turn it was to take out the garbage. They didn't fight much. Paul worshiped Will too much, and Will was too protective of Paul.

Now there seemed no more hope of salvaging this relationship than there was of healing the rift with his son.

WILL STOPPED BY the cemetery on his way back to the house. He sought out his mother's grave, marked with a small slab of granite. Her name. Nadine Connor Travers. The year of her birth and the year of her death. That was it. Nothing else to remind future generations of her shame.

He wanted to kneel, to say something to set things right. He wanted to cry and promise to make it up to her. But he knew none of that could ever make a difference to his mother again. He'd lost his chance

with her. Thrown it away, just as he'd thrown away
what he had with Ginger, because he didn't know
how to overcome his own past.

But maybe if he could clear his name, his past
would no longer hurt his son or his brother.

He turned from the grave and walked back to his
truck, head down. He didn't realize he wasn't alone
until he discovered someone propped against the
door of his truck. An imposing black man in a uniform.

His heart lurched, the way it always did when he
saw a law-enforcement officer.

"You Will Travers?"

Anxiety shot through him. "That's right."

"I'm Al Tillman. I'm sheriff here now."

Will remembered Al Tillman. He'd been a rookie
deputy when Will was arrested. He'd been nice, too.
Will was surprised how many people he remembered being nice to him all those years ago. The
young reporter who was now editor of the *Courier*,
the attorney who had defended him, even the lanky
kid in the sheriff's department.

"I understand you've been harassing Libby Jeffries."

Will's mouth went dry. Yep, he'd already
screwed up. "No, I—"

"You saying you haven't been over there, Travers?"

"No, I... I just... I didn't mean to frighten her."

"Listen, Travers, the jury said there was enough
reasonable doubt to let you walk. You're a free man.

I'm not going to hassle you, 'cause you've got every right to be here in Hope Springs.'' He shoved a finger in Will's chest. "But I don't want any trouble. This is a nice, quiet town full of nice, quiet people, and I don't want any of them getting jumpy. Can you appreciate that?''

I didn't do it. "Yes. I can appreciate that.''

"Then we've got an agreement. You stay out of trouble and I won't have to hassle you.'' The sheriff paused; his eyes seemed to turn to stone as he studied Will. "You don't stay out of trouble, all bets are off. And this time we'll nail your ass. I promise you that.''

WHEN THE FULL-PAGE AD seeking information about the attack on Mrs. Esterhaus was repeated in the Saturday paper, Libby had the strangest thought.

She was preparing Mrs. E's morning medications when it came to her, and it startled her so she jabbed the plunger of the hypodermic needle and squirted most of the medication into the sink. She had to start over, but her fingers were less than steady the second time.

What if Will Travers hadn't done it?

She banished the thought. She'd seen him. Known exactly who he was. She of all people in town had no reason to doubt.

But the thought continued to nag her as she administered Mrs. E.'s medications, gave her a sponge bath and started their morning physical therapy.

If Will Travers is guilty, why is he wasting money

on advertisements asking for information about the attack?

"I don't have to figure out the way a sick mind works," she said to Mrs. E. as they finished up therapy. "I should certainly know that. Wouldn't you say, Mrs. E.?"

Mrs. E. gave her a benign look, which Libby took as support for her position. Of course that was it. He was back in town, who knew why, trying to throw people off and to get them thinking just as crazily as she was thinking right now. He'd mentioned his son. Maybe it was just some grandiose scheme to look good in his son's eyes.

As she did every week, Libby took Saturday afternoon off when a nurse came up from Roanoke to take over for the rest of the day. She seldom had big plans. Sometimes a hike through the woods, an idea that made her feel edgy today. Sometimes shopping or a game of tennis with Meg. She and Meg had been in high school together, went off to college together and came home together. The difference between them was that Meg still had high hopes for the future. Libby had accepted the fact that her future was likely to be a lot like the present. That suited her. It didn't suit Meg. Meg's unwillingness to settle for what life seemed to have brought them sometimes made their friendship uncomfortable for Libby. But Libby was loyal and she did appreciate the breaks in routine her friendship with Meg afforded her. Meg supervised the spa facilities at Heritage Manor and could usually line up a court.

This afternoon Libby put Meg off.

"But it's going to be a perfect afternoon," Meg said when she called. "Come on. One set. We won't have too many more days like this before winter hits."

"I know," Libby said. "But I need to do other things."

That wasn't true, and Libby didn't like to tell even little white fibs. But she knew why Meg was so insistent. Meg proved her right with her next breath.

"Then let's meet at Sweet Ida's after your errands," she said. "We need to talk."

"No, we don't."

Sweet Ida's Tea Room would be full on a Saturday afternoon, and Libby didn't feel like seeing anyone. Didn't feel like having them see her. Stare at her.

"I knew it," Meg said. "You're fretting about that thing in the paper. Libby, you already stay cooped up in that house with that crazy old lady ninety percent of the time. I can't—"

"She's not crazy."

She heard Meg sigh. It was an irritated sigh. Meg was often short on patience. She said Libby was a good influence that way.

"I know she's not crazy," Meg said. "She's impaired. She's disabled. And you're her angel of mercy. But you don't have to bury yourself down there with her. You could get temporary nurses to fill in more often. You could get the estate to hire a night nurse. Libby, you do this on purpose."

"I do not." But in her heart Libby knew it was true.

"The heck you don't. Now listen, you can't let this guy scare you just because he's back in town and getting everybody worked up."

"I won't."

She had made up her mind about that. He could only frighten her if she allowed him to. And she had no intention of giving him that kind of power over her. She'd worked too hard all these years to get rid of her fear.

"Good. But we still need to talk."

"I'm going over to Dad's," she said. That wasn't true, either, but the excuse worked. Meg gave up her efforts to coerce Libby into an outing, although she did promise—threaten, actually—to come by one evening the following week.

"We *will* talk," Meg vowed.

As Libby hung up, she noticed that her hand was still trembling. It had been ever since Meg mentioned going to Sweet Ida's, ever since she'd thought about all the people who might be staring at her. Would they expect her to react the way she'd reacted all those years ago when she'd seen Will Travers on the street after the trial?

Her parents had been pretending that everything was back to normal. They'd taken her to the afternoon matinee—the Bijou was still open on weekends twenty years ago. The dark theater had made Libby feel fidgety, but she hadn't said anything. She didn't want to worry her parents any more; she knew they'd already worried plenty.

When they walked out of the theater, the first person she'd seen had been Will Travers. He was waiting in line to buy a ticket, his hands shoved into his pockets, that glare still on his face. Libby had frozen.

Then he'd looked at her, his gaze making her weak-kneed with terror all over again. But this time there was no judge, no lawyer, no Ozzie Wiedermann to protect her.

She'd tried to move, to run, to look away. But she'd only been able to cry. All those tears she'd bottled up since the night Mrs. E. was hurt had spilled out, turning to hysteria as she gave up the control that had seen her through the trial.

Everyone in town, it seemed to Libby, had seen her out of control and hysterical in front of the Bijou Theater. For years the kids at school hadn't let her forget the humiliation.

Libby shivered. What if she lost control again? The notion had haunted her for years. And now, thanks to Will Travers, the fear was back. Maybe Meg was right. Maybe she did need to talk to someone about all this, make sure there wasn't something else she needed to do. Maybe she could swear out a warrant of some kind, requiring Will Travers to stay away from Mrs. E.'s house. Keep him off Old Oak Street entirely. Her dad would know. And if she saw her dad, she wouldn't even have been fibbing to Meg.

Noah Jeffries still lived next door, although the old house was way too big now that his daughter stayed with Mrs. E. and his wife was no longer living. But he spent less time alone now than he had right after Charlotte Jeffries died. Now he spent more of his free time with Vera Templeton.

Like this afternoon.

"I'm sorry," Libby said when she followed her dad into the kitchen and saw Vera puttering around, pulling a bag of flour and a bottle of vanilla flavoring out of a cupboard. "I can come some other time."

"Oh, no," Vera said, stopping in the middle of the kitchen with the flour and flavoring in her hands. She looked at Noah. Vera rarely looked directly at Libby.

"No need for that," Noah said, pulling out one of the kitchen chairs and gesturing to it. "Vera's making a pound cake. You should hang around. Hers are worth waiting for."

Libby sat, hoping the action would hide the misgivings that crossed her face. Pound cake. Noah Jeffries shouldn't even be eating pound cake, not with his cholesterol level. Then there was the last comment. *Hers are worth waiting for.* Mom never could make a pound cake that was fit to eat.

But Libby refused to let herself bristle. Vera Templeton, who had been a widow better than ten years, had made her dad happy this past year. Vera was slender and well dressed, even if her smile was a little timid and her hair a little determinedly black for someone who must be closing in on sixty.

While Vera beat eggs and creamed sugar and butter, Libby and her father made small talk. The early fall, the prediction for winter—heavy snow was coming, said all the woolly-worm watchers—the outlook for the high-school football team.

"New quarterback," Noah said, shaking his head and dribbling extra cream into his coffee. "A rebuilding year. We could lose a lot of games."

Libby took the cream out of her father's hand and shook her head at his wheedling expression.

"But he was strong on the junior varsity team," she said. She always made a point of reading the *Courier* sports pages; she'd started that in high school. Noah Jeffries had taken his daughter to work with him one day, and she'd realized how much he liked talking sports with the guys in the warehouse.

She would never forget the delight and surprise on his face when she'd asked him, a week later, who he thought would win the baseball playoffs and wind up in the World Series.

Noah waved a dismissive hand. "JV—it's a whole different ball game. If he thinks he's got what it takes against an experienced defense, they'll kill 'im."

Libby smiled; she knew what was coming next.

"And if he lets them intimidate him, they'll kill 'im then, too."

The small talk continued as the fragrance of baking cake started to fill the kitchen. If it had been anyone but Vera Templeton, Libby would have thought it odd that no one had mentioned Will Travers's return. In fact, Libby caught her dad's worried glance once and knew he wondered how both his daughter and his lady friend were reacting. But he wouldn't bring it up any more than either of them would.

After all, Vera was one of the members of the jury that had set Will free.

Libby had never been able to ask Vera about the trial, and Vera never talked about it, either.

When the cake came out to cool, Libby stood and began saying her goodbyes. But Noah waved her back into the chair. "Not yet, Lib. Stay a few more minutes."

"I'd like to, Dad, but I've got to do a few things before I go back to Mrs. E.'s."

"Just a couple minutes, okay? We've...we've got some news, Vera and me."

A little bubble of apprehension welled up in Libby's chest. Noah looked embarrassed. Vera bit her lower lip and clutched her coffee cup.

"Oh?"

"Yeah. Well." He reached over and awkwardly took Vera's hand in his. "We're going to get... engaged."

The little bubble expanded. Libby looked at her dad's dear face and saw the worry there as he studied her face in return. She didn't have the heart to show anything but support for what he wanted. She might have mixed feelings about having anyone take her mother's place, but the most important thing was seeing her dad happy again after five lonely years.

"Oh, Dad," she said softly, "that's wonderful. I'm so happy for you."

He looked delighted. "Yeah?"

"Yeah."

She gave him a big hug, followed by a more reserved hug for Vera Templeton. They chatted a few more minutes, long enough for Libby to learn that they hadn't yet set a date and hadn't yet decided whether to live in Vera's house or Noah's house or sell them both and get one that was exclusively their own. They looked shyly excited as they talked about the possibilities, and Libby ignored the void in her heart as she considered the possibility of seeing strangers move into the home where she'd grown up. Actually, she told herself, it might be nice to see kids running in the yard again. Maybe they would spruce up the old swing set in the backyard. That might be nice. She smiled.

"Why don't I cook you dinner next Saturday night to celebrate," she said as she moved toward the front door.

"Sure, sure," Noah said. "That'd be great."

Noah followed Libby out. He caught her on the porch, his hand on her elbow. "You're really okay with this?"

"I promise."

"I mean, I know Vera may not ever be like a mother to you, but—"

"Dad, she's a nice lady and she makes you

happy." It was true. Noah looked years younger than he had fourteen months ago, before another couple at church fixed him up with Vera in a bridge foursome. Being with her had restored him.

"Okay. If you're sure." He gave her another hug. "Say, there's something else, too. About this guy Travers. I hear he's back."

She nodded.

"You worried about it?"

Her need to talk to him about it, to find out what he thought she should do, surfaced. But this wasn't the time. Not with Vera here. Not as a follow-up to their happy news.

"Dad, it was a long time ago."

Noah gave her a long, hard look. A skeptical look. "You need anything, you call. I'm right next door, you know, little girl."

She smiled. He always called her "little girl" when he was worried about her, even though she was twenty-eight.

She waved goodbye and started toward Ridge Lane. It was late afternoon, a cloudless, crisp autumn afternoon when the sky was so blue it wouldn't have been believable in a watercolor. The shops would be closing soon, but she had a few minutes to wander around, peek in windows, give her legs a bit of a workout.

She stopped for a half pound of melt-away mints at the candy store, Mrs. E.'s favorites. She bought muffins for the week at the bakery and checked out three historical novels at the library, also Mrs. E.'s favorites. She ran into Clem Weeks in front of her garage and stopped for a chat.

"Seems strange to see you in civilian clothes," Clem said, gesturing to the creased navy slacks and matching cardigan Libby wore. "About as strange as I'd look without my overalls, I guess."

Libby smiled and nodded. It was hard to imagine Clem without her grease-streaked overalls and baseball cap. It struck her for a moment that Clem might be cute if she weren't such a grease monkey.

"But it does make life simple, doesn't it?" she said. "Not worrying about fashion, I mean."

Clem nodded and slapped a wrench against her palm. "Yeah, that's for sure."

Libby could tell that Clem was working up the courage to suggest they get together sometime and wondered how she could avoid it. Granted, they had plenty in common—Clem's childhood had been as tough as Libby's. And they both hid behind their work and their shyness. She knew Clem must be hungry for a friend in a town that still remembered the details of her unhappy upbringing. But Libby couldn't imagine being that friend, told herself she didn't feel that hunger at all. Besides, what in the world would they talk about? Carburetors and cardiograms?

Then again, it might be nice to have a friend who understood her, someone different from Meg. Meg drew her out, but sometimes her inability to understand how Libby felt about things frustrated Libby.

With that thought in mind, she latched onto the

first idea that came to her. "Say, Clem, I was wondering. I know you're busy, but..."

She hesitated. Clem looked hopeful. Libby
plunged ahead. "About a car. I don't have one. And
I was thinking maybe I should."

Clem's eyes brightened. "Sure. That's a swell
idea, Libby."

"But I don't know much about cars. And I was
thinking, maybe you could look around for me. I
mean, I'm not in any hurry." The truth was, she'd
never had the least interest in a car. But maybe it
would smooth the way, give them something to talk
about for a while. "But if you ran across something,
well, you could let me know."

Clem fidgeted with her wrench. "Yeah, I could
do that."

So they talked a few more minutes, and when
Libby walked away, she didn't feel so guilty. Or
quite so alone.

She debated going to the chapel in the woods near
Heritage Manor for a few minutes before the sun
went down, but she still felt uneasy about being
alone in the woods. A week ago she'd never worried
about being alone anywhere in Hope Springs.

She reminded herself of her determination not to
give Will Travers any power over her. She headed
up the steep, narrow steps to the cobblestone path
that ran parallel to Ridge Lane. A few hundred yards
along the path and she would be at the trail leading
to the old chapel. The chapel, built during the Civil
War so the young daughter of the town's most

prominent family could pray for the safety of her lover, was mostly in ruins now. But Libby liked the quiet and the peace of the spot. This time of day she would likely find it empty.

Before she reached the top of the stairs, she saw a pair of boots ahead of her, poised to leave the cobblestone path. Smiling, she let her gaze travel up the boots and jeans and workshirt to see who was waiting for her to pass before starting his descent.

The man at the top of the steps was Will Travers.

She gasped, almost lost her balance on the narrow stairs and swayed backward. She dropped her packages when she grabbed for the handrail, and they tumbled down the stairs. She couldn't take her eyes off him.

The path was shadowy; the sun was lower than she'd realized. He loomed over her, dark and forbidding. She took a step back, concentrating on placing her foot carefully. *No need to panic.* She was only a few feet off Ridge Lane. Keys jangled as shopkeepers closed up. Last-minute shoppers scurried along the sidewalk. *No need to panic.*

He took a step in her direction. Her heart pounded painfully.

"I'm not going to hurt you," he said. "There's nothing to be afraid of."

His voice sounded almost pleading. Once again she found herself wondering, doubting what she knew to be true.

Mrs. Esterhaus had trusted him, too.

"You'd be a fool to lay a hand on me," she said

as firmly as she could manage. "You'd never get away with it."

He almost seemed to smile then, a wry twist of his lips that held no humor. "I don't hurt people."

A flash of anger overpowered her fear. She tossed her head defiantly. "Tell that to Mrs. Esterhaus."

"I'd like to. I want to see her."

"Never."

He moved then, so swiftly she didn't have time to react. His hand shot out, trapped the fist still clutching the railing. His palm was warm, tough with calluses. His flesh on hers made her shiver.

"She was good to me," he said.

The simple words had the effect of defusing her intense fear at his touch. His words, and the electric current in his touch, almost stripped her of her anxiety. She looked up at him and saw something she'd never before noticed in his brooding gaze. Pain. Anguish. She couldn't look away.

Libby knew his words were true, because she'd been on the receiving end of Mrs. E's goodness herself. And she knew the emotions she saw in his eyes were true, too. Because... She didn't know why. Logic insisted otherwise. But she knew. And wanted to understand.

"All these years," he said, his voice suddenly gruff, "it's killed me to think she believed I would do something like that to her."

Libby felt the most insane urge to comfort him, to reassure him that Mrs. Esterhaus didn't believe anything, couldn't believe anything. She wanted to

soothe that deep furrow off his brow, to comfort that
hoarseness from his voice.

Then she remembered Mrs. E.'s agitation when
she'd mentioned Will Travers. Even in a mind that
had no conscious thought, the unconscious obviously never forgot.

She had no intention of allowing him close
enough to Mrs. Esterhaus to dredge up more memories of pain and fear.

"Stay away from her," she said. "You owe her
that much."

Then she snatched her hand back, turned and hurried down the steps.

CHAPTER FIVE

RELIEF AND GRATITUDE flooded Will as he took the list of addresses from his new boss. Both emotions were shortlived. As soon as he looked at the addresses where he was expected to work that day, he knew he was in trouble.

Second on the list was the home of Alice Esterhaus.

He nodded, shoved the list in his shirt pocket and walked out the door of Preston Realty.

What now? he wondered.

The job offer had seemed like a godsend, a message meant to counteract all the other messages he'd received since returning to Hope Springs. He'd answered every Help Wanted ad he was remotely qualified to fill, from clerking at Hurd's Hardware to driving a delivery truck part-time for the consortium of galleries and antique shops along Ridge Lane. Everywhere he'd applied, someone knew him. He recognized the look as soon as he saw it.

Lainey Waterson, who ran Antique Alley and headed up the loose-knit consortium of small-business owners in town, had at first looked startled, then sympathetic. She'd been in high school with him and had become an elegant-looking woman.

"Will, I'm going to level with you," she'd said
without even passing him a copy of the job application. "There's no way I could convince the consortium to hire you. You'll be wasting my time and
yours even filling out the application."

"That's probably illegal," he said stiffly.

"I know. But it's also reality." She'd followed
him to the door of her little shop. "Somebody will
give you a chance, Will. Hope Springs is like that.
But the person we need will be going into people's
homes. Even if we gave you a chance and someone
found out…"

She shrugged and held the door open as he left.

Not everyone was as nice as Lainey. And by the
end of his first full week back in Hope Springs, Will
was discouraged. At least in D.C. he'd been able to
support his son. Here, starvation looked like a dis-
tinct possibility.

So the night he let Kyle talk him into dinner at
the Tex-a-Tavern restaurant, Will was wondering
what his next move should be.

The people who ran the restaurant were nice to
them; their children knew Kyle from school. Will
saw the curious stares from others in the restaurant,
but tried to focus on the friendly familiarity of Luisita Mendoza and her family as they ate tacos and
refried beans that were better than any he'd had in
Washington.

"You have a good boy," Luisita said. "My Juan
tells me he is the pet of the teacher."

"Is that so?" When Luisita went to refill tea

glasses at another table, he looked at his son, whose eyes were trained on his plate. Kyle began to pick at his taco. "So, the teacher likes you?"

"No."

"According to Juan, she does."

"That's 'cause Juan doesn't understand."

"Doesn't understand what?"

"Nothing."

Will clenched his teeth. Just once he'd like to have a conversation with the boy that didn't require a court order to get a simple answer to a simple question. "Doesn't understand what?"

Kyle heaved an exasperated sigh. "Mrs. Foster, she put my desk right in front of hers. That's all."

"Were you misbehaving?"

"No."

"Then what was it?"

Kyle shoved half the taco into his mouth.

"If you don't tell me, I'll have to ask Mrs. Foster myself."

Kyle glared at him as he chewed the oversize bite of taco. When he finally swallowed, he said, "The other kids were bugging me. That's why."

"Bugging you how?"

"Just bugging me. I'm gonna play the machines, okay?"

Without waiting for his father's reply, Kyle jumped up from the booth, fished a quarter out of his pocket and dropped it into one of the arcade games lining the far wall. Although he itched to know what kind of "bugging" from other kids had prompted a teacher to single out his son, Will decided not to push it. There was only so much he could expect to learn from Kyle. The more he pushed, the more Kyle shut him out.

Besides, he knew without asking why the kids were bugging his son.

He finished his meal in silence, then stood in line to pay. He ended up behind Lainey Waterson and a friend, who spotted him when they turned around to leave. Lainey smiled at him, a welcome surprise.

"Hi, Will. Any luck yet?"

"Not yet."

"Soon," she said.

"Sure, soon."

Then her gaze strayed over his shoulder. She hesitated. "Say, Bama. Are you and Torrence still looking for someone to handle maintenance for the properties you manage?"

And that was how Will Travers ended up working for Preston Realty. Bama and Torrence Preston were new to Hope Springs, which meant they'd only been in town nine years. But Will made sure they knew he'd once been charged with attempted murder. It seemed pointless to hire on only to have them hear about him from someone else a week later and have to fire him. So he told them about the trial. Bama heard the story, shrugged and said, "And they found you not guilty? Is that what you're saying?"

"That's right."

"And you didn't do it. You said yourself you're

hoping to find out who really committed the assault now that you're back in town.''

''That's right.''

Bama plucked off an oversize earring as the phone rang. ''Then I don't see the problem. It's ancient history for one thing. And you're an innocent man for another.'' She answered the phone with a wave that said his worries carried no weight with her.

Will would never have believed how his heart contracted just to hear someone call him an innocent man. He'd harbored the words in his heart for so long, always afraid to speak them for fear that whoever heard them would reject them. The way Paul had. To hear them spoken aloud by someone else was almost painful, so deeply and unexpectedly did they strike him.

And now this. Alice Esterhaus's home was on the list of properties they managed. With a sick feeling, Will realized the only information he'd failed to include when he told Bama Preston about his history was *who* he'd been charged with assaulting.

Maybe he should walk right back into the office, give the list back to Bama Preston and resign before he created any trouble for her and her husband.

He postponed a decision. He went to the first job on the list, telling himself he could decide later what to do about the house on Old Oak Street. He was to install storm windows on the first job. Wrestling with the heavy windows alone wasn't easy and served as a good distraction. Physical labor had al-

ways been that way for him, a sort of moving med-
itation. He tuned out everything but his body, then
he listened to it and flowed with it. Nothing mattered
but the fluid strain of muscle and bone and tendon.
His mind emptied and left him free. Free of doubts,
free of anger, free of his past.

It was like that today. He almost regretted the
moment the windows were in, clean and secure and
ready to face the winter.

He looked at his list again. Mrs. E.'s house was
next.

He skipped to the third place on the list. The funeral home had a leak in the roof that needed patch-
ing. He worked through lunch.

No more stalling. He had to either go to Mrs.
Esterhaus's or go back to Bama Preston and resign.

THE BLUE RIDGE ACADEMY for Girls had no classes
on Wednesday afternoons. The time was set aside
for extracurricular activities, which were strongly
encouraged for the 323 girls who came to the academy from moneyed families up and down the East-
ern seaboard.

Those extracurricular activities—things such as
the drama club and the debating club and the literary
society—were organized by different teachers. So
even though there were no classes, most of the
teachers hung out in the lounge until it was time for
their club or organization to meet. While they
waited, they played at grading papers or finishing up
lesson plans. But their main activity was rubbing

elbows with the other instructors—comparing notes on the girls, complaining about stiff-necked headmaster Larry Templeton and generally gossiping about anything that came to mind.

Paul Travers was the only teacher at Blue Ridge Academy who didn't head up one of the organizations intended to turn out well-rounded young women. He refused and Larry Templeton didn't push it, which had caused some resentment and much surprise among the rest of the staff. So Paul never stuck around on Wednesday afternoons. It sometimes occurred to him that it made him a prime target for their gossip.

He was used to that.

Sometimes, as he cleared his desk and hefted his frayed canvas backpack, he heard the staff head down the hall toward the lounge, chatting and laughing like a gaggle of the adolescent girls they taught. Sometimes he longed to be part of it. To have someone to laugh with and joke with and just feel connected to somehow.

He hadn't done any of those things in so long he wouldn't remember how even if he'd had the chance. He rarely missed it anymore.

Today was one of those rare days when he did. Probably because Will was back, bringing old wounds to the surface again. Damn Will, anyway.

Unsettling things clattered around in Paul's head as he exited the building and unlocked his truck. He watched the others leave sometimes and had noted he was the only one on the staff who locked his vehicle. The necessity to lock up hadn't reached Hope Springs yet.

That didn't stop Paul, however.

Unsettling things continued bumping against each other in his head. He plugged in a cassette of Motown hits from the sixties and cranked up the volume. Most of the time he would sing along.

Today he barely listened.

He hadn't imagined Will would look so old. Creases in his forehead, fine lines around his eyes. Rough and weathered for a thirty-eight-year-old.

The image he always conjured up of Will—on those rare occasions when he couldn't keep the images at bay—was always the young, stormy-faced Will who had stared out over the courtroom so belligerently. He'd hated that Will. It helped to keep that Will in mind.

He turned up the music.

Or there was the Will who taught him how to box when they were fourteen and eleven, respectively. Will's face still round and smooth, his eyes still clear and bright. No frowns, no darkness.

He'd loved that Will. He couldn't bear to let that Will in for long.

He punched the button to eject the cassette and started station hopping, listening for a better distraction.

Paul's pickup was like a cowboy's horse. If he gave it its head at the end of the day, it found its way home automatically. But he looked up now and realized he was nowhere near his isolated cabin. He was parked in the gravel drive in front of the old house where he'd grown up.

His heart leaped. He glanced around for signs of Will, saw none. He was alone, at least.

He was tempted to kill the engine, to swing out of the truck and walk around. The place looked ragged at the edges. His fault, he supposed. He should've been keeping it up.

To hell with that, he thought, hands still clamped on the steering wheel. *It should've been mine. I was the one who stayed. I was the one who stood by her and kept my nose clean and tried to give her a son she could be proud of.*

Look where that had gotten him. In the same boat as the son who'd cut her life short.

It broke her heart seeing the rift between you two, son. That's what Melvin Guthry had said when Paul had demanded an explanation of his mother's will. *She hoped it'd mend things, bring you two together again.*

Paul slammed the gearshift into reverse and gunned the engine. *To hell with that.*

LIBBY KEPT ONE EYE on the windows and doors.

No matter where she was in the house, no matter what she was doing in the days that followed Will Travers's return, she remained alert to any noise, any movement outside the house on Old Oak Street. For years the house had been her haven. A safe place. With Will Travers's return, it had become the place where she was incarcerated with her worst nightmare.

The thump of the newspaper on the front steps was ominous. The noisy engine of a passing vehicle gave her pause. A clumsy bird bumping a window stopped her heart.

When someone pounded on her door, she had to force herself to walk down the hallway and peer through the white lace curtains. This afternoon it was Meg, standing there in a warm-up suit, glancing around impatiently. She looked relieved when Libby opened the front door.

"What took you? I thought maybe you'd flown the coop."

Impatient herself with the intrusion, Libby invited her friend in. She saw no reason to tell Meg that she was simply being cautious. It rankled to admit she felt the need to be cautious here in Hope Springs.

"I *am* working, you know," she said.

Meg walked toward the kitchen. "Got coffee?"

Libby double-checked the dead bolt and followed Meg, who had already located a mug and was pouring a cup of coffee. "That's left over from this morning," she warned.

Meg shrugged, but grimaced as she took a swallow. "Girl, this is strong enough to stop a cat fight."

Libby sat at the kitchen table. She always felt uneasy at disruptions in her routine; she sometimes felt uneasy having people in the house with her. She was accustomed to the solitude. But she knew Meg would come out quickly enough with her reason for being here.

Meg boosted herself onto the counter and looked down at her friend over the rim of her coffee mug. "He's looking for work, you know. All over town."

Libby didn't have to ask whom Meg was referring to. She pursed her lips and tried not to react. "I guess that means he's staying."

"He's not having much luck."

Libby nodded. Her shoulders began to tense, despite her efforts to remain calm.

"What'll you do if he stays?"

The idea of Will Travers in town to stay snapped sharply in Libby's head. She couldn't think clearly for a moment; so many feelings and impressions were suddenly colliding in her mind.

"He can't do that." Her voice sounded hollow and far away to her. She realized, in some vague way, that Meg was studying her intently.

"Are you okay?"

Libby intended to nod. But she found she couldn't. All she could think of was the glowering look in Will Travers's dark eyes.

"Maybe you ought to ask your dad to move over here for a while," Meg said. "Just until you see how things shake down. Or you could have an alarm system installed. You should definitely do that."

Meg went on, ticking off ideas. Libby didn't register them. What was the point? She couldn't quite imagine safeguarding herself from Will Travers. Whatever she did, he could overcome it. She'd believed that for so long it was impossible to think otherwise now.

"Libby, are you even—"

Another pounding on the front door. Libby jumped. She looked at her friend. Meg seemed spooked, too, then she grinned sheepishly. Libby forced herself up out of her chair and down the hall. Meg was right behind her.

The hulking shadow beyond the lace curtain was Will Travers. She knew it right away.

"Omigosh." Meg's breathless whisper reflected the fear running cold in Libby's veins. "Is that him? Libby, that's not him, is it?"

Libby nodded.

"You don't have to answer," Meg said, still whispering. "We can call the sheriff. Libby, don't..."

Refusing to give in to her fear, Libby swung the front door open. He stood there, a slip of paper in his hand. He was trying his hardest to terrify her.

She wasn't having it.

"I told you to stay away," she said, stepping toward him, making eye contact, the way the self-defense expert on "Oprah" had said to do. "What are you doing here?"

She heard Meg's gasp behind her.

He wouldn't meet her eyes. He held out the paper in his hand. "I'm working for the Prestons."

"So?"

"I'm supposed to do yard work here today. And tomorrow—"

"Bama Preston *sent* you? Sent you *here?*"

She was incredulous. She snatched the paper from his hand, proud of herself for having the gumption to get that close to him. Sure enough, what he had was a piece of Preston Realty stationery with instructions for work at three locations around Hope Springs. One of the locations was right here at 23 Old Oak Street. She felt violated. The violation fed her anger.

"Bama Preston hired you?"

He nodded. "I wanted to let you know before I got started."

"You wait right here." She pointed at his feet. "Don't move."

She backed into the house, bumping into Meg in the process, and locked the door behind her. She went for the portable phone and dialed while she walked. The phone rang. Meg stood at the door, frozen, her tanned face drained of color. Libby walked back and peered through the curtains. He still stood where she'd left him. She let her breath out. She'd stood up to him. No more running.

Bama Preston confirmed that Will Travers was working for them, doing maintenance and landscaping at the properties they managed in the county. Libby felt her anger rise, but reminded herself that the Prestons were new to Hope Springs.

"You probably don't know this," Libby said, trying to keep the quiver out of her voice, "but Will Travers is the man responsible for the condition Mrs. Esterhaus is in."

There was a brief silence on the line. "That's who he was accused of assaulting? Mrs. Esterhaus?"

"He tried to kill her," Libby said tightly.

Bama sounded horrified. "I am so sorry, Libby. It was our understanding that Mr. Travers was acquitted."

Libby went hot all over. Her fault, her fault, her fault. She could barely swallow the rage that choked her in order to reply.

"He did it."

"Listen, if we've been misled, I'm terribly sorry. But Lainey Waterson and Mr. Travers both said he'd been acquitted. Are you saying he was convicted?"

"That doesn't matter. He did it."

Another silence. "By law, I can't discriminate against a man because there are people in town who don't like the verdict of a jury. Miss Jeffries, this was twenty years ago, wasn't it? Isn't it time to let it go?"

Libby punched the off switch without a reply. It all sounded reasonable. She knew better.

She looked outside. He had turned to the banister, leaned against it and was staring toward the street.

"I'm stuck with him," she said to Meg, keeping her voice as firm as possible.

"That can't be, Libby!"

Maybe Bama Preston was right, she thought, studying once again the way he held his ground there on the porch, like a wild animal on alert, ready for instant flight. Maybe the law said Will Travers had every right in the world to be here on Mrs. E.'s property, scaring the living daylights out of Libby, but if that was his plan, she had no intention of giving him the satisfaction.

She opened the door and walked out, ignoring the hand Meg reached out to block her. He turned to face her, slowly.

"Do your work," she said. "And be quick about it."

"There's a lot to be done. The yard. Roof work. It may take several days. A week."

Her insides cringed. "Then you'd better get busy."

She watched him walk down the front steps and out to the dusty black truck parked in front of the house. He retrieved some tools and came back through the gateless fence. He looked up at her and said, "I'm going to show you that you can trust me, Libby Jeffries. I'm going to show you I'm not somebody you have to fear."

She wanted to tell him it would be a cold day in the netherworld before she ever trusted the likes of him, but she didn't. Not, she told herself, because she was afraid of his reaction. But because she had made up her mind not to let him provoke her. She'd show him a cool, unperturbed exterior. Maybe if there was no thrill to be had from frightening her, he'd lose interest and take his game somewhere else.

Meg at first refused to leave her alone with Will Travers on the property, although she had an appointment at the spa in half an hour. But Libby assured her she would be fine. "He's just trying to scare me,'' she said firmly. ''I'm not giving in to that, Meg.''

''But—''

''You have work to do. Go. I'll be fine.''

''But—''

''He wouldn't dare do anything. Not now. You know he's here. Bama Preston knows he's here. He's not stupid, Meg.''

''Libby, I—''

''Go. I'll be fine. I'm not going to let him throw my whole world into a tailspin.''

Meg left. Libby watched her go, wondering if her show of bravado would come back to haunt her. From safely behind the locked windows, she kept an eye on him the rest of the afternoon.

He started in the back, clearing the row of hedges that had grown into a wild tangle of vines and briars around the perimeter of the yard. The hedges where she'd seen him ditch the fireplace poker on that spring night twenty years ago. Her heart pounded unsteadily when she thought of it.

He worked hard, his body in continuous motion, his movements methodical but fluid. After the first hour he took off his sweat-drenched shirt and she could see that he was all lean sinew. His back and chest and arms were golden, despite the fact the summer was long gone. His hair was dark with perspiration, his torso slick with it. But he never slowed down, never paused to rest.

When she realized there was something in her that admired the way he worked and the picture he made while he did it, she turned away from the window and forbade herself to return.

But she continued to be aware of his presence, the way you knew a blizzard was bearing down from the smell in the air, the color of the sky.

He knocked on the door at the end of the afternoon. She hesitated. She had no choice. Unless she wanted him to know he still terrified her.

"Yes?"

"I finished the back hedge."

That needed no reply that she could see. Did he expect a thank-you? Praise?

"I'll be back in the morning to finish up the yard work."

"There's more?"

"Is eight too early?"

"I'll be ready." His T-shirt was streaked with dirt and perspiration. His hair was slicked back, also damp, his face ruddy from exertion. His arms seemed to have swelled with his efforts. Libby felt as if a flock of hummingbirds had been unleashed high in her chest. Light-headedness overtook her. She tightened her grip on the door. She wasn't accustomed to being around men.

He nodded. "Thanks."

"Thanks?"

He rubbed at the soil caked around his short, neatly trimmed nails. "For not getting me fired."

"Yet," she said sharply.

His eyes met hers now. Challenging her. "You'll see."

She didn't flinch from his gaze. "Don't waste your time, Will Travers."

He drove off. She felt the tension she'd been carrying in her neck and shoulders ever since he'd arrived; it didn't dissipate. She was worn-out. And she still had to run to the drugstore.

Maybe, while she was at it, she would stop by the municipal building and have a word with Sheriff Tillman. She would do whatever she had to do to get Will Travers fired. She would take out her own full-page ad and remind everybody in town what he'd done. She would go to the town council. She would raise such a ruckus Will Travers would have to get out of town again.

Mrs. Ryan came from across the street to keep an eye on Mrs. E. Libby promised to return within the hour. Then she marched toward Ridge Lane, refusing to give in to her urge to look over her shoulder, behind every shrub. Voices startled her as she passed the schoolyard. She realized quickly they were the voices of children, but the tone of those voices still made her pause. They sounded ugly and mean.

"He's a jailbird," taunted one of the little boys.

"Is not!"

"Is, too. And you're just a jailbird's kid."

The taunting made Libby uneasy. She remembered taunting from her own childhood. Adults had never spoken against her for her inability to tell a jury what she'd seen, but children had not been so compassionate. She peered over the fence.

Four little boys stood in a semicircle in the basketball court. Backed up against the pole, glaring at them with dark venom, was a little boy she recognized as Kyle Travers. Her heart gave another jolt. Will's son.

"He's a killer and a jailbird, and you'd end up just like him except you're such a chicken."

With those words the little boy who'd spoken gave Kyle a shove. Kyle raised his fists. The foursome advanced menacingly.

"Kyle!"

Libby's voice froze the little boys bent on terrorizing Will's son. Four mean little faces turned toward the grown-up voice and became masks of unconvincing innocence before they took off in a cloud of playground dust.

Only Kyle remained. He still looked venomous, or as venomous as an eight-year-old with silky blond hair, freckles and a missing front tooth could look.

"I was gonna kick their butts," he declared.

"I see." She bent to pick up a red vinyl windbreaker fluttering in the schoolyard dust. "I'm Libby."

"I know. You're a nurse."

"That's right." She smiled at him. He didn't smile back. "I need somebody to help me carry things home from the drugstore. Interested in earning a dollar?"

He shrugged and leaned over to gather up the things that had spilled out of his schoolbag.

"I'm not scared of them," he said when he reached her side.

"Good. They're just bullies."

He walked beside her. He smelled faintly of grape soda and chalk dust. She smiled. His hair was like corn silk, so long it covered his eyebrows. She wanted to brush it back. She wasn't sure how old he was, but he'd been smaller than the other boys. He might like to think he was tough, but they could've made mincemeat out of him.

Maybe they had, anyway. Without ever laying a hand on him. She remembered how that was, how much it hurt.

He stared at the ground as he walked. She remembered his mother's funeral. He'd worn a little black suit and a clip-on bow tie that sat askew on a collar that swallowed his thin neck. It had broken her heart to see him.

Maybe there was no justice, not in this world, at least. Maybe Libby was responsible for that. But she didn't have to add to the ugliness and in the process guarantee that this motherless boy became one more victim of his father's crime.

She wouldn't cause more trouble for Will Travers. She wouldn't talk to Sheriff Tillman. She would hang tough. She would keep her eyes open. And she would do what she could to see that nobody else got hurt. Not Mrs. E. Not herself. And certainly not a little boy who didn't know he hadn't a prayer of kicking butt.

CHAPTER SIX

WILL WAS ENCOURAGED as he went up the walk to the Esterhaus home, hedge trimmer dangling awkwardly from one hand. He'd talked to Melvin Guthry during his lunch hour.

The attorney who'd represented him at his trial was retired now, living in a farmhouse at the foot of one of the many waterfalls spilling and trickling through the woods surrounding Hope Springs. He'd been fishing from the creek bank when Will drove up.

He hadn't looked surprised or alarmed when he saw Will. His eyes had crinkled in pleasure as he set aside his rod and rolled down the sleeves of the old blue oxford-cloth shirt he wore.

"Mr. Travers," Melvin said. "I'd shake your hand, but I've been baiting hooks. Quite a messy business."

"I remember." Will wasn't sure where to begin. "You must be used to messy business."

"Oh, indeed. And that brings us to the reason for your visit, I presume."

Will remembered liking that about the old man. He hadn't played games. He'd been straightforward. He'd told Will right from the get-go that having a little girl testify she'd seen him leaving Mrs. Ester-haus's at the time of the attack made the likelihood of an acquittal very slim.

"You helped me all those years ago," Will said. "I wasn't feeling very grateful at the time. I don't think I ever thanked you."

"No need. I was doing a job."

Will remembered that, too. Melvin Guthry had made no pretense of believing Will's story. But he'd still been fair and kind and compassionate to a kid who was in a whale of a lot of trouble. He hadn't been judgmental. Will hadn't understood that at the time. Now he knew that some people were simply good-hearted. Melvin Guthry was one of them.

"No, you were kind to me. Not everyone was. I should've been more appreciative."

Melvin put his hand on Will's shoulder and they walked toward the porch of his farmhouse, which looked out over the base of Deep Cove Fall.

"Fear brings out the worst in people, son. Hope Springs wasn't accustomed to violence. Nobody knew how to handle the fear."

They sat in cane-bottom rockers. The water bab-bled sweetly in the distance, answered by a flock of geese making its way south from Canada. For the second time since coming back, Will remembered how soothing nature could be. He felt himself begin to relax.

"Anyway, I've thought lately about how kind you were to me. It only seemed right to say." He gripped the armrests of the rocker. Melvin had already started up a gentle rhythm; Will kept still. "I wondered...is there any way, anything I could do... I want to clear my name."

He felt the old man's assessing gaze focus on him; he remembered how unsettled people on the witness stand had grown under that unyielding stare. He didn't mind it.

"The jury found in your favor."

"But that wasn't enough to clear my name. Not then. Not now. Ask my son."

A shadow of regret passed over Melvin's face. "Ah, yes. Young Kyle. He's finding things difficult."

"Yeah."

Melvin nodded, and Will felt that the old gentleman understood all the things he'd left unsaid.

"You want your son to believe in you."

"Wouldn't you?"

"Indeed I would."

"What can I do, Mr. Guthry?"

Melvin steepled his fingers and brought them to the tip of his nose. He stared out over them at something far beyond the woodland area before them. Will remembered that pose; it always preceded a particularly tough question to someone on the witness stand.

"Did you hurt Mrs. Esterhaus, son?"

The question startled Will. So few people had ever asked. A few, like his mother, had assumed the answer was no. Most, like the police, had assumed the answer was yes. They asked *how* he did it. *Why* he did it. Never *if* he did it.

"You never asked before."

Melvin's smile was wry. "A good attorney never asks if his client is guilty. A good attorney's job is to make sure his client gets the full benefit of his expertise, guilty or not."

Will didn't like that rationale. He knew what it meant. It meant Melvin had likely been in the camp that assumed the answer was yes.

"I didn't do it," he said. "I never raised a hand to Mrs. Esterhaus. I..." He realized there was little he could say to convince someone who didn't want to be convinced. "I could never do that. Especially not to her."

Will's mouth had gone dry and his heart thudded uncomfortably. What if this nice old man rejected his claim of innocence? What if he stated unequivocably that no one in Hope Springs was likely ever to believe him? What if he dashed Will's hopes for good?

When Melvin spoke again, it was gently. "It's been a long time. Records get lost. Memories grow fuzzy. If there had been some tiny bit of information that pointed in another direction, chances are slim today that information would still rise to the surface."

"I have to try."

"I understand. And you're wondering if I can help?"

"I thought... Maybe in your records. Or you might have some ideas what else I could do."

"You've had no response to your advertisement, I take it."

Will shook his head.

"All right. Let me see what records I still have in storage. And I'll talk to Sean Davenport, the young man who's taken over my practice. Sean may have ideas about other avenues we can pursue. But, Will, don't get your hopes up. After all this time, finding the truth will be nothing short of a miracle."

Will got up to leave, but before he walked off the porch, he hesitated. He didn't want to ask the question, but he had to. He had to hear the answer, no matter what it was.

"Does that mean you believe me?"

He couldn't even look at Melvin as he asked. The weight of looking someone in the eye and seeing doubt was more than he could stand right now.

Melvin walked over and put his hand on Will's shoulder again. Even so, Will couldn't bring himself to look up.

"Look at me, son." Then he waited until Will reluctantly complied. "I know people. Too well sometimes, I'm afraid. I never could imagine you doing something like that. I'm glad you're not going to run from it anymore."

So Melvin's kindness, his promise of help and—most of all—his apparent belief in Will's innocence all added up to a heart that was filled with hope by the time Will drove back into town to complete his day's work for Preston Realty.

He put the hedge trimmer on the steps and bounded up them to knock on the front door. Today he would spruce up the front, where shrubs had grown up to obscure the windows and even the front porch. Soon he would install a new gate, then paint it and the picket fence. He looked around. There was no rocker, no porch swing, no sign whatsoever that anyone in this house ever ventured out to enjoy the sunshine, the fresh air, the smell of grass and winter daphne or summer jasmine.

Because of him, he supposed. Because of what everyone believed he did.

Everyone but Melvin Guthry.

Will smiled. It was a start.

The lace curtain over the front door fluttered. He saw the tips of pale fingers, the nails clipped short. Utilitarian hands. A nurse's hands.

The front door opened just enough to frame her face.

He looked at her, really looked at her, for the first time. Her skin was pale, flawless but pale, except for the hint of shadows collecting under her wide eyes. Her eyes were hazel, rimmed in brown. Her lips were a pale pink bow, tipped slightly down at the corners. Her neck was a long, pale column, her shoulder-length hair the color of moonlight. And she was thin. She didn't look up to handling the demands of an invalid.

But her eyes and her jaw were set in a way that

said she wanted him to know she was up to handling him.

"I need to plug in the hedge trimmer," he said, although his head filled with a dozen other things he wanted to say. "Sorry to bother you."

He watched as she slowly drew in air, filling her lungs, then expelled it deliberately.

"I have something to say to you."

Will felt some of his upbeat mood slip away. He doubted Libby Jeffries had anything good to say. "I'm listening."

She glanced back, then opened the door another few inches. Enough to slip out, then she closed it again decisively. She stood with her hand on the doorknob. She looked, he thought, as if she might keel over if she let go.

"I want you to know I understand what you're doing here," she said. "Back in Hope Springs, I mean. I know you're here for Kyle's sake. And I think that's commendable."

Will felt another faint flicker of hope in his chest. What was she telling him? This was the person who'd convinced everyone in town that he was Mrs. Esterhaus's attacker. Maybe if she could be convinced, if she changed her mind...

"I believe in second chances and I believe in rehabilitation," she continued. "Maybe that's why Kyle was put in your life. To give you a second chance. It's not my place to stand in the way of that."

"Listen—"

"I'm not finished," she said, and she seemed to straighten. "I know what you did. But I also know that a jury decided to let you go. Society gave you the benefit of the doubt. I can't prosecute you all on my own. I'm going to leave you alone to get on with your life. Not for your sake, but for Kyle's. He needs this town on his side."

A thread of righteousness ran through her words and her tone of voice, spoiling Will's hopefulness and bringing anger back into his heart.

"Well, isn't that big of you, Miss Judge and Jury."

She flinched visibly. But she stood her ground.

"What you mean is, you won't try to have me run out of town on a rail."

"If that's how you choose to view it."

"As long as there isn't a rash of people getting their heads bashed in in Hope Springs."

She flinched again, but again she didn't back off. "That wasn't necessary."

"And your holier-than-thou little speech wasn't necessary, either," he said, even as he admired her courage.

"Yes, it was," she said. "I wanted you to know where I stand. I wanted you to know that I'm not...afraid of you. This is about Kyle, not about you or me."

He saw from her hesitation that she might be claiming not to be afraid of him, but it was a lie. She was terrified of him. She believed he was a would-be killer, yet she was standing here face-to-face, confronting him. Challenging him, even.

For the sake of his son.

For a moment his anger yielded to his appreciation for anyone who would stand up for his son. And he had to admit, her courage impressed him. He'd been impressed with her courage before, when she was just a little girl. She'd been wrong, but she'd been brave.

But as he studied her again, it occurred to him that Libby Jeffries was no longer a child. She was a woman, pretty in a quiet way. A woman he ought to be ashamed of terrorizing and snapping at.

She was still wrong, but she was brave nevertheless.

And he might still be right, but that didn't make it any easier when people looked at him and saw a monster. It made him frustrated; it made him angry. Sometimes it almost made him want to be exactly what they expected.

He forced himself to forget that urge, that impotent rage that made it seem so imperative that he do *something*. He once again swallowed his anger, tamped down his frustration. He wouldn't become the monster, no matter what.

"I appreciate your concern for Kyle," he said slowly.

She nodded.

"I promise you, I mean no harm. Not to Mrs. Esterhaus, not to you. Not to anyone."

He watched the way she refused to let her eyes

change; she didn't accept what he was saying. He told himself that was okay. It had to be okay. He couldn't change it. For a moment he was tempted to tell her what he'd told Melvin Guthry, that he hadn't hurt Mrs. Esterhaus, couldn't hurt anyone, but that was pointless, a waste of breath.

He would have to prove that before anyone, especially Libby Jeffries, would believe him. Maybe he could. Maybe Melvin would help him. Maybe things could change. In the meantime he would do what he did best. Keep to himself. Contain his anger. Let no one close enough to stir him up, as Libby Jeffries had just done.

''Tell me where to plug in the trimmer.''

She looked startled that he'd let it go so easily.

''I'll show you,'' she said.

He noticed, when the trimmer was plugged in and he was set to begin his work, that she stood at the door for a moment, the back of her hand pressed to her lips, her eyes closed. She was deathly afraid. Realizing his presence did that to her made him almost physically ill. Knowing she'd stood up to him anyway made him admire her more than he could ever remember admiring anyone.

LARRY TEMPLETON liked to maintain a presence in the halls of the Blue Ridge Academy for Girls. An omnipresence, actually. He liked his instructors and his students to keep in mind that there was no predicting when and where the headmaster might show up. Things stayed more orderly that way.

He had another purpose today, but he didn't want that purpose to be obvious.

He made his usual meandering rounds, sticking his nose into this room or that, pausing occasionally at the back of the classroom to observe one of his instructors who tended to be a tad too iconoclastic. Larry finally wound up where he'd been headed all along, in Paul Travers's classroom, just as the students were filing out at the end of fourth period.

Paul looked up as Larry came in, then turned his attention back to the desktop he was straightening. He didn't smile, gave no sign of welcome to the headmaster.

That annoyed Larry, as it always did. He felt Paul should acknowledge his indebtedness a little more. After all, Larry had helped Paul get his start. He'd helped procure young Paul Travers a scholarship to Larry's own prestigious alma mater, and later lined up a job for him at the girls' academy when Larry was still a teacher himself.

"How are you getting along?" Larry asked, walking over to perch on a student desk.

"Fine."

Larry managed a tight smile, even though Paul wasn't looking in his direction. "I thought you might be a bit disturbed these days."

"I'm not disturbed."

"Good. That's good to hear. I should have known you'd be fine, even with Will back in town."

He took some satisfaction in watching Paul pause,

head still down. At least the coldhearted so-and-so reacted to something.

"Actually I wanted to assure you that Will's return in no way jeopardizes your position here."

Paul at last looked up. His dark eyes bore into Larry, hard and cold. Larry thought, as he had plenty of times, that he should never have gone out of his way to lend a hand to someone as problematic as Paul Travers.

"I never thought it would," Paul said.

"Good. Good." Still, Larry didn't move. Neither did Paul. "What are his plans? He's not really going to stay, is he?"

"I don't know what his plans are. It's none of my concern. Or yours, either."

Larry bristled. After all he'd done for Paul, he had a right to a little courtesy, a little cooperation. "You're as uncivil as ever, I see."

There was no reply.

Larry finally got up and walked out when it became apparent that Paul had no intention of saying more. Larry had hoped for a pipeline to Will, a way to keep track of what Will was up to. He would have to think of something else.

KYLE SLAPPED the soapy towel against the whitewall tire, less concerned than his slave driver that the tires look spotless. What was the point? They were all going to get muddy again, anyway.

Will was on the opposite side of the truck scrubbing the tires, the last step in washing the pickup.

A radio sat on the porch, screeching out some dumb country music. Will had pretended it would be fun, the two of them washing the truck together. That was dumb, too, Kyle thought.

Will tried too hard. Kyle could see that. But no matter how hard he tried, Kyle had made up his mind. He wouldn't give in. He wouldn't be nice in return. He wouldn't pretend that it no longer hurt that his mother was gone and was never coming back.

He hated the way everybody sort of pretended his mother had never existed. It made him want to smash something. It made him want to scream until he couldn't make another sound.

Kyle thought about his mother a lot. The way she laughed, giggly and loud, like she was a kid, too. The way she smelled, like the dusting powder in her bedroom, when she kissed him good-night at bedtime. Sometimes she would wink at him when just the two of them knew something nobody else knew.

It hurt too much to think she was never coming back. Hurt more than he could stand.

Sometimes he knew from the way other women acted that they wanted to treat him the way a mother would. Like they thought that would make him feel better. They patted his head and mooed over him like silly cows, and he hated them all. Even Aunt Becky sometimes made him feel smothered when she tried to act like his mother.

His mother was gone. She wasn't coming back.

He wiped his cheek, leaving a smear of soapy water.

The only one who hadn't made him feel that way was the nice nurse. Libby. The way she smiled was nice. Her voice was nice. And she didn't smother him the way the others did. That was good.

At least it should have been good. Somehow, though, it just made thinking of his mother even harder. Like there was suddenly a big hollow spot right in the middle of his chest, and he couldn't fill it no matter how deeply he breathed.

Will sure couldn't fill it. Nobody could. And Kyle wanted to make sure nobody got close enough to try.

CHAPTER SEVEN

EACH DAY PRESENTED Libby with a distraction called Will Travers.

Sometimes, like this morning, Will had arrived by the time she poured the morning coffee. She watched him out the kitchen window, bringing around bales of pine needles. Yesterday he'd cut back and moved a couple of shrubs, a task that seemed completely unnecessary to Libby. And now this. Pine needles. Not a single pine needle had been brought into this yard in all the years she'd been caring for Mrs. E. She didn't know why the yard needed pine needles now.

She walked to the back door, hesitated over the heavy dead bolt, then opened it and stepped out.

Cool, damp morning air wrapped itself around her, curling around her neck, her bare arms, her ankles. Winter was on the way. Will, however, was lightly dressed for a day outdoors. Jeans and a short-sleeved T-shirt, no cap. The sun wasn't bright enough yet, she noticed, to bring out the glints of gold in his hair. She'd noticed them the day before, only because she'd wondered where Kyle got his blond hair. She tried to imagine Will as a gap-toothed, towheaded youngster. It didn't compute.

She cupped her hands around her coffee mug. "Is all this really necessary?"

He dropped the two bales beside the row of hedges and looked at her. He was frowning. He always seemed to be frowning, no matter when Libby caught herself looking at him. She realized that frown didn't frighten her the way it had at first.

"Yes."

He bent over the bale, already going back to his work. Libby pursed her lips. Irritating man. "Why?"

He clipped the wire binding the bale and tossed aside the cutters he'd used. Libby saw the gesture and flashed on a memory. Her heart jumped in her chest. She forced herself to hold her ground.

"Holds the moisture in," he said. "So it doesn't evaporate before the roots have a chance to soak it up. Makes for healthier bushes."

Libby wasn't sure why healthier bushes mattered, frankly. Mrs. E. couldn't enjoy them anymore. Yet Will had spent days nurturing and babying things that had hung on for years without a bit of tending.

Watching the way he handled the bushes and plants reminded her of the way she handled Mrs. E. With loving care. As if the effort meant something to him. She might have thought it was an act, but he couldn't have known she was watching him. So why would he bother?

"It's a lot of effort just for bushes," she said, taking another sip of her coffee. It was cooling quickly in the chill morning air.

"They're living things," he said sharply. "How much effort is too much for a living thing?"

His question seemed an accusation, charged with a touch of hostility. His reaction reminded her of her own reaction when she sometimes realized that the sub nurses who came in on weekends to spell her occasionally treated Mrs. E. like something less than one hundred percent human. They thought Libby strange for talking to the old woman, for using a gentle voice and an even gentler hand. Libby sometimes wanted to snap at them, the way Will had just snapped at her.

But it was hardly the same thing.

Suddenly angry, she emptied her mug with a jerking motion onto the ground at her feet. "Whatever."

Before she could get in the door, Will had her by the wrist, restraining her, forcing her to look back at him. Libby felt her anger grow in response to the sudden fear that electrified her.

"Why did that make you angry?" he demanded, letting her go almost as abruptly as he'd grabbed her.

Libby's wrist felt as if it were on fire where his fingers had encircled her flesh.

"Maybe if you cared half as much for people as you seem to care about a row of old camellia bushes, neither of us would even be here this morning," she said, astonished at her boldness even as the cutting words spilled out.

His face went cold and vacant. He looked as if he was struggling to keep from speaking. Libby dashed into the house and locked the door behind her, not interested in whatever he might have had in mind to reply.

So his presence around the house became a distraction, a blip in her routine. She kept a close eye on him, watching him work, ever mindful of precisely where he was and what he was doing. For safety's sake, she had to do that.

He created a new bed around the shrubs in back, a curving bed where he planted flower bulbs. He lined the edges of the bed with decorative stones, and even with winter coming on, Libby could see the improvement. He cleaned the gutters. He worked on the listing arbor. He patched a small spot under the roof where squirrels had burrowed into the attic to hide their winter stash. He wrapped the outside pipes in preparation for the cold and replaced the rotting third step on the back porch. He started scraping the trim where it peeled and flaked. She guessed that meant he would paint next—a chore that could take days.

Every day, it seemed, he was at the house for a few hours doing something, doing things Libby hadn't even realized needed doing.

She talked to him as little as possible, but found as the days passed that it was often impossible not to talk to him.

She enlisted his help when the washing machine overflowed. She sometimes had to unlock the shed for him. He even needed to use the phone once. She handed the cordless to him through the back door and waited while he checked on his son, who had complained of a tummyache before leaving for school that morning.

When he finished, she took the phone and prepared to close the door again.

"I'd like to see Mrs. Esterhaus," he said as casually as he had asked to use the phone.

"That's out of the question."

"Why?"

"I should think that would be obvious."

She expected that to be the end of it. But he brought it up again the next day, and the next. On the fourth day he said, "I've been coming over here every day for almost two weeks. Have I given you any reason to believe I'd hurt you?"

She didn't like answering that question. It seemed to absolve him of things she wasn't willing to absolve him of. "No."

"Then why can't I see Mrs. Esterhaus?"

"Because I don't think it's in her best interests."

"You think it's in her best interests to stay cooped up in that house day after day with nobody but you to keep her company?"

The words stung, criticizing of her professional judgment. "What I think and what I do are none of your business. You gave up the right to judge anybody else twenty years ago."

He slammed the screen door with a fury that should have frightened her. "The jury said I have the same rights as you!"

"And the jury was wrong, wasn't it! You and I

may be the only people who know how wrong they were. But we know, don't we?''

Libby was astonished to realize, as she stood there watching him struggle to control his rage, that she wasn't afraid of him. She had no fear that he would harm her, even as the darkest of angers clouded his face. The realization disconcerted her. Did it mean she had finally worked free of the hold of the past?

Or did it simply mean that Will had accomplished what he wanted, to get her to let down her guard?

He turned and left that day without saying more. He didn't come again for two days, and she thought perhaps he had realized he would get no further with her.

But on the third day she came up from the laundry room in the basement to the sound of a deep voice drifting in from the front of the house. First startled, then galvanized by the fear she'd thought she'd banished, she dropped the basket of clothes on the kitchen table and started toward the sound of the voice.

There was no question it was Will's. But how could that be? She thought back and could only assume she'd forgotten to lock the door after taking a load of clothes outside to hang for drying. Wishing she had a weapon, wondering if she should call the sheriff, instead of handling this herself, Libby realized she couldn't wait for help to come.

Will was sitting beside Mrs. E.'s bed in the chair where Libby usually sat. And he was holding Mrs. Esterhaus's hand. But before Libby's protective instincts could kick into action, she noticed one more thing. She noticed the look on Mrs. Esterhaus's face.

Mrs. Esterhaus was smiling. A contented smile. A smile of fondness.

Ridiculous, of course, but Libby thought she had never seen such a pronounced expression on the old lady's face in all the years she'd been caring for her. Her patient's reaction arrested her.

"I would have come by long before now," Will was saying, a softness in his voice Libby had never before heard. "I know I should have. But I've been gone. Living in Washington, D.C., all these years. Remember when you told me all about the trip you took to Washington, Mrs. E.?"

And Libby could have sworn Mrs. E. nodded.

That was ridiculous of course. Mrs. E. didn't understand anything anyone said. Libby supposed she'd been playing her little game of talking to Mrs. E. and pretending she responded for so long that she'd forgotten, for the moment, it was impossible.

"Anyway, I've been fixing up a few things in the yard, Mrs. E. I planted twenty-five tulip bulbs for spring. I remembered you liked tulips."

Libby wanted to make a move, to run him out of the room. But she couldn't make herself act. She was so astonished by Mrs. Esterhaus's reaction to him she couldn't decide what to do. Mrs. Esterhaus always grew agitated with visitors, with strangers. Especially with men. Libby had learned years ago that Mrs. E. wouldn't tolerate male nurses.

But here she was, smiling at Will Travers, gazing

at him with the fond expression she usually reserved for Libby.

"When spring comes," Will said, "I'll take you out so you can see them all in bloom. We'll sit out by the arbor again. Did I tell you I'm fixing it up? And the tulips—they're yellow and red. Isn't that what you liked best, Mrs. E.? That's what I seem to remember."

"That's right," Libby said softly.

He didn't look back at her, didn't remove his hand from Mrs. Esterhaus's, didn't take his attention away from the woman in the bed. "Good. I'm glad I remembered. Listen, Mrs. E., I don't want to tire you out, so I'm going to go for now. But I'll come back. I'll bring a book. I could read to you. Would that be okay?"

Then he patted her hand and backed out of the room, smiling at Mrs. Esterhaus the whole time. His expression didn't change until he stood in the hallway out of sight of the old woman. Then he slumped against the wall, closed his eyes, let out a shuddering breath.

Libby thought she ought to shove him out the door right then, ought to give him a piece of her mind, ought to threaten him with dire consequences if he ever set foot in the house again. But she kept seeing how pleased Mrs. Esterhaus had seemed by his presence.

Thank goodness she apparently didn't recognize her attacker. Blessedly that memory seemed to be wiped out with all the rest.

But if the visit had cheered Mrs. Esterhaus, it was apparent it hadn't done the same for Will. He looked as if he'd seen a ghost.

Good.

"Seen enough?" she said.

He opened his eyes. Sure enough, they looked haunted. Libby held her breath, waited for some indication of remorse from him. But he merely dragged himself away from the wall that propped him up and walked unsteadily out the front door.

FOR TWENTY YEARS Will had carried a memory of Alice Esterhaus. He should have been satisfied with the memory. He would have given anything to wipe out what he'd just seen.

Will had been fifteen when he first walked into an American-literature class taught by Alice Esterhaus. His father was dead, his mother had her hands full, and Will had a chip on his shoulder. He'd already had more than one run-in with the law, mostly for driving without a license and a little petty vandalism. Hope Springs was too uptight for Will. And so was Mrs. Esterhaus.

A stocky, square-faced woman, she had appeared to lack one iota of warmth and kindness. She'd prodded him every day in class, staying on his case, asking him questions she surely knew he had no clue how to answer. Her biting reaction to his indifference to her subject had finally provoked him.

He would show her.

He'd started reading the dumb stuff she assigned

the class just to prove she didn't have his number, after all. He came to class with answers. He started acing her tests just to prove he was no dummy.

And somewhere along the line he'd started almost enjoying the stuff she assigned. Somewhere along the line he started enjoying—then craving—her attention. He discovered that she wasn't cold and hateful, after all. Once she had his attention, she always had a smile for him, a pat on his shoulder, an ear for listening when nobody else in Hope Springs had time for a kid who had already gotten off on the wrong foot.

"You don't have to be who they expect you to be," Mrs. E. had said to him. "You can take a turn in a different direction, you know."

College was what she meant. She'd talked to him about it plenty. She'd told him what college was like and what he could do with his life with a college education. She'd made him believe it was possible.

She'd made him want it, and even convinced him he deserved it.

Will wasn't the only one she helped, either. He discovered that as he spent more time with her. She gave encouragement to anyone who needed it and made the effort. She had helped countless kids in Hope Springs make it into college.

Alice Esterhaus had the biggest heart of any person he'd ever known.

And now all that was gone.

Today she was a wisp of a woman, her smile faded to a ghost of what it had once been, her eyes barely alight. She would never inspire another kid to reach for something beyond his or her grasp. Today she didn't know him.

But that was just as well. She didn't have to realize that he'd let it all go, that he'd turned his back on all the dreams she'd helped him uncover in his heart. He could be glad, he supposed, that he wouldn't have to disappoint her.

Part of him wanted to flee Hope Springs once again, to get as far away as possible from the discovery that his wasn't the only life ruined by a cowardly assailant twenty years ago. But the other part of him, the part of him that was tired of running from something he couldn't escape, anyway, knew that seeing Mrs. Esterhaus had simply given him one more reason to stay in Hope Springs.

He had to clear his name for Kyle's sake. But he had to find out who the real guilty party was for Mrs. Esterhaus's sake.

LIBBY HAD BROUGHT Mrs. E. her morning coffee when she heard pounding outside the bedroom window.

"What in the world?" She rose from her chair and set her own cup on the bedside table. "On a Saturday morning, that wouldn't be him, would it?"

She didn't like to mention Will's name in front of Mrs. E., even though it had been clear the day before that Mrs. E. didn't remember him. If the name triggered something in some small part of

Mrs. E.'s mind, Libby didn't want to be responsible for that.

Pulling back the curtain, she saw him, hammer in hand, frown firmly in place as he studied the placement of what appeared to be a new window box. He nodded to acknowledge her. Libby shook her head and dropped the curtain. Surely to goodness nobody was paying him to come out on a weekend to hang completely unnecessary window boxes.

She was restless while she helped Mrs. E. drink the rest of her coffee. The pounding moved to the next bedroom window, then the final one. Libby cut short the reading of the Saturday-morning paper. She could save the notices of church activities for this afternoon.

Shrugging into her navy cardigan, she went out the front door to see what Will was up to and instead found herself staring at Kyle. He sat on the top step, feet pulled up under him, a coloring book in his lap. He looked up as she walked out.

"I remember you," he said. "You're the nurse lady who let me be a delivery boy."

"That's right." She smiled even though he hadn't. Kyle Travers didn't look as if he smiled much, which didn't strike her as natural for an eight-year-old. But she remembered being an eight-year-old who didn't smile much, either, so she knew how it looked from the inside out. "I'm Libby. And you're Kyle."

"Yeah."

"Yes, *ma'am*." The deep voice came from

around the corner of the porch. "Isn't that what you mean?"

"Yes, ma'am, I mean." Kyle's voice grew softer and he lowered his eyes.

Will appeared at the corner of the house. "Didn't mean to disturb you."

Looking at them almost side by side, Libby was struck by the subtle changes that transformed the boy into the man. The same features were already in place on Kyle's young face—the straight narrow nose, the dark eyes, the finely shaped lips, the square chin. That chin even jutted out precisely as it did on the father's face. Libby could already see the man the boy would become. And even more disconcerting, she could see the boy the father had once been.

That upset her emotional equilibrium. It stirred in her feelings of sympathy and compassion that she didn't like having for a would-be killer.

It also startled her to realize that the leap from troubled boy to would-be killer might not be so great. Her heart hurt with the realization. People who were hurt themselves were often the ones who grew up to hurt others. She hoped that wouldn't be Kyle's fate. It made her want to sit down beside him and pull him against her side while he colored and tell him one of the stories Mrs. E. had told her when she was about Kyle's size.

Did Will Travers ever tell stories to his son? she wondered. Had anyone ever told stories to Will Travers?

She walked off the porch toward Will. "No trouble," she said. "Window boxes?"

He shrugged and hooked his claw hammer through his belt. Libby thought she should be troubled being so close to him while he was in possession of such a weapon—and realized she wasn't troubled in the least.

"Thought she might like seeing flowers through her window."

His admission pulled Libby in two directions. Her heart melted when anyone thought of a kindness for Mrs. E., but it hardened with the realization that, if it weren't for Will Travers, Mrs. E. could enjoy her flowers on her own.

"It's winter," she said. "Or will be soon."

"I know. I'm planting bulbs. They need to go in now." A satisfied air settled over him as he looked at the boxes. "In a few months she'll have winter crocuses—purple and white."

"You aren't getting paid to do this, are you?"

He turned away and busied himself with the bag of bonemeal and the sacks of bulbs on the ground below the window boxes he'd just installed. "Hope you don't mind the boy being here. He's usually not much trouble."

"I don't mind."

"We'll be out of your way before lunch."

"I'll take him in for hot chocolate if that's okay."

He looked at her sharply. "No need for that."

"I'd like to."

"Suit yourself."

So she did.

Kyle was as reluctant to accept her hospitality as his father had been, but the lure of hot chocolate on a chilly October morning was powerful. The added inducement of marshmallow topping made it an offer he couldn't refuse.

He sat at the kitchen table while she heated milk and cocoa. She watched him surreptitiously as he did the same with her. She longed to trim the silky blond bangs that obscured his dark eyes. A mother would never let his hair get that long, she thought.

"You like to color?" she asked.

He'd brought the oatmeal box full of crayons and his coloring book in with him. They were stacked neatly on the table in front of him. He nodded.

"Me, too," she said.

He shot her a skeptical look.

"I do."

"You're a grown-up," he said.

"Don't you know any grown-ups who color?"

"Nope."

"Then it's a good thing you met me, isn't it?"

She set the hot chocolate with its generous dollop of marshmallow topping on the table in front of him. His eyes grew wide in anticipation. She could tell that, despite the hair. She joined him at the table with her own hot chocolate.

"I guess you're glad to be back home in Hope Springs," she said.

A chocolate-and-marshmallow mustache appeared on his upper lip. He shrugged, his father's version of

"I ain't talking," Libby decided. She smiled.

"Where did you and your dad live before you came back?" she asked, even though she knew the answer from overhearing Will's conversation with Mrs. E the day before. She wanted to draw the boy out.

"Washington. That's the capital." He sipped his hot chocolate. "Of the whole country."

"Wow. I guess that was pretty neat, huh?"

He looked at her as if he should have known better than to expect a rational response from an adult. "I had to ride a bus to school."

"I see. Then I guess you *are* glad to be home."

"And they didn't have the Tex-a-Tavern, either."

Libby smiled again. She couldn't remember the last time she'd been around a child. He had a little dimple at the lower right corner of his mouth; it quirked into place when he talked.

He drank the hot chocolate. Then he showed her the Mighty Morphin Power Rangers picture he'd been coloring with his stubs of crayons. He colored very precisely for a boy his age, taking great pains not to go outside the lines. Libby wondered what a child psychologist would say about that. She wondered what the child psychologist her parents had taken her to after the trial had said about her.

At least Kyle was coloring. And at least he had enough trust to sit down with a stranger to drink hot chocolate and talk about important issues like coloring books and the superior food at the Tex-a-Tavern.

Libby almost forgot her routine, almost forgot it was her afternoon off in the simple pleasure of getting to know Kyle Travers.

She was sorry when Will knocked on the back door and said it was time they left.

Over the week that followed, however, Kyle became as much a fixture in her routine as his father had become. Kyle took to walking over to the house after school to wait for his father to finish his work. He would sit on the porch, as he had on that first Saturday morning, and do his homework—tasks like coloring in the pictures that corresponded with his spelling words. Then Libby started inviting him in, and he would sit at the kitchen table and have an afternoon snack with his schoolwork spread out before him. Or Libby helped him when arithmetic had him stumped. Sometimes they talked. Sometimes he wanted to help her read to Mrs. E.

And that was when Libby fell in love with eight-year-old Kyle Travers.

Children, Libby knew, didn't always like old people. Especially old people who were sick in ways they didn't understand. Sickness frightened children. But not Kyle. He couldn't wait to bring in his book from school and read to them about Bongo the dog. His eyes began to gleam as he read. He even picked up on the way Libby talked to Mrs. E. and took her replies for granted.

''I'll bring my computer and show you tomorrow,'' he promised Mrs. Esterhaus as one afternoon came to a close. ''It's just a kid's computer, not a real one like grown-ups use. But it's so cool. You can pick the word that goes with the picture, and if you pick the right one, it makes whistles and bells and lots of cool noise.''

And he seemed satisfied with the enthusiasm he read into Mrs. Esterhaus's slight nod.

Libby watched him follow his father down the front sidewalk that afternoon and marveled at how abruptly and completely her world had changed with the return of Will Travers. A few weeks ago her world had been caring for Mrs. Esterhaus. Today she had expanded the circle just enough to take in a man and his son.

She might not care much for the man, but his son had opened her heart. Given her history with the man, Libby knew she was in dangerous territory. But she had no choice. She'd fallen for a pair of dark brown eyes that she'd made up her mind to save from ever becoming as wary and haunted as the eyes they mirrored.

She sighed. She was making a habit of taking on the people Will Travers had scarred. Understandable, since she was one herself.

But she had to be careful. Sometimes she even thought of taking on Will Travers himself.

CHAPTER EIGHT

WILL GLARED at the sheriff over the waist-high counter that separated the public from the inner workings of county law enforcement. Al Tillman looked as intractable and unappeased as Will felt; the dispatcher sitting at the console looked uncertain the barrier that separated them was sufficient to protect her.

"I have a right to see those records," Will insisted for at least the third time.

"That's an open case," the sheriff said, losing the patience his voice had held when Will walked in ten minutes earlier. "We don't go passing out files on open cases to anybody who walks in the door."

"It's *my* case."

"Not anymore it's not. Unless you got something you want to say after all this time."

Will seethed. He could feel the urge to smash his fist into something—something like Al Tillman's nose—and knew he was going to have to get out of here before he screwed up majorly. He was also acutely aware of Walker Shearin, who stood at the end of the counter perusing the daily reports. If Will was going to make a scene, he really should be smarter than to do it in front of the editor of the paper.

He'd come in with every intention of being calm and reasonable. The day before, he'd learned from Melvin Guthry that his law firm's records from the trial—which would have included the sheriff's investigation and arrest reports—had apparently been lost or disposed of years earlier. Melvin had been apologetic, but suggested that the courthouse and the sheriff's department might be convinced to give Melvin access to their files, since he'd been the attorney in the case.

Will was too impatient to wait for the attorney to go through channels. He'd wanted to do it now.

He should have waited.

The woman who worked in the courthouse had looked positive that Will was deranged. "Twenty years ago? Do you have any idea how much time it would take to find those records? Do you have any idea how much work I already have to do today?"

He'd offered to look himself, and her belief in his mental instability had grown.

Al Tillman, on the other hand, made no excuses. He'd said no, plain and simple. No room for negotiation. After ten minutes of arguing, he now looked at Will as if he sincerely hoped Will had something very interesting to say about the old case.

"Yeah, I've got something to say," Will said, jabbing his finger in Tillman's direction, barely able to restrain himself from giving the sheriff a sharp poke in the chest. It would have been a poor substitute for a punch in the nose, anyway. "Somebody else did this, and you guys weren't competent enough to figure out who."

"Now, listen, Travers—"

"So it looks like I'm going to have to do the job myself."

"If I catch you so much as—"

"I'll do what I have to." Will leaned over the counter, so close he caught a whiff of coffee on Tillman's breath. He knew he was skirting dangerously close to the far edge of good judgment.

Tillman stepped closer. "Don't tempt me, Travers."

"I—"

Will felt a hand on his arm and whirled. Walker Shearin looked concerned and conciliatory.

"Come on, Will. Let's talk."

Will pursed his lips tightly. He was so angry he even wanted to lash out at the editor. Walker had been nothing but nice to him since he'd come back to Hope Springs, but Will would have welcomed the least provocation to include him in his fury against Al Tillman.

He nodded abruptly. He glared at Tillman, then stalked out ahead of Walker. The newsman caught up with him in front of the power company and fell into step beside him.

"You're not doing yourself any favors when you turn the sheriff into your enemy, Will."

Will crossed Ridge Lane without bothering to check for traffic. He knew he'd made an ass of himself, but he couldn't let go of it yet. How could he make a calm and rational man like Walker Shearin understand how it felt to have the world label you a criminal? To know you were powerless to ever be rid of that label? To see it in the eyes of everyone you met?

It was why he'd left Hope Springs. Why he should never have come back.

"I didn't do myself any favors the day I drove back into town," he snapped when he realized Walker was still beside him.

"Let me buy you a drink. We'll talk."

As if talking—or even drinking—would make things better. "Why would you want to be seen with me?"

"Cut it out, Will." Walker put a hand on his arm and steered him back across the street to the Nineteenth Hole tavern. "I'm on your side."

Willing himself to calm down, Will followed Walker to the tavern. Maybe Walker was right. A shot of whiskey, a quiet talk, a few minutes to get his temper back under control. He could figure out what to do next, how to keep from screwing things up any worse than they already were.

LIBBY TOOK THE TICKET for her winter coat from the clerk behind the counter at the dry cleaner and tucked it into the zippered change compartment of her wallet.

"I can't believe I almost forgot it's going to be coat weather soon," she said.

Mandy Powell attached the identifying tag to the gray wool coat and gave Libby a speculative look. "I suppose you've had a lot on your mind."

Libby told herself she was reading more into Mandy's look than was actually there. "There's always a lot to keep me busy."

"Especially now."

Libby didn't know how to answer. She didn't like talking about her personal business, but she wasn't used to being evasive.

"They say he's stalking you."

The ludicrous comment and the greedy interest in Mandy's eyes fueled Libby's irritation in an instant. "Why, that's ridiculous."

"Well, excuse me, but *I* didn't make it up. And I only wanted you to know that we're all concerned."

You're all nosy, Libby thought. *That's what you really are.* "Nobody's stalking me. Nobody needs to be concerned about me. I'm just fine. And so is Mrs. E."

Then she whirled and left, the jingle of the bell over the shop door punctuated by an indignant grunt from Mandy Powell. Libby kept to herself so much she tended to forget the power of the grapevine in a small town. Of course people had been talking about Will Travers's return. And of course somebody had noticed him spending time at the Esterhaus house.

And by the end of the day plenty of those same people would have heard what she'd just said to

Mandy Powell—at least they would have heard Mandy's version of it, embellished with every telling by the next person in the gossip chain.

She was still steaming and wondering why it had piqued her so when she saw the knot of men gathered in front of the Nineteenth Hole. Voices were raised. They sounded heated. Libby was ready to scurry away when she realized one of the men—the man whose voice was raised the loudest—was Will Travers.

Alarm rushed through her. She told herself to keep walking, to go straight home to the little house on Old Oak Street and forget she'd seen anything. But she couldn't. She inched closer, straining to hear what was being said.

"...your kind."

Libby flinched at both the tone and the words. They'd been spoken by one of the men who worked on maintenance at Heritage Manor, and she didn't need more information to know exactly what he was getting at.

Will Travers wasn't welcome at their bar.

Her anger swelled again and made her bold. She moved toward the men, listening as their words grew uglier. Will's as ugly as any of the rest.

"...and you can't stop me."

Libby saw that one of the men was being restrained by his friends. Standing close by with his hand on Will's arm was Walker Shearin from the *Courier*. But neither Will nor the maintenance worker was paying attention to voices of reason. The air around the entrance to the tavern felt heavy with the threat of violence.

Kyle's face flashed into Libby's mind. What would happen to him if Will raised his fist to someone else, even if it was justified? How would Kyle feel? What would he have to take from the other kids?

Her heart in her throat, Libby marched right up and stood beside Will. She put her hand on his other arm and realized he didn't even notice.

"Will," she said softly, "isn't it time we picked up Kyle from school?"

She felt some of the tension go out of his arm. It was only then that she realized how taut his arm had been, already tensed with his intention to take a swing.

"Get out of here, Libby," he said gruffly, not taking his eyes off the man he confronted.

"But it's time, Will. For Kyle. Remember?"

He took a deep breath then, and as he did, Libby let out the breath she'd been holding.

"Kyle," he said. "Right."

It took a few moments, but the tension finally seemed to ebb out of everyone. People backed away. Libby noted from the corner of her eye that Walker Shearin closed his eyes and stood for a moment with his hand against the brick front of the tavern. Will took a couple of steps away from the Nineteenth Hole, then seemed to spot the flight of steps that led to the woods above the street and the cobblestone path that ran parallel to Ridge Lane. He walked toward it. Libby watched him, trying to fathom what he was feeling.

"Will he be all right?" she said softly.

The only one left to respond was Walker Shearin. "I don't know, Libby. I honestly don't know."

The concern in Walker's voice once again triggered her own worry. As foolish as it seemed to follow a man like Will Travers into the woods as the sun lowered on a late fall afternoon, Libby started after him. A man like Will Travers. A sour feeling seeped into her stomach. The way they'd treated him didn't sit well with her. But was she any better?

When she reached the top of the steps, she saw him headed along the path away from town, toward the World War I memorial and the spa. She hurried after him. It wasn't hard to catch up. He walked slowly, heavily, apparently in no hurry to get away from the demons that drove him.

Maybe, she supposed, because the demons were within. Maybe he already knew he couldn't move fast enough to escape them.

He didn't look up when she reached his side. "I told you to go home."

"I was worried."

"About what?"

"About you."

His jaw muscle worked. "Shouldn't you be worried about yourself? Up here alone with me?"

Maybe she should be worried to hear he was thinking along those lines, too, but somehow that reassured her. If he wanted to hurt her, he surely wouldn't be warning her, would he? "Should I be?"

"You're the one with the answer to that. You're the *witness*. Remember?"

She flinched. "I remember."

"Then leave me the hell alone, Libby Jeffries. You'll be better off."

"What about Kyle? Will he be better off?"

"Kyle isn't your concern, either."

"Well, I can't turn that kind of thing on and off."

He headed off into the woods. Libby hesitated, then followed. He made his way to the war memorial, a stone column that rose ten feet in the air and listed the names of the men from Hope Springs who had died in World War I. Will sat on the wide base of the memorial, elbows on his knees. His entire body had the slack look of abject hopelessness. Fool that she was, Libby felt her heart go out to him. She knew her hands couldn't heal, but as a nurse she'd learned long ago how much comfort patients sometimes drew from a simple tender touch. She wanted to give that to him right now. Her touch along the carved length of his face, across his slumped shoulders.

She must be crazy.

She sat on the wooden bench that faced the memorial and hugged her cardigan close against the chill. "I'm sorry coming back has been so hard."

"I knew it would be."

"But you came, anyway."

"I had to. For Kyle."

"But now too many people here won't let you forget."

He looked at her for the first time. Looking too deeply into his eyes was painful; she could only imagine how it felt from inside.

"People like you," he said.

"Especially me," she admitted.

"You must really hate me."

She didn't know how to answer that. She never thought of herself as the kind of person who hated other people. In fact, she couldn't think of a single other person she would say she hated. But how else could she describe the way she'd felt about Will Travers all these years?

"I don't know how I feel right now," she said. "All that really seems to matter at the moment is Kyle."

"Why does he matter so much to you?"

More things she shouldn't say to him. "Maybe I understand what it's like to be a kid who's carrying too much baggage."

He sighed deeply. "I'm sorry for what all this has done to you."

It was the only remorse she'd ever heard him express. It was a start, she supposed. But it wasn't nearly enough.

"Be sorry for Mrs. Esterhaus."

He got up and paced halfway around the base of the memorial. He looked at her twice as if he wanted to say something, but bit it back. When he finally spoke, he said, "Thanks for saving me from doing something really stupid back there."

"I didn't do it for you," she said.

He nodded and gestured in the direction of the path. "We'd better go back. They'll be worried about you."

She walked ahead of him through the woods, wondering at her lack of fear. She felt instinctively that whatever he might have been twenty years ago, he was no longer that person. Nevertheless, she remembered the unyielding tension she'd felt in his arm just half an hour earlier. What was it about him that made her want to forget what she knew to be the truth?

He brought out her caretaking nature. She had to be careful of that. Had to be careful of him and her tendency to be her own worst enemy.

LIBBY SAT ON THE TOP STEP of the porch enjoying the swirl of dead leaves along the sidewalk in front of the house. It had been a windy day, followed by a windy night. The leaves that had been left on the trees the day before had mostly fallen in the past twelve hours. They crackled and whisked along the sidewalk.

Libby's shoulders ached; her hands felt cramped. On the days Mrs. Esterhaus didn't feel well, Libby always spent extra time massaging the muscles that threatened to atrophy from disuse. The intense work was a physical strain. Today was one of those days.

She closed her eyes, listened to the leaves and let her mind drift.

She wondered if Will Travers's hands and shoulders ever ached from the work he did. A massage would probably seem like indulgence to a man like Will. And a man like Will probably didn't allow himself much indulgence.

Frowning, Libby opened her eyes. She wasn't accustomed to having her mind drift to useless things. She had decided to go back into the house and start supper when she noticed her father headed up his own sidewalk next door. Noah saw her, waved, hesitated. He turned in her direction and walked toward her.

The cheerfulness on his face looked forced. He greeted her and sat beside her on the step.

"Things going okay, Lib?"

"Fine, Dad. How are the wedding plans coming along?"

He gave a short nod. "Oh, fine, I suppose. I'm leaving all that to Vera."

"Have you set a date?"

"A date? Oh, maybe before Christmas. You think that'd be okay?"

She wanted to tell him she didn't want to feel left out at Christmas, this Christmas in particular, but she didn't. "Sure. Whatever the two of you want is fine."

"Been thinking, Lib. About this business of that Travers boy coming home."

An uncomfortable rush of adrenaline went

through her. She thought of saying that Will wasn't a boy anymore, but she didn't say that, either.

"I've been noticing he's around here some. I don't like that much."

"It's okay, Dad."

"Okay?" He turned startled eyes on her. "How can it be okay?"

"He's just helping out. He's not... I don't think he'd hurt anybody."

"I can't believe I'm hearing this."

Noah stood and backed down the steps, his eyes snapping at her.

"Dad, he's got his son to think about now. And you should see the way Mrs. E. reacts to him."

"You've let him see Mrs. Esterhaus?"

His incredulity told her how everyone else in town would react to the revelation. In fact, it helped her see just how strange her defense of Will Travers must appear.

"It was a long time ago, Dad. People change." Didn't they?

He grunted. "Evil doesn't change that much, Elisabeth Anne Jeffries."

She caught herself on the verge of saying that Will Travers wasn't evil, and then couldn't believe her part in this conversation. Had her concern for Kyle taken her this far?

"Vera said he ought to be run out of town. That he ought not be living here among decent people."

Libby stood, suddenly angry. "Then Vera should

have done something about that twenty years ago. Don't you think?''

Noah's face turned red. ''All she meant is—''

''She was one of twelve people who voted to acquit Will Travers,'' Libby said. ''He's a free man, and nobody has the right to condemn him anymore. The people of this town need to think twice about their holier-than-thou attitude.''

Noah stared at his daughter. He shook his head, then turned his hands up in a gesture of surrender. ''I better go. But, Lib, you be careful. You don't know what you're dealing with here. You hear me?''

He waited for a moment, and when she didn't reply, he shook his head again and left. Libby watched him go home and wondered what in the world had come over her. She and her father never argued. And now she'd lit into him because he was warning her that Will Travers was a dangerous man. What in the world was wrong with her? Nobody knew better than she how dangerous Will was.

Why couldn't she seem to remember that?

THE CRAZY THING WAS, the only two places in town where Will didn't feel self-conscious about the past were his own house and Mrs. Esterhaus's.

He climbed down off the extension ladder and eyed the new four-by-four he'd installed to replace a rotting brace under the eaves. It would need painting now, and that pleased him. One more excuse to be here.

Everywhere else he felt eyes on him. He felt the sharpness of words he didn't even hear. Most of it could be his imagination, he knew, but it felt real nevertheless. Walker Shearin, to whom he'd apologized the day after the incidents at the sheriff's office and the Nineteenth Hole, had assured him that most people in town weren't as quick to condemn as the one man they'd encountered the day before. But Will felt what he felt.

"Hope Springs is a fair town, Will," Walker had said. "That doesn't mean every individual is fair. But on the whole, folks here will give you a fair shake."

Will thought of Melvin Guthry and Bama Preston and Walker himself. Even Libby Jeffries, though God knew why. He thought of Luisita Mendoza and Kyle's teacher and Mrs. Haigler, the minister's wife, inviting him and his son to services. Plenty of people in Hope Springs had been kind to him since his return.

But he still felt the weight of the judgment against him.

Will retracted the aluminum ladder and headed for the shed. He would soon have to start rebuilding the whole damn house to have an excuse to spend time here. But if he had to, he would come over on his own time. Just to see Mrs. Esterhaus.

And Libby.

He stashed the ladder and tried to stash his thoughts about Libby, as well. He glanced at his watch. Suppertime. He supposed Kyle was in the kitchen pestering Libby. She helped Kyle with his homework sometimes, he knew. He felt a little jealous, because Kyle always refused Will's help with his schoolwork. And Libby let him visit with Mrs. E. anytime he wanted to. It was helping his reading, Will thought, because he'd listened in a couple of times when he'd gone inside to drag the boy home at the end of the afternoon.

Kyle never wanted to leave and Will couldn't blame him. Who wouldn't rather stay in a warm, cheery house that smelled of mashed potatoes and stewed apples and hot cocoa, instead of a house where the best you could hope for was canned chicken noodle soup?

He should learn to cook if he was going to raise the boy. That would be better use of his time than hanging around the house on Old Oak Street, he told himself.

He opened the back screen door and stopped in the mudroom to examine his boots to make sure he didn't track in dirt. He heard voices in the kitchen.

"I hate Halloween," Kyle was saying vehemently.

"Why on earth would you hate Halloween? It was my very favorite holiday."

"'Cause it's stupid."

Will grinned wryly at his son's truculent tone.

"Don't you think it's fun to dress up and get a bag full of candy?"

Will waited for the reply and apparently so did

Libby. But the next voice, a few moments later, was also Libby's, filled with concern.

"Kyle, honey, what's wrong?"

Will let the screen door close softly and moved closer to the door into the kitchen. He peered in. Libby had pulled a kitchen chair into place beside Kyle's chair. She sat with her arm around him. Kyle had buried his face against her shoulder. Will fought the impulse to dash in and demand to know what was going on.

Kyle sniffled and hiccuped, then began to mumble against Libby's uniform. Will strained to hear.

"They're mean."

"Who's mean, honey?"

Her voice was so tender, and her head, bent close to his, was almost the same dandelion-soft corn-silk color as Kyle's. They could have been mother and son. Will felt his heart lurch in his chest. Libby Jeffries, the woman in town with the most reason to hate and mistrust him, was more a parent to his son these days than he was.

"The kids at school. They're mean. They..."

He sobbed for a few minutes and Libby began to rock him back and forth, crooning something soft and motherly. Kyle's sobs subsided.

"They said, some of the boys in the f-fourth grade said they were g-going to dress up like...like a killer. They said they were g-going to dress up and be...Will Travers."

Will's heart broke clean in two. He didn't hear what Libby said to his son, although he heard the murmur of her voice even through the buzz of hurt that filled his head. Here he'd been telling himself how many good people there were in Hope Springs, and yet there were enough small-minded ones that even the kids in his son's class had picked up on their parents' fears and prejudices.

Will hated having to pay the price for that himself; it killed him to realize his son was paying it, too.

No wonder Kyle hated him.

He slumped against the door frame and closed his eyes against the impotent anger flooding him. How could he hope to reach the little boy who sat in the next room crying to a woman who probably felt no different from the people who were causing Kyle's tears?

But at least she had a heart.

He began to focus on the soothing timbre of her voice. She was telling his son that he could find the courage to ignore their hatred and fear. The words she said, Will thought, seemed less important than the gentleness of her voice and the warmth of her arms around Kyle's shoulders. It was hard for him to imagine where she found enough love to do that for his son, believing what she believed.

Then he remembered what she'd said about understanding what it was like to deal with tough stuff as a kid. Reality sank in for Will. This woman wasn't the person who had dragged him through the humiliation of an accusation that he'd never quite shaken. That person had been a child, no older than his own son was now. He imagined, for a moment, Kyle witnessing what Libby had witnessed. Imagined how traumatized Kyle would be. Imagined how easy it would be for a child so young to make a mistake.

And to be haunted for years to come.

Yet Libby Jeffries wasn't haunted. She was brave and tender and possessed of love for Mrs. Esterhaus and Kyle Travers.

Will's heart felt suddenly full.

Now he had three reasons to find out the truth. For his son, for Mrs. Esterhaus and for the woman who also deserved to be free of the past.

CHAPTER NINE

EVERY TIME WILL THOUGHT he had the people of Hope Springs figured out, someone surprised him.

T. J. Crichton stepped out of the bakery on Ridge Lane one day as Will passed, carrying a loaf-shaped package. He pressed the package into Will's hands. T.J. had been on the football team with Will before T.J. was cut because of his size and Will was cut because of his unacceptable extracurricular activities.

"Just wanted you to know," T.J. said, "I always did think the jury did the right thing. Letting you off and all."

Another time he saw Marcia Moondancer coming out of the post office. He'd passed her quickly, but she turned and came after him. She put her hand on his arm—she had a ring on each finger, he noticed—and said, "You did the right thing, coming home to set things straight. There are people in this town whose lives will be cosmically unbalanced until the truth is known."

He hadn't been sure how to respond to that, but she smiled and didn't seem to need a response. "You're a brave man to take it on. The universe will reward you."

Then she left him standing there. He supposed that was her way of stating her support for him.

Others' support came in more concrete ways. People like Cindy Martin and Bertie Newsome, who invited Kyle to play with their children and grandchildren, and Ester Hurd, who brought a tunnel of fudge cake and told him how much she missed his mother in their Sunday-school class. Those gestures sometimes brought a lump to his throat and reminded him of all that was best about small towns like Hope Springs.

Other times the ugly thought came to him that somebody in this town might be nice to him only because he or she knew with absolute certainty that Will Travers had never hurt Alice Esterhaus. Somebody in Hope Springs had attacked Mrs. Esterhaus, and Will's presence might just activate a guilty conscience.

Will knew it had to be true, but he tried to concentrate on the neighborliness of most people in Hope Springs. They were nice folks. He told himself that over and over. But as soon as he got comfortable with the notion that people in town might not condemn him as much as he supposed, another incident like the one in front of the Nineteenth Hole occurred.

Across the street from his mother's house, which he'd already painted and patched so that it looked plenty respectable on the outside, the family that had lived in the little bungalow for six years stuck a For Sale sign in the front yard. The only people who showed an interest in the house were flatlanders, people from out of town who presumably hadn't heard about the would-be killer who lived across the street. One day an old woman with a walking stick stopped dead in her tracks when she saw him coming in her direction on Ridge Lane. Then she crossed the street, her cane clicking rapidly. And, of course, Kyle's teacher had confirmed that the other boys gave Kyle a hard time about his father's history. The young teacher was nice enough, but she clutched the sides of her chair so tightly her knuckles were white for the duration of their after-class conference. Will took pity on her and kept it short.

The day he went into Fudgie Ruppenthal's barbershop for a trim, he was of a mind to pack it in. Maybe he *should* leave Kyle with his aunt so the boy could have a normal life. He could go back to Washington and sink into obscurity again. It had worked for twenty years; it could work for twenty more.

But the thought of losing Kyle again ripped his gut out.

He could hear the laughter and the buzz of conversation before he even opened the door to Fudgie's. The barbershop had an official name, of course—Blue Ridge Barbershop. But it had been called Fudgie's so long most people didn't remember the real name without looking up at the sign over the red-and-white-striped barber pole. Inside the long narrow shop, Fudgie's was exactly what you'd expect. Two metal-framed chairs, two mirrors, two marble-topped shelves in front of each mirror, with glass canisters of combs and razors and scissors. A glass-topped oak case that held cigars and gum and candy bars so musty and old they probably qualified as antiques. There was a shoeshine chair, used almost exclusively by Tood Grunkemeier, the farmer who owned apple orchards south of town. A nest of straight-backed wooden chairs and a matching bench offered a place for a group of aging regulars to get off their feet.

It had looked exactly the same when Will was growing up. Some of the faces were new, but most were just more lined.

When Will stepped into the shop, the laughter stopped. The man in Fudgie's chair, a past-middle-age man Will didn't recognize, froze with his mouth open.

Fudgie nudged him. "Go on, Leland."

"Don't reckon so." Leland clamped his mouth shut and glared at Will.

Will stood inside the door, his hand still on the knob. He didn't have to get a haircut at Fudgie's, he supposed. There was always the shop a few miles up the road in Browerton.

"Aw, hellfire, Leland, don't leave us hangin'," Tood Grunkemeier said, his raspy voice impatient.

"I'll tell you later."

Fudgie folded his arms across his chest, scissors sticking out beneath one elbow. Leland glanced over his shoulder at the barber.

"Well, come on, Fudgie, let's get on with it."

"What's your hurry?"

"I told the missus I'd run her down to Roanoke this afternoon—she thinks we need a new dishwasher."

Fudgie glanced up at the clock with its yellowing face and the slogan for Electro-Sol shaving cream circling the numbers. "You better get a move on, then. Don't want the shops closing up before you get down the mountain."

Leland was turning the shade of one of Tood Grunkemeier's ripe apples. "I'll get going as soon as you finish up my cut."

Fudgie studied Leland's head, which had been sheared close to the scalp on one side. "Don't know as I have time to finish it right this minute, Leland."

"What!" Leland jumped up, snatching off the white coverup that protected his clothes from snipped hair. He tossed it into the chair. "Francis Ruppenthal, are you telling me you'd run *me* off and not *him?*"

Fudgie studied his scissors. Will stirred at the door and said, "Listen…"

Fudgie gestured in Will's direction and Tood Grunkemeier jumped up and put a hand on Will's forearm.

"Don't mind serving gossips and troublemakers," Fudgie said slowly, looking around the room with a sly grin. "Reckon that's clear. But pure-T meanness…well, a man's gotta draw the line somewhere. You come back after you've had time to think on it, Leland."

"Don't hold your breath."

Leland took two steps, then came face-to-face with Will. Will stepped aside, feeling as if he should apologize. His presence had come between this man and a haircut. This man and his old friends.

"We all know you're guilty as sin," Leland said as he left. "They should've locked you up and pitched the key off Confederate Cliff."

Then he was gone. Will still stood in the room, which felt hot and close. He looked around awkwardly. "I'm sorry. I didn't mean to cause a scene."

"Aw, hell," Tood said, returning to his seat, "he always was a horse's rear end."

"Better watch your tongue, Tood," a wiry old codger said. "Fudgie'll run you off, too."

Everybody cackled over that. Then Fudgie gestured at the recently vacated chair. "Looks like you need a trim, young feller."

With a slight hesitation Will settled into the chair. The leather seat was cracked and worn nearly flat from fifty years of backsides.

"So, Will, how're you finding Hope Springs? Things changed much?"

Will relaxed. The gossipy group drew him into their discussion of the high-school football team's losing streak, the bumper crop from Tood's orchard, who was marrying whom and where they predicted imminent divorces. They chuckled and grumbled and made Will feel like one of the guys. Maybe things would be all right, after all.

When his cut was finished, Will almost hated to

leave the place where he'd been able to forget for a few moments that he wasn't accepted by everyone in Hope Springs. As he left, Tood Grunkemeier took a faded denim jacket off the hook by the door and followed him out.

"You never mind about folks like Leland, young feller," he said, slipping stiffly into the jacket as they walked into the blustery day. "He was a buddy of Virgil Esterhaus's, you know. Thinks he's being loyal by throwing off on you like that."

"Thanks."

"How's that boy of yours doing?"

"Okay."

Tood studied him; Will studied the sidewalk.

"You bring him out to my place sometime. I've got a few horses. A dog or two. Stuff a boy might like."

Will tried to imagine his prickly son accepting the old farmer's hospitality. He couldn't, but he still appreciated the offer. "That's good of you."

Tood waved a leathery hand. "Ain't good of me at all. Just plain selfish. Get lonesome out there. Got nobody, you know. Except a nephew I can't get word of. Rest of the family's dead and gone. Keep hoping the boy'll turn up. He's supposed to have a kid of his own. But so far, no luck. You and your boy, you'd be doing me a favor."

Will thought for a moment that was just Tood's way of making him feel less beholden. Then he caught a glimpse of the look in the old man's eyes and knew what he'd said was true. Tood Grunkemeier was lonely and alone. Will understood that. It was a revelation to him that others were in the same boat.

"We'd like that."

Tood smiled. "Yeah. Me, too."

THE PERSON WHO CONTINUED to surprise Will the most—and give him the most hope—was Libby.

Like his moods, his feelings about Libby swung wildly. Sometimes he could still feel a lot of anger for the part she'd played in ruining his life. But he had only to stop and picture her as a frightened little eight-year-old and his anger dissipated. She'd been just like Kyle.

And that, of course, was what kept his feelings for her swinging more and more away from anger and toward... He couldn't decide how to label his feelings for her. He was forgiving her, that was obvious. He had some sympathy now for what the nightmare of the attack on Mrs. Esterhaus had done to her. But there was more.

He shook his head as he knocked on the back door at Mrs. Esterhaus's. He'd insisted that Kyle go straight home after school because he didn't want the boy bothering Libby on a day when Will would be working elsewhere. But Kyle had been just as insistent that he had to see Libby after school today. Will had relented.

The door was opened by a three-and-a-half-foot-tall superhero with blond hair that Fudgie Ruppenthal would love to get his hands on.

"Look!" Kyle, a broad smile on his face, soared around the kitchen, arms outstretched. "I'm Superman!"

Libby, who was on her knees in the middle of the floor wearing a smile as broad as the boy's, said, "Not yet you're not. Stand still for five minutes while I measure the hem of this cape."

Kyle had to demonstrate his superhero abilities for thirty more seconds, then came to an abrupt stop in front of Libby. While Kyle chattered away, she pinned the cape to the right length.

Will stood in the doorway, hardly trusting himself to speak, hardly knowing how to interpret his feelings. This woman who had spent twenty years hating him was making a Halloween costume for his son. Will had let the event approach with no notice. If Kyle had been depending on him, he would have ended up sitting home in a pair of jeans a couple of weeks from tonight while every other kid in Hope Springs dressed up as witches and pirates and knocked on doors demanding candy.

But Libby had seen to it that Kyle wouldn't miss out.

His chest felt tight as he thought about it. He watched her nimble fingers pluck straight pins from a tiny plastic box and found himself caught up in the radiance of the smile she bestowed on Kyle. Her eyes glittered and her laughter echoed in the high-ceilinged kitchen.

For a moment he wished she would turn that smile, those eyes, the song of her laughter, on him.

Can the sentimental crap, Travers. This town'll vote you in as sheriff before that happens.

Libby announced that the costume would fit perfectly with a nip and a tuck done on Mrs. Esterhaus's sewing machine, then sent Kyle off to the bathroom to change back into his jeans. She stood.

"I hope you don't mind," she said.

Her face was so sweet, so innocent, glowing with the pleasure of what she'd just done. Libby, he realized, was happier with the costume than Kyle was.

"I'm grateful," he said, not trusting himself to say more.

He wanted to approach her. He wanted to look deeper into those warm hazel eyes. He wanted to breathe in her sweetness.

Oh, Lord, he was wading into deep water here.

"Kyle means a lot to me," she said. "I...you know, not having any of my own and not... Well, anyway..."

From the tone of her voice, it sounded as if she thought of herself as an old maid. She must be all of twenty-eight, and so fresh-faced, so young herself. She bit her lower lip and looked down. He realized he'd been staring, had made her nervous.

"He likes you," Will said. "A lot. I'm glad."

"Are you?"

He started to reply, but realized his throat was tight now, too. His whole body was pounding with some kind of expectation. He simply nodded. He had to get out of here. If he didn't, he was going to do something he would regret. Something...

He might kiss her.

Startled by the sudden awareness, he backed away, bumping into a kitchen chair. It scraped across the floor, teetered. He grabbed it and righted it and took another step backward in the direction of the door.

"Kyle!" His voice came out tinged with desperation. "Make it snappy! We've got to get home."

His fingers ached to touch her, to feel skin that must be softer than anything he could imagine. Panic welled up. What was happening to him? If he so much as laid a hand on her, all hell would break loose.

He started to yell for his son again when Kyle reappeared.

"Okay, okay," Kyle said, handing the red-and-blue costume to Libby. "I'm ready."

Will put a hand on his son's narrow shoulder and pointed him toward the door.

"Will I see you tomorrow?"

It was Libby, close behind them, her voice as soft as a whisper in his ear. He couldn't catch a full breath. He had to remind himself that she wasn't talking to him. She was talking to his son. He hurried out the door.

The cool early-evening air helped clear his head.

Libby Jeffries was not a woman he could want to kiss. Libby Jeffries was kind to his son but she damn sure had no reason to be kind to him. If she even had a hint what he'd been thinking, she'd call Al Tillman and they'd bring out the tar and feathers.

Wanting to kiss Libby Jeffries was the worst kind of insanity. If he thought people came down hard on him now, he could just imagine what kind of hell would break loose if he laid a hand on the town's very own Florence Nightingale.

LIBBY FELT UNSETTLED.

She liked her life in perfect order. Nothing in her world out of place, everything secure under her gentle control. Things felt safe that way.

On the surface things still looked pretty orderly. Mrs. E.'s routine was still inviolable. Libby still rose every morning at six-thirty, ate her own lunch at eleven-forty-five, took Saturday afternoons off. The mail still came on time each day, and the paychecks from Mrs. E.'s estate arrived like clockwork.

But there were hitches in the plan, hesitations in the second hand of Libby's inner clock.

There was Will and there was Kyle, and mostly there was what was happening in Libby's head and heart. None of that was under her control, and sometimes that made her breath run shallow and her heart pump from someplace deep within. Someplace she wasn't accustomed to going.

Libby didn't trust what was happening to her.

She listened now as Kyle giggled from Mrs. E.'s bedroom, telling a joke he'd remembered because of the new word he was learning to spell on the toy computer. He was bright and funny, and Mrs. E. seemed to bring that out in him even if she couldn't speak or respond.

The way she'd always brought it out in Libby.

"And then," Kyle was saying with barely disguised excitement, "you'll never guess what the walrus said!"

Libby smiled and walked on to the kitchen. The smell of baking cookies filled the house. Oatmeal and spices and raisins. A lot like the ones Mrs. E. had always baked for her. She checked the clock over the refrigerator. Two minutes. Maybe she would peek.

As she reached for the pot holder, the back screen door creaked. That would be Will. She wasn't even afraid anymore, she realized. She trusted the man he seemed to have become.

But she didn't trust herself, or her reactions to him.

She turned away from the oven toward the noisy screen door. She watched as he came in from the mudroom. He wore jeans and an old gray sweatshirt, frayed at the ribbed cuffs and collar. His boots were scuffed. All of Will, she realized, looked a little battered, even his dark, guarded eyes.

Seeing him like this still set her heart beating at a different pace. If it wasn't fear, then what?

"They smell like the ones Mrs. E. used to make," he said.

"Do they?"

He nodded. He still spoke little enough, and Libby realized she sometimes said things in hopes of getting a response from him. His voice seemed to curl up somewhere inside her, brushing against her like a kitten, appealing in its softness. She bit her lip.

"I saw the recipe on the back of the oatmeal box," she said. "I thought I'd try it. See how close it comes to the real thing."

"Smells close to me." He almost grinned. "Brought me all the way in from the shed."

Libby smiled, continued studying him. Why did he draw her so?

Then she remembered the cookies and glanced up at the clock with a little gasp. "It's time."

She took the cookie sheet out and turned off the oven. Will walked over and studied the oblong pan of golden-brown cookies.

"They have to cool first," she said.

He was close. She surprised herself, sometimes, how close she let him get. Close enough, sometimes, that they could have touched if that had ever been on their minds. Close enough that sometimes their shoulders brushed or her hand grazed his arm. Close enough that she knew he smelled of the outdoors— fresh air and burning leaves and newly turned soil. The smell of a man.

Her mouth went dry.

She backed away.

He was looking at her oddly, she thought. Those eyes of his coming out of his own private hell just long enough to look into hers. She couldn't seem to turn away, just stood there captured by his searching gaze. His mouth was set in the hard lines she'd grown so familiar with. His hair was windblown.

She thought of brushing her hand through it, learning its texture, the way she sometimes did with Kyle.

The feeling sparked by the thought was nothing like the feeling she got when she brushed Kyle's hair out of his eyes.

If she didn't know better…

"You took him by the graveyard," he said, looking away as abruptly as he spoke.

"We were passing on the way to the library Saturday. He said he hadn't been since the funeral. I hope you don't mind. I should've asked. I—"

"I don't mind. I should've thought of it myself." He ran his own hand through his sun-kissed hair and brought another reaction lurching to the surface of Libby's consciousness. A spark. A jolt. A wave of desire. "I'm not real good at this father business. Not much practice."

She thought again of touching him, a comforting hand on his shoulder. A way to sympathize. What was happening to her?

"It takes time. He's not used to you yet."

"He got used to you in a hurry."

She shrugged. "I'm a woman."

Like Kyle's mother. That was all she'd meant. Wasn't it? But she realized even as she rationalized that she'd been hoping to make Will notice.

"I know," he said.

When he looked at her again, his eyes weren't riveted on hers. Instead, they made a slow intimate study of her face. She told herself she should move, look away, do something to break the spell. But she couldn't. She simply stood there, accepting the gaze that was as real as a touch and feeling herself go soft and weak.

She felt a sigh rising to her lips. A sigh that seemed like an admission of surrender.

"Let's…ah… The cookies. They're probably cool enough."

After a moment he nodded. But he appeared to move only under protest, just like Libby. She'd heard about women who came under the spell of men with evil intent and wondered if this was what it was like.

Ridiculous, she told herself as she began to lift the cookies off the baking sheet. Her fingers trembled. *Will Travers isn't a man with evil intent.*

Of course a woman falling under that kind of spell would think precisely that.

She and Will and Kyle ate oatmeal cookies and drank milk at the kitchen table. She studied Will closely, looking for the telltale signs that marked him as evil. She didn't see any, but that could hardly be called conclusive evidence.

She watched him closely after that, labeling her feelings for him dangerous even as those feelings began to spiral out of control.

One afternoon she watched him waylay Kyle as the boy darted into the yard after school. Kyle brushed him off, beating his father back with that unyieldingly petulant look children master so easily. Kyle came in and lavished his need for attention on

Libby and Mrs. E. Will, Libby noticed, stood at the back fence for a long time, not moving, looking down, his shoulders slumped.

Her heart broke for him. She wanted to go to him, give him comfort. But she knew that wasn't wise.

Another afternoon she watched as he discovered an injured squirrel in the yard. She almost turned away, assuming he would put it out of its misery and unwilling to witness the violence that would nevertheless be an act of mercy. He pulled on his work gloves, brought a box from the shed filled with clean rags. Then gently he picked up the squirrel, placed it on the bed of rags and got into his truck.

It was two days before she ran into the town vet on the street and learned that Will had taken the injured squirrel in to be treated. The squirrel would be ready to be released soon, Aggie Treadaway told her.

The spell around her heart grew stronger every day.

That was why, on her next Saturday off, she marched into Al Tillman's office.

The sheriff looked surprised. "Libby. Something wrong out at Mrs. E.'s?"

She read in his eyes the expectation that he knew exactly what was wrong. Others in town had questioned her with that same certainty in their eyes. Sometimes she had agreed with the look; more and more she found she was angered by it.

"I want you to tell me what you know about Will Travers. About what he's been doing all this time."

"Well, Libby, we don't exactly keep tabs on people like Travers, you know."

"But you could find out if he had a record. If he's...done anything else."

The words stuck in her mouth like sawdust. She hated asking them, regretted asking them, before they were even out. She wasn't sure what answer she hoped for. Something to get her back in touch with reality, maybe.

Or something that would give her permission to keep feeling what she was feeling.

"Well, we can't find any record. No sign of trouble from him since he left here."

Libby felt the relief ease through her and had to admit to herself precisely what her motives were.

"I told you, if he's a problem, all you've got to do is let me know."

"No. No, he's no problem." She shrugged. "It just seemed smart to ask."

Actually it felt backhanded and small-minded to ask.

As she turned to leave, the sheriff stopped her. "'Course, he could have a record in another state. Under another name. We may never know that."

A frisson of disappointment skittered down her spine. She nodded. And as she walked back to Mrs. Esterhaus's home, she reminded herself of the old woman's frail body and broken mind. No matter what Will had done or not done since, the thing that made it wrong for Libby to care about him was waiting for her at Old Oak Street every day.

She had to watch herself. She had to stop the way she was beginning to think and feel. She had to remember the truth about Will Travers. Twenty years might have changed him, but it didn't change what he'd done.

WILL SAT IN HIS living room, lights turned low, a chill in the air. He would turn the heat up soon so things would warm up a little before Kyle got home.

He'd had more than a moment of uneasiness when Kyle drove off to the movies with his aunt and her two kids. It had been a while since Kyle had begged to live with his aunt and cousins. But Becky hadn't stopped telling Will that Kyle would be better off with her. *He's lived with us most of his life,* she reminded him. *Ever since Ginger came home. We're his family.*

Will found that hard to dispute, especially when things were still so stiff and unsettled between him and his son.

Kyle still didn't call him Dad.

Will tried not to think about that, tried not to feel the sting of knowing that, of all the people in Hope Springs who still condemned him, Kyle led the list. He picked up the mug of coffee from the table beside the old recliner that no longer reclined and drew it to his lips. It was cold. Like the house. Like Will's heart.

Except when he thought of Libby.

He swallowed the coffee. Bitterness coated his mouth. He grimaced, uncertain whether the bitter-

ness came from the coffee or from thinking about
Libby.

He didn't have time to figure it out. Headlights
flickered across the front window. They were back
early. He switched on another lamp, stopped by the
thermostat to crank up the heat. But when he opened
the front door, it wasn't Kyle walking up the front
steps.

It was his brother.

Paul stopped on the top step and cast him a challenging glare. Will wondered if that was the look
people saw on his own face much of the time. The
deeply creased forehead, the eyes in shadow, the
grimly set mouth. No wonder they believed the
worst about him.

"Come on in," he said.

"Stay away from Mrs. Esterhaus and Libby Jeffries."

Paul's voice was implacable, carrying a hard edge
that brooked no argument. Will felt suddenly pee-
vish. Oh, they were too much alike. He should close
the door in Paul's face right now before the argument began. But he didn't.

"It's none of your business."

"You made it my business when you drove back
into town."

Anger rising, Will barely took notice of the other
set of headlights, the noise of other car doors slam-
ming at the end of the driveway. Paul was advancing
on him, getting in his face, the way the man had in

front of the Nineteenth Hole a week ago. Will's chest grew tight.

"Don't make me forget you're my little brother," he said.

"She went to the sheriff, you know."

"Who did?"

"Libby Jeffries. Filed some kind of complaint, I guess. Listen, you son of a—"

Will grabbed his brother by the front of his shirt and pulled him up. "You're lying. And I don't have to listen to it here on my own front porch."

"*Our* front porch," Paul spit. "And I saw her with my own eyes, looking like somebody had her good and spooked. I don't suppose there's much doubt who that somebody is."

Will shoved his brother away from him. Paul stumbled backward against the banister. When he did, Will saw Kyle and Becky standing at the foot of the steps, staring up. Kyle's eyes were wide with fear.

The anger blackening Will's soul fizzled out at the look in his son's eyes.

Becky put her hand on Kyle's shoulder. "Come on, Kyle. You can stay over with us tonight."

"No!" Will said automatically.

"You hurt Libby," Kyle said, his voice trembling. "You hurt Libby."

"Kyle, I—"

"I hate you! I hate you and I never want to see you again!"

Kyle turned and ran back to his aunt's car. Becky

glared at Will a moment, then followed. Will stared after them, drained.

Paul smoothed his shirtfront. "Listen to the boy."

He left, too. Two sets of headlights swept over Will, then he was alone on his porch.

His brother hated him. His son hated him. Half the town hated him. Libby Jeffries had done this to him twenty years ago. She was still doing it to him.

He reached inside the door, grabbed his coat and stalked off in the direction of Old Oak Street and the woman who was responsible for ruining his life.

CHAPTER TEN

FROM HER BEDROOM WINDOW Libby glanced toward the street, expecting Clem Weeks and trying not to be anxious. After all, she was the one who had opened the door to a friendship when she asked Clem to help her find a car.

But she was nervous about the idea of a visitor tonight. She didn't like worrying about making small talk and trying to be sociable, things that other people seemed to do so effortlessly.

"She's doing you a favor," Libby muttered. "Don't be such a crab."

She had untied her robe to change back into street clothes when she saw the man stride up the street. He caught her eye and she paused. Even before he passed beneath the halo of the streetlight, she knew from the rigid angle of his shoulders that it was Will and that he was coming for her.

She wasn't sure why he'd be coming for her, but she knew it was so. She knotted the tie of her terry robe again and started downstairs in her fleece-lined slippers. The pounding on the front door had already begun by the time she reached the bottom of the stairs.

Sticking her head into Mrs. E.'s room, she whispered, "It's only Will. Don't worry."

The comment struck her as odd, all things considered. Her own lack of concern as she opened the door for him also struck her as strange. But she knew the truth of what she felt. It was Will. It was nothing to worry about.

"What's wrong?" she asked gently.

His face shifted and softened as he looked at her. Libby realized he was struggling to hang on to whatever fierce emotions had driven him here. But it was too late. He looked defeated and weary, confused by his presence at her door.

She reached out, took him by the arm and led him into the house.

"Want coffee?"

He nodded and followed her to the kitchen. She turned on the light and in minutes had a pot of coffee brewing. He stood beside the table, staring at the floor. In the bright kitchen light, the circles beneath his eyes were pronounced, testimony to the fact that the things troubling Will Travers were things of long standing. A good night's sleep, Libby suspected, was a rare commodity for him.

She urged him to sit, then took out cups and milk and spoons. His shoulders sagged, the way they had the day Kyle brushed him off.

"Is Kyle okay?"

He nodded. His voice was barely audible. "With his aunt."

Libby wondered at that. She knew Kyle liked his

aunt; he and his mother had lived with Becky Marr and her children for years. It was home to him. She also knew, without anyone telling her, that his son's allegiance to Becky's family must feel threatening to Will. But his reaction tonight…it seemed to be more.

The coffeemaker gurgled to a stop and she filled two cups. She doctored Will's the way he liked it, with a touch of milk and plenty of sugar. She sipped at hers, black.

"What's wrong, Will?" she asked again.

He nursed his coffee for a long time, stirring, sipping, staring into it for answers. She waited.

"He thinks I hurt you."

She sighed. "Why on earth…? Who would have said such a thing?"

"My brother. Paul. He came to the house. Told me to leave you alone. You and Mrs. Esterhaus. Kyle came home in the middle of it. He…" Will's face twisted bitterly. "I guess it wasn't such an unlikely leap for a little boy to make, was it?"

She covered his free hand with hers before she realized what she was doing. "We'll both talk to him. We'll explain."

He studied her, then pulled his hand back. "Explain what, Libby?"

"Well, that you wouldn't hurt me."

"Wouldn't I?"

The edge was in his voice again. Libby sat back in her chair, inching away from him. "Of course not."

"Then maybe you could explain why you went to the sheriff about me," he said.

Libby's heart grew heavy. "Will—"

"Or you could explain to him how you know now that what you said all those years ago isn't true." His voice and his eyes were sharp with bitterness. "How you know better now. How you know I never hurt Mrs. Esterhaus. Right, Libby?"

"Will…"

But there was nothing to say. She *had* gone to Al Tillman. And she still knew what she'd seen twenty years ago. There was nothing she could say to Kyle about that. Or to Will.

"I wish things weren't so tangled up," she said.

His anger ebbed. "So do I."

"I'll make it right with Kyle."

He shook his head. "It's my problem."

"You're not the only one who cares about him."

Will toyed with the coffee cup. It was too small, too dainty for his workman's hands. He needed a mug, she decided, not this bit of delicacy that was Mrs. E.'s everyday china.

He set the cup down. "When he came to live with me, I really believed he'd come around. That some kind of father-son thing would happen and—" He broke off. "He said he hates me."

"He loves you or he'd never say that."

Will grunted his skepticism. "I was so tired of being alone. I wasn't glad Ginger died—never that. But it felt like a reprieve with Kyle. A second chance." He shoved the coffee cup away. "What a joke."

Libby hurt with him. She could hear the anguish in every word. She had nothing but compassion for Will Travers. No more anger, no more blame, certainly no more fear. He had served time in hell for what happened in this very kitchen twenty years earlier. He deserved to be released.

How could she be thinking these things?

Looking at his somber face, at his tortured eyes, how could she not?

She touched him again.

He gripped her hand.

His flesh scraped against hers, heated and hard. She began to tingle with the contact. She groped for something to say, some way to break the spell of this connection and her reaction.

"I'm sorry about the sheriff."

She realized too late that the words had come out in a whisper.

"You filed a report?"

"No." Still whispering, unable to bring her voice back to normal, she said, "I just asked if you'd been...if anything else had happened since you were gone."

She saw the injured pride flicker in his eyes.

"He said no." She saw no point in telling him what else Al had said. "I knew that's what he would say."

"Did you?"

She nodded.

"Then why?"

"Maybe...if... I don't know. Maybe I could help..." She stopped short of saying the words she was tempted to say. *Maybe I could help prove you're innocent.* Because she would only be saying the words to comfort him. So she said nothing, because something less than the truth would, in the long run, be no comfort to him at all.

He watched her for a moment, as if he knew what she was thinking. When she could no longer look him in the eye, he pulled away and stood.

"I'd better go."

"Wait."

She rose, searching for a reason to keep him here. Her mind wasn't functioning. The only reason she could think of for keeping him with her was that she wanted to feel his touch, to hear his voice, dusky and tender in the night. She reached for him, put her hand on his chest.

"Libby, don't."

She looked into his eyes. She wanted to ease what she saw there, but didn't know how.

"Oh, Will..."

She leaned close. To kiss him on the cheek, the way she would his son. But that was a lie and it took only a split second for her to realize the truth. She pressed her lips to his. They were hard, full, his breath hot. Her head began to spin as a tempest of yearning and desire whirled up inside her.

"Don't do that, Libby. Ever."

His voice was gruff, a low growl of a warning.

She felt her body spring to life as if she'd just been hooked into a source of power. She brushed her lips over his, willing his to soften and accept her. He grabbed her then, pulling her to him, covering her lips with his. A hard, hot, brief kiss. Something in her expanded and exploded. It was over too quickly. He thrust her away and glared at her, a look she knew intimately after all these weeks. It made her smile.

"I'm going."

"You'll come back," she said.

"You don't know what you're doing."

That much was true.

He stalked out, almost ran out, as if he were afraid of what had happened between them.

Libby wasn't afraid. She still didn't understand why this was happening. She *had* to be crazy. But she wasn't afraid. She had been all her life, it sometimes seemed. But not any longer.

She went after him, hoping to catch him and make him understand how things were changing. But when she reached the front porch, Clem Weeks was coming up the walk as Will retreated. Clem watched him hurry away, then glanced back at Libby.

Libby caught the lapels of her robe and clutched them to her throat. She knew her face was red, and she could still feel his kiss like a vivid brand on her lips.

Clem walked up the steps. "You okay?"

Libby nodded. She needed to explain. But how?

"You want to look at this car?"

"Not...not tonight, Clem. I'm sorry."

"It's okay. Tomorrow's soon enough." She jingled the keys in the pocket of her overalls. "I guess I feel sorry for him."

"You do?"

Clem gave her a faint smile. "I know what it's like. Feeling you don't fit in, that people are always talking about you."

Libby saw the forlorn look flicker across Clem's girlish face. She was lonely, too. Libby remembered all the talk about Clem's mother, the reputation that must have haunted Clem her whole life. And Libby hadn't been able to reach out in friendship before because of the things that haunted *her*. She realized Clem couldn't know that Libby's aloofness had nothing to do with the young mechanic's family baggage.

"People don't talk about you, Clem," she said softly.

"Sure they do." She smiled again. "Anyway, I think I understand how he feels. You do, too, don't you?"

"No, I..." Libby felt the heat rising in her face again. "It's his son. Kyle. I worry about Kyle."

"We misfits have to stick together."

Libby wanted to deny it, but it was true. She was a lot like Clem, retreating from the mainstream of life in Hope Springs so people wouldn't see her emotional scars. Will's return was forcing her out of her hiding place.

She returned Clem's smile. "I have fresh coffee. You could tell me about the car."

"Yeah?" From the tone of her voice, Clem couldn't believe she was being invited in.

"Yeah."

WILL SPENT the next few days trembling inside.

He felt as bad as he had at eighteen, sitting in the city jail cell, wondering how he could be in the fix he was in. Knowing he'd done nothing wrong but certain he would have to pay for what had happened regardless.

Charged with anxiety, he took his son to school and picked him up. They talked little. He'd given up trying to explain to Kyle that he hadn't hurt Libby Jeffries.

"Then why can't I go over there anymore?" Kyle said one drizzly morning on the way to school.

"Because I said so."

The knowing sneer on his son's face seemed to Will a harbinger. Things would only get worse. His own son didn't believe him, and everything conspired to keep it that way.

Everything except Libby. And she was off-limits.

And why is that? he asked himself as he drove away from the elementary school.

Because they had a history. Because she didn't really believe in him. Because she was the reason his life had been such hell. Because she was naive and gentle and touched a place in his heart he'd kept sealed away from the rest of the world for years.

Because she stirred his blood. And if he didn't stay away, he would lose his mind with wanting her.

Paul was right. He had to stay away from her.

He thought about her when he picked up his paycheck, about the way her pale skin glowed with the faintest hint of color in her cheeks. He almost told Bama Preston right then and there that he could work anywhere but at the Esterhaus home.

He thought about her when he deposited his check, about the shiny hair that drifted around her slender neck, kissing her cheeks.

He thought about her when he gassed up the truck, the bewilderment in her hazel eyes when she'd leaned in to touch his lips with hers, the soft, searching curiosity of her kiss.

My God, she'd kissed him! How could he have let that happen?

His fingers fumbled with the gas cap when he tried to replace it on his truck. Cold sweat, colder than the spitting rain, dampened his T-shirt. When someone called his name, he jumped guiltily and dropped the gas cap. He turned toward the voice. A vaguely familiar-looking man stood on the other side of the gas pumps beside a big shiny sedan. The man thrust his hand between the pumps; his smile struck Will as determined to prove a lack of prejudice.

"Larry Templeton, Will."

He remembered now. Templeton had been in his graduating class. Valedictorian or student-body president or something. Maybe both. Larry Templeton hadn't given Will the time of day back then. Cocksure and spotless, he was far too good for the likes of Will Travers.

Will nodded and took his hand.

Larry still looked spotless, from his razor-cut hair that had never been touched by Fudgie Ruppenthal to the black sedan that said he'd lived up to every ounce of his youthful potential.

"How's it going, being back home?" Larry asked as Will retrieved the gas cap that had rolled under his pickup.

"Pretty good," Will said. *Pretty good if you don't count the fact that Hurd's Hardware sold out of dead bolts the day after I rolled into town.*

Larry finished pumping his own gas and walked with Will to the cashier. "Heard you're working for the Prestons. You worked in landscaping before you came back if I'm not mistaken."

The inquiries were genial; Will tried not to bristle at the implication he'd been talked about plenty, his entire life rehashed at dinner tables all over town.

"That's right."

Larry peeled off a twenty-dollar bill, passed it through the window to the cashier and shook his head. "Too bad. Sounds like you're exactly whom I need."

"Oh?" Small talk. Will knew small talk when he heard it.

"I'm headmaster at the Blue Ridge Academy. And we sure do need a groundskeeper."

Will remembered the Blue Ridge Academy for

Girls. A private prep school for bluebloods, the pre-Vassar crowd. His brother taught there—another reason Will couldn't imagine fitting in. And he doubted that the Blue Ridge parents would look favorably on having a man with his reputation hanging out around their daughters. Small talk.

He paid. Larry had waited. They walked back to their vehicles together.

"Don't suppose you'd consider making a change?" Larry said.

"The Prestons were good to hire me." Will tried not to think about his conviction that he had to get away from Libby Jeffries.

"Pay's good at the academy," Larry said.

Will hesitated. That would simplify everything. The academy was out of town a few miles. Out of sight, out of mind. He would be out of sight of the townspeople. And Libby would be out of *his* sight. It made sense. It might even give him a chance to see Paul, to figure out a way to mend fences with his angry brother. But...

"I don't imagine my background would stand up to much scrutiny," he said finally, reluctantly.

Larry put a hand on Will's shoulder. "Listen, Will, you've had a tough break in life. No reason that ought to haunt you forever. You let me worry about your background."

Larry's support lightened the load on Will's shoulders. It still surprised him how often people in Hope Springs expressed that kind of belief in him.

Even Libby.

Her lips had been so soft. So trusting.

He had to do something. Fast. He felt her tugging on him right now. If he wasn't careful, he'd be there before the day was over. Touching her hair with his big rough hands. Touching her life with his, spoiling hers in the process.

"If you're sure…"

Larry beamed. "When can you start?"

LIBBY HADN'T SEEN Will for almost a week. It felt like a lifetime.

She hadn't seen Kyle, either, and that left an empty place in her day—in her heart—too. Even Mrs. E. seemed listless and cranky, as if she were expecting something that never happened.

Libby told herself that was her imagination.

She didn't know what she had expected to happen after she and Will kissed, but it wasn't this. Abandonment. It stung. It became a tender ache in her heart. She'd been abandoned before, when her old boyfriend left for Arizona. When she thought about it happening again, it was all she could do to catch her breath.

The night of a howling, driving rainstorm, when she found herself without power, she did what she'd told herself all week she wouldn't do. She picked up the phone and dialed his number.

His voice had the ability to touch her even over the telephone line.

"Will…I… The power went out."

There was a silence. She could almost sense the

rhythm of his breathing. She could see the way his frown would deepen, the shadows descend over his eyes.

"The electric company will come soon."

"But..." Of course, he was right. "I think Mrs. E. is afraid."

"I don't work for the Prestons anymore."

So he *had* abandoned her. She felt as if the ground had been snatched out from under her. "Oh. Still..."

"I can't come, Libby."

She hated herself for feeling so weak and needy, and for her willingness to let him see it. "Why not?"

There was a long silence. She thought of hanging up, saving him the embarrassment of finding an answer.

"I don't want to screw up your life, Libby," he said at last. "I couldn't handle it."

"It won't be that way, Will."

"I don't need the guilt."

Libby closed her eyes. She thought of a million ways to plead with Will, and none of them seemed fair. It was too complicated. It would hurt them both. She was crazy to think otherwise.

She hung up, feeling the ragged rhythm of her heartbeat.

He was right. But it didn't help.

CHAPTER ELEVEN

KYLE KNEW HE WASN'T supposed to be here. But he didn't give a poop. He didn't have to do a thing Will told him unless he felt like it.

And what he felt like was seeing Libby and Mrs. E.

But Libby didn't seem especially glad to see him. She set out a brownie and a glass of milk when he showed up after school, but she sat there looking at him and frowning and shaking her head. The brownie was gooey and extra good. He smiled at Libby and hoped she'd smile at him.

"I don't think your father wants you to be here, Kyle," she said when he finished the last bite of brownie.

Kyle contemplated his chances of getting another; better than his chances of taking Libby's mind off what she was saying, he thought.

"That sure was good," he said. "Better than Aunt Becky's, even. Aunt Becky's brownies are never that gooey."

Libby didn't smile at that and Kyle's heart began to sink. He'd counted on Libby being a softy.

"Kyle?"

He thought of another tactic. "I had to make sure he didn't hurt you."

"Well, he didn't hurt me. I promise you that." She stopped peeling a potato from the metal bowl on the table in front of her. "Now, don't you think you should go over to your aunt's house? Isn't that where you should be this afternoon? Won't she be worried?"

Kyle felt uneasy. He hated people worrying about him. He hated the way Aunt Becky looked at him sometimes, like she knew he liked being at Libby's better than at her house. He couldn't tell her it was because being with his aunt reminded him of his mother and he knew now that no matter how much he wanted his mother back, she wasn't coming. Not even now that they'd moved back to Hope Springs.

Life stank that way.

So he didn't want to think about it right now. He didn't want to sit in the kitchen where Mom used to make the best macaroni-and-cheese in the entire world or walk by the bedroom door where she used to have all her stuff. Now it was his cousin Moira's room. Moira was fourteen and too grown-up to sleep with her sisters anymore. So she'd taken over Kyle's mother's room.

He hated cousin Moira. Her hairspray smelled yucky. And she wore too much gunk on her eyes. Not like his mom.

Not like Libby.

So how was he going to fix it so that he could visit Libby again, instead of having to sit there and remember his mom when nothing would ever be the same again?

"She won't worry. I told my cousin what to tell her."

"You told her you'd be here?"

Kyle hesitated. "Sort of."

Libby sighed and made a mother-frown. He wondered how she knew how to do mother-frowns when she didn't even have kids of her own.

"Kyle, I'm going to have to call your father or—"

"No!" He jumped up, knocking over the plastic tumbler and spilling the rest of his milk all over the table. "Please don't call *him.*"

Libby took a paper napkin from the wooden holder on the table and wiped up the milk. She looked at him—not a softie look, either. "Why don't you call him Dad?"

Kyle scrunched up his face in a deep frown. He didn't have to answer that question. "Don't make me go to Aunt Becky's. I... It makes me remember stuff."

He saw the way Libby's eyes melted when he said that and figured he'd finally said something right. But before things had a chance to work out, he heard the knocking on the front door. It sounded like an angry man's knock to Kyle.

"I better go," he said, edging toward the back door.

Libby put a hand on his shoulder. "No, you'd better come with me."

LIBBY'S HEART was racing. There they sat, the two of them, on the sofa in the living room. The two people she'd missed so desperately this past week. They both looked miserable. Kyle sullen, Will thunderous. She wanted to pat their heads, smooth their hair, feed them brownies. She wanted to give them back to each other, but that was impossible, she supposed.

"Sorry he bothered you," Will said. "It won't happen again."

He looked with firm determination at his son, who stared at the scuffed sneakers he raked back and forth on the cabbage-rose rug.

"He's no bother," she said.

Will didn't seem to welcome her comment.

"See?" Kyle muttered.

"Don't give me another good reason to ground you."

"I'll run away."

Libby studied the two stubborn faces and saw the fear and uncertainty beneath their mutual belligerence. How could they both hurt so much, she wondered, and turn *on* each other, instead of turning *to* each other?

"Go sit in the truck," Will said to his son. "I'll be out in a minute."

Kyle looked primed to rebel.

"Kyle, I can tell you right now that Mrs. E. and I won't have anyone around the house who doesn't follow the rules," Libby said. "Privileges carry certain responsibilities. One of your responsibilities is to do what your father tells you.''

The boy kept a defiant look on his face, but he picked up his jacket and schoolbag and trudged out the front door to Will's truck. Will stood at the front window and watched to make sure his son did as he'd been told.

''Thanks,'' he said without turning away from the window. ''He won't listen to me.''

''You're too much alike,'' she said gently. ''Neither one of you bends much.''

''I'm not supposed to bend. I'm the parent.'' He sighed heavily. ''At least that's the way I see it. I suppose I'm wrong about that, too.''

She wanted to go to him and touch his shoulder. The need to do so was a physical ache.

''I'm glad to have him here, you know. So is Mrs. E.''

Will shook his head. ''It's better this way.''

''Why?''

He didn't answer.

''Better for you?'' she prodded. ''Easier for you if you just put me out of your mind?''

He hunched his shoulders against her question. She got up and walked over to him. The scent of the outdoors that always clung to him assailed her, filling her head. Her body responded automatically with sharp yearning.

''Is it really so easy to run away, Will? Was it easy all those years you turned yourself into an exile? Did that really solve anything?''

He whirled to face her. "I don't know. Does it for you?"

She snapped back from the angry accusation in his voice. "For *me?*"

"Holing up like this with an invalid, living your life with somebody who can't give back to you. If that's not running away, I don't know what is."

"We're talking about you, not me," she said, refusing to acknowledge the bruised part of her life that he'd called to her attention. Clem Weeks had seen it, as well, so it must be true. But if she'd turned herself into an outcast, too, what of it? She wasn't hurting anyone with her choices. "You and Kyle."

She watched the fight die in him at the mention of his son.

"What am I going to do with him? I came back here because of him, you know. And it's…it's all been pointless. If anything, things are worse."

She did touch him then. She put her hand on his arm and tried to ignore the reactions that shot through her. "He's lost his mother. He's not sure he has a father."

"What the hell does that mean?"

"It means he only knows what he's heard about you. And every time you speak in anger or impatience, it reinforces everything he's been told. He wants to believe something else. Any boy would."

"But I don't give him much choice. Is that it?"

"Maybe."

Will ran his fingers through his hair, a frustrated

gesture. "I don't know how to... I've gotten hard, I know that. What the hell am I supposed to do?"

"Show him you love him."

Will drew a ragged breath and she realized he was close to tears. "He'll reject me."

"Keep doing it."

He shook his head and closed his eyes tightly. "I'm so afraid of that. Of having him turn me away. You don't know."

She laughed softly. "Yes, I do."

He looked at her then, studied her for a long moment. "It's not like that."

"Isn't it?"

He took her in his arms, tentatively and gently. He didn't pull her close, just held her in a loose embrace that still felt warm beyond belief. His lips trailed tenderly across her forehead, her cheek, her jaw, barely missing her lips. Then he pulled away.

"Why?" she said.

He looked at her as helplessly as Kyle had looked at her in the kitchen, as if explaining what was inside him was a task beyond his ability. "Because you're right. It's easier not to. It's easier not to let myself...wish."

"Wishing isn't so hard."

"It is from where I sit."

Then he walked toward the front door. She followed him into the hall, wanting to call him back, wanting to find a way to give him back his wishes and hopes and dreams.

After all, wasn't she the one who'd robbed him of them?

He paused at the door but didn't turn around. "You don't mind if he comes?"

"I don't mind if both of you come."

He nodded. "I'll tell him it's okay."

She watched him make his way down the sidewalk. He looked whipped, overwhelmed by the burden he carried. She tried to figure out whether he had taken that burden on himself with his own actions, or if an unreliable little girl had placed that burden there for him.

She thought back. It had all been so clear. How could she have been wrong?

But it was either that or she was wrong now. And somehow she knew that was impossible.

WILL DIDN'T LIKE battling with himself. He didn't like the way he vacillated between listening to his heart and listening to his head.

His head told him that hanging around Libby Jeffries was asking for trouble.

His heart told him her presence in his life was healing.

Back and forth he warred with himself.

The only thing that successfully distracted him was his stepped-up efforts to find someone who knew something about the attack on Alice Esterhaus. After weeks with no success, he was fairly certain he was tilting at windmills. But every time he thought of giving up the search, he remembered

Kyle. He remembered Mrs. E. And he remembered Libby.

Will could survive the way things were. But *they* deserved to learn the truth.

So he poured over the trial records Melvin Guthry helped him obtain from the courthouse. He studied every bit of testimony, looking for some elusive fact that might be the key to that truth. He made a list of everyone who had testified. He stared at the pages that were the history of his downfall as if they might suddenly yield something new, something that would set him free of the past. Something that would win him his son's love and justice for Mrs. E.

Something that would bring him back into the fold so he could love a woman like Libby Jeffries.

He slammed the file shut, sending papers fluttering, and jumped up from the kitchen table, frustrated with the world and irritated with himself. He didn't love Libby Jeffries. He was grateful to her for the way she treated Kyle. He longed for normalcy and she was it, even while she was the very reason he hadn't had normalcy for most of his life. He longed for absolution, and she could provide it.

He was simply obsessed with Libby Jeffries.

He swore and left the papers scattered on the kitchen table. He wandered toward the back of the house. The light in Kyle's room was still on, but a peek revealed that the boy was asleep, sprawled almost crossways on the narrow bed. His feet hung off, uncovered and bare. He hugged his pillow to his chest. His pale hair shone in the faint light from the moon.

Will ached with the yearning to be a father to his son.

But in that way, too, he was an outcast, rejected by his own flesh and blood.

He nudged Kyle's feet under the covers. He almost gave in to the urge to kiss the boy's cheek, hoping to get away with it while sleep claimed his son. But if Kyle awoke, if he flinched away in fear or loathing...

Show him you love him. He remembered Libby's words. The parameters of his inner battle extended. Was he really such a coward that he would rather rob his own son of his love than risk rejection? He had been. But Libby was challenging him to go beyond his fear. To face it.

Gulping back the anxiety, he leaned over the sleeping boy and brushed his forehead with a kiss. Kyle stirred only slightly, then cuddled his pillow more tightly in his arms. He smelled of cherry-flavored toothpaste and baby shampoo. Will backed away quietly. His throat felt thick and his eyes stung. He told himself he couldn't afford these emotions.

He feared that the truth was he couldn't afford to ignore them any longer.

The next morning he started visiting the people who had testified at his trial. He knocked on doors and pleaded with them to talk to him. He asked questions and learned that memories grew fuzzy with time. People *wanted* to forget. Nobody wanted to look back.

"Young man," said Jewell Northrop, who had taught high-school math in the classroom next door to Mrs. E.'s, "you need to let this go."

Miss Northrop shared a house with another retired teacher on the edge of town, and she still stood erect and wore the forbidding expression that had made her so unpopular with students like Will. He'd caught her planting daffodil bulbs and had taken the trowel out of her knotted hands and dug himself while they talked.

"I can't let it go," he said as he mixed bulb food into the soil he'd just dug.

"Why not?" Her tone demanded an answer as surely as if she'd still been standing in front of a blackboard and asking the formula for figuring square roots.

Will would rather answer the square-root question. He reached for a bulb and placed it gently in the soil.

"The jury found you not guilty," Miss Northrop said. "Why isn't that enough?"

"Nobody believed it." He plunged the trowel into the soil again and found it cool, crumbling easily at his touch. He concentrated on the feel of it. The earth was easy, welcoming, ready to yield up its gifts to anyone with patience.

"You are a gardener if I've heard correctly."

He nodded.

"So the grapevine is sometimes correct." She sat

on a concrete bench that curved along the edge of the flower bed. She crossed her ankles. "Have you ever noticed how much good comes out of the darkness?"

He glanced up at her. Her piercing eyes were fixed on him, but a calm certainty played over her wrinkled face.

"Like the bulbs you're planting," she continued. "We place them in the ground, where they'll winter in the cold and the dark. But their time in the cold, in the darkness, is what transforms them from odd-looking knots into something of beauty and grace in a world that sometimes seems to have too little of either."

Her words jangled around in Will's head, knocking against his skepticism and his bitterness.

"That seems to be the way of it in this world of ours," she said. "Babies, butterflies, even a loaf of bread. Have you ever smelled bread dough rising? Smells funny, that yeast does. Ah, but what comes later is divine."

He planted the last of the bulbs and stood, dusting loose soil from his fingers.

"You've spent a lot of time in the dark, Will Travers."

"I'm not exactly divine yet, either."

She laughed, and suddenly her face was delightful, lit with a joy he wished he could find.

"But you can be transformed," she said, smiling as she rose. "Even the homeliest caterpillar becomes a butterfly, young man."

He gathered up her basket of garden tools and followed her to her back door.

"I could let it go if it was just me," he said. "But there's my son. And there's Mrs. E. She deserves justice."

Miss Northrop nodded. "Indeed she does."

"You were her friend. You said so at the trial. You must know if there could have been anybody else who would have hurt her, who was angry with her."

She put her garden basket on a deep shelf on her screened back porch. "She helped so many people."

"Who? Who else?"

"So many. With no children of her own, it was a need she had. Who could keep track of all she did? But Alice was meticulous. She wrote it all down. I guess everyone she came in contact with was somewhere in those notebooks of hers."

"Notebooks?" He'd seen no mention of Mrs. E.'s records in any of the court documents.

"Heavens, yes. She wrote everything down. I don't know what happened to all her paperwork."

"Where did she keep it?"

"She had a big file cabinet in her classroom. I remember the day they came to clean it out. It was all locked up and there was quite a bit of agitation because no one had a key except Alice, and of course she couldn't tell anyone where it was. I'm not sure what happened, but I suppose the school eventually disposed of everything."

Knowing this was a very thin thread, Will nevertheless set out to find out about Mrs. E.'s records. He doubted they contained anything helpful; he doubted they still existed. But they were the only thing he'd heard about so far that hadn't been covered at the trial. Maybe, just maybe...

He ended up talking to the head of the local school board, who promised to do her best to find out what had happened to Alice Esterhaus's records. Probably destroyed, she said, or given to the family. Will pressed her to find out soon. He could tell she thought it was a waste of time, but he didn't care. He would clutch at straws if he had to. Something had to give.

He never expected to become a butterfly, but he was tired of living in the darkness.

LARRY TEMPLETON liked his position as an elected official on the local public school board even more than he liked his position as headmaster of the Blue Ridge Academy. It wasn't a paid position of course, but being elected to office carried prestige and the illusion of power. It added another layer of respectability to the life of Lawrence Albert Templeton.

The meetings were boring, but Larry liked sharing his opinions and sometimes seeing those opinions quoted in the local newspaper.

Tonight's meeting, however, had not been boring. Tonight, he had heard something that had him jumping out of his skin. Will Travers had asked Judy Manicioto, head of the school board, for help finding the old records of Alice Esterhaus. That revelation was mentioned in passing. No one else paid it much attention. But for the rest of the meeting Larry had trouble concentrating on whatever topic the board was addressing. He was short on opinions tonight; he wasn't likely to be quoted in the *Courier* this week.

After the meeting adjourned, he worked his way to Judy's side, trying not to look as urgent as he felt.

"What's this business about Will Travers?" he said, keeping his voice casual.

"Nothing big. He seems to think Mrs. Esterhaus kept a bunch of records that might reveal something about that old assault case."

One of the other board members looked up from the sheaf of papers she was stuffing into a briefcase. "He doesn't give up, does he?"

Larry frowned at the intrusion. "What makes him think Mrs. Esterhaus had records in the first place?"

Judy shrugged. "I think he talked to one of her old friends. He said he heard she wrote everything down. I don't know. I talked to Randall Hamm—he was the principal then—and he said he did remember a file cabinet full of stuff in her classroom. But he didn't think it was the kind of stuff the school would have stored. He said the family probably took it."

Larry's skin grew tight. He remembered the file cabinet. An ugly gray metal monster, it sat in the back of Mrs. E.'s classroom. She kept master copies of her tests in it—at least that was the rumor, because it was always locked. What else, he wondered with a thin spike of dread, had she kept there?

"He's asking questions all over town," the other board member said. "I heard he's talked to everybody who testified at the trial."

Larry refused to react, but the words sliced through him.

"A lot of people are saying the jury must've been right all along," someone added. "He wouldn't be asking all these questions if he did it, would he?"

"Unless that's exactly what he wants everyone to think," Larry said.

Judy shrugged and shouldered her briefcase. "Which brings up a very interesting question." Everyone looked toward her. "If Will Travers didn't do it, who did?"

She looked around the circle of board members. A few heads began to nod. Someone laughed nervously. Larry struggled to hang on to his composure.

Who, indeed.

He had to find out if Mrs. Esterhaus's files still existed. And if they did, he had to get his hands on them before someone else did. Because if Mrs. Esterhaus, as Judy said, had written everything down, his name would be there, too. He hadn't been willing for all that to come out then; he'd thought he had too much to lose.

Today he could lose far more.

CHAPTER TWELVE

WHAT A DIFFERENCE five minutes could make.

Kyle had been flitting about Mrs. Esterhaus's living room in the Superman costume Libby had made him, laughing and excited about the Halloween carnival at the school. Libby was sitting on the footstool beside the fireplace, her delicate features marked with fondness as she watched Kyle's excitement.

Will had been trying hard to keep his face expressionless. He'd never seen his son so happy, so utterly little boyish.

Now Kyle stood in the middle of the room, all boyish enthusiasm gone, replaced by the truculent defiance that was so familiar to Will. Libby, who had worked so hard on the costume, still sat on the footstool, her face downcast.

"Five minutes ago you couldn't wait to get to the school carnival," Will said. "You want to tell me what changed your mind?"

"I don't feel like it."

Will was losing his temper, and fast. He struggled to contain it. "Libby worked hard so you'd have a nice costume for Halloween. You're going to have to do better than that, young man."

Kyle looked up, anger flashing in his dark eyes. "I'm big enough to go by myself."

"No, you're not."

"I don't have to go with you." The little boy's defiant words sank in. Kyle was ashamed to go to the school carnival with his father. "I want Libby to take me."

Anger seeped out of Will like a tire with a fast leak. His own son was that ashamed of him. And what could he do about it? Walk out? Let someone else raise his son? Run some more and expect his son to run with him?

Libby's soft voice broke through the tension between father and son. "What if all three of us went?"

"You don't have to do that," Will said. He didn't want her to do it, didn't want her even making the offer. He didn't want—didn't need—another reason to feel hope in her presence.

"It would be fun," she said. "How about it, Kyle?"

"You'd go with *him?*"

Will's insides constricted as he, too, waited for the answer.

Libby got up and walked over to Kyle. She knelt in front of him and took his hands in hers. Will's heart ached with wanting to be part of their closeness. Was he destined, he wondered, to always be on the outside looking in when people drew close and gave from their hearts? He'd started doing that with Ginger, he supposed, withdrawing when she expressed her longing to go home so it wouldn't hurt as much when she finally left.

"Kyle," Libby said, "I know there are people in this town who judge your father for something that happened a long time ago. Good people try not to judge at all, but none of us is perfect. Sometimes the best we can do is judge people by their actions today."

Kyle frowned.

"Today," Libby continued, "your dad is working hard to take good care of you. He's kind to me and Mrs. Esterhaus and probably other people, too. He doesn't do anything mean to anybody. Does he?"

Kyle stared at his feet. "Sometimes he yells at me."

Libby ruffled his hair. "Maybe sometimes he needs to get your attention."

Kyle shrugged.

"Does he hit you?" Kyle shook his head. "Starve you? Make you sleep on the porch where the birds can nest in your hair?"

Kyle giggled. "No."

"Well, then, he's not so bad. And I know that from personal experience, because my dad was the same way." She stood up. "I'll call my dad. He can probably sit with Mrs. E. for a few hours. While I do that, you run and show her your costume."

She went to the phone in the kitchen, leaving the two of them alone. Will looked at his son, who was glancing up through his too-long bangs, a doubtful expression on his face.

"It's up to you," Will said. "We can have fun with Libby tonight or we can go home and feel bad because we're the only ones in town not having fun."

Kyle bit his lower lip. It was clearly a tough decision. Will could appreciate that. Sometimes pride dictates that you hold on to your bad feelings no matter what the consequences.

"I'll go show Mrs. E." Kyle paused on his way out of the living room. "Once I have my mask on, nobody'll know who I am, anyway."

The victory was hollow. Will tried to console himself with the idea that being with Libby would make up for saddling his son with his unwelcome presence.

VERA TEMPLETON listened to Libby's instructions. Then, her heart tripping uncomfortably, she saw them out the door. Libby, Will Travers and the little boy. A very unlikely trio.

As unlikely as her becoming Alice Esterhaus's caretaker.

What had she been thinking, volunteering to come over when Libby called Noah looking for someone to sit with the old woman? Noah could have come, had said he'd be glad to come. But, no, Vera had insisted.

She stood in the foyer, reminding herself that she'd had a pressing reason for insisting.

Vera took three steps toward the bedroom, where the lights were already out. Libby said she'd given the old woman her evening medication before she left. She would no doubt sleep until Libby returned. Libby had said so. There was no reason for Vera to venture in that direction.

The doorbell rang, startling her.

A clutch of tiny goblins demanded their booty. She passed out candy bars. Another group came before she could return the bowl of candy to the table. Then another.

When Vera finally closed the door she was impatient. She walked to the bedroom door without hesitating this time. The light from the foyer brightened the bedroom. It was the first time she'd seen Mrs. Esterhaus since before the attack. Mrs. Esterhaus had been younger then than Vera was now, a sturdy woman with a strong voice. Vera understood that voice hadn't been heard since. And she was no longer a sturdy woman. She was frail.

The old woman's eyes were wide open. She wasn't sleeping at all. That startled Vera. What if she sensed Vera's presence in her house? What if that troubled her? What if she knew more than people thought?

"Mrs. Esterhaus?"

The old woman didn't move, didn't so much as twitch. Vera wasn't reassured. She needed to convince herself that Alice Esterhaus was as unaware as everyone said.

"Mrs. Esterhaus, do you need anything?"

Still there was no response, no flicker of reaction.

Vera let out the breath she'd been holding and backed out of the room.

The doorbell rang again. The silhouette against the circle of glass was tall and broad-shouldered, not a pint-size goblin. She opened the door to her son. Her heart was a painful weight in her chest.

"I took the kids next door so you could see their costumes," Larry said. "Noah said you were playing good Samaritan."

She nodded. She noted her son's fine clothes, the educated way he spoke. He was a son to make any mother proud. Unless that mother knew.

"Noah's giving them hot chocolate," he said. "Going to invite me in?" He stepped past her, overlooking her lack of response. He gazed around curiously. "I could stay here for a few minutes if you want to run over and see the kids."

Of course she wanted to see her grandchildren. Of course she could leave her son, her only son, here for the few minutes it would take.

"No, I...I don't think Libby would like that."

Larry gave her the look he reserved for those times he didn't think she was making the smartest decisions. Like marrying Noah Jeffries. "Mother, don't be silly. The kids want to see you. I can look after things here."

She wanted to insist that he bring them over here instead. She wanted to stand firm.

"Besides," he said when she hesitated, "you shouldn't be here alone. Not with Will Travers running around town."

Her response caught in her throat. Her son was afraid of Will Travers. Not in the same way others were, but afraid nevertheless. It struck her suddenly. She had to do something. She had to get Will Travers to leave town before her son did something himself.

Unable to look her son in the eye, she left him alone with Mrs. Esterhaus, using the excuse her grandchildren offered. She rushed down the front steps. She would hurry. There was no reason to worry. No reason to feel guilty about leaving Mrs. Esterhaus for a few minutes. No reason at all.

THE HIGH-SCHOOL GYMNASIUM was full, echoing with the squeals and laughter of children, the rumble of their parents' voices. Libby noticed how tentatively Will followed his son into the melee. He looked around furtively, waiting to be seen, waiting for the reaction.

The community carnival was in full swing. The gym was set up with games—apple bobbing, cakewalk, ring toss. Along the darkened corridor, classrooms had been turned into haunted houses. Children and adults alike were in costume. Devils and angels, pirates and war heroes, princesses and ballerinas. Libby wondered what it would be like to be in costume herself, to feel as loose and carefree as these people seemed to feel.

Libby wasn't comfortable with crowds. Being with Will in public wasn't terribly comfortable, either.

She was conscious, as they made their way through the gym, of the eyes that turned in their direction. Libby felt her cheeks go warm, her mouth go dry. Will would notice, too.

Even Kyle, as young as he was, probably felt the surreptitious attention.

They made the rounds in the gym quickly. None of them bobbed for apples. Kyle didn't want to participate in the cakewalk. He threw a few darts at the balloons and won a fistful of candy, but he didn't seem to enjoy being the center of attention even for those few minutes. He didn't want to go through the haunted houses.

"Let's go," he said. "It's too loud."

Libby glanced at Will. If she could only save these two from the past that still hurt them. The past that she'd helped create the minute she pointed a finger at Will Travers.

"But, Kyle—"

A ruckus at their side interrupted her. Two little boys ran up to them, shuffling into them and giggling. One was dressed as Count Dracula, the other as a space alien. The alien looked up at Will and said, "Will you autograph my Halloween bag?"

Count Dracula rolled his eyes as if he couldn't believe his friend's words. Will looked confused. Kyle looked mortified.

"I don't understand," Will said. "I'm nobody. You don't want my autograph."

"Sure I do, mister." The alien thrust his bag and

a crayon at Will, who refused to take his hands out of his pockets.

By now, Libby realized people nearby had noticed that something strange was happening. They stopped to look.

The little boy didn't waver in his determination. "You gotta sign it, mister. I've got a collection. Okay?"

"A collection?"

"Serial-killer cards. So sign my bag, okay?"

Libby reached out to pull the boy away, but another adult beat her to it. Someone called the boy's name in horror. Will went white. Kyle froze, his face suddenly anguished.

"Travers, don't mind him, he's—"

Will didn't wait for the rest of the explanation from the mortified parent. He grabbed Kyle by the hand and rushed through the crowd to the door. Libby looked around her, wanting to say something to the clutch of people who were watching, wanting to bring them to their senses. But she didn't know what that would take. She was prepared to turn away when Lavinia Holt, the town gossip, put her hands on the shoulders of her granddaughter and said, "I don't know what he expected, coming back here like this."

Someone else nodded. "Hanging around our children."

"There ought to be a law…"

"Sounds a mite small-minded to me," Eben Monk, one of the barbershop regulars, said.

"He ought to be in prison!"

Amidst the rumble of assent, someone said, "He was found not guilty. And even if he'd been found guilty, he would've served his sentence already—he'd probably be free by now. Don't forget that."

"Mrs. Esterhaus isn't free," came a clipped retort.

Libby's outrage grew as she listened to the divided townspeople.

"Stop it!" she said hoarsely and loudly. "Just stop it! What happened twenty years ago ruined a dozen lives—Mrs. E. and her family, my family, Will's family. Can't we spare one life? One little boy who shouldn't have to pay the price for something that happened before he was born?"

She looked around the crowd. Plenty of people nodded. Others looked away, ashamed. Some maintained a righteous silence.

"Now, Libby…"

She turned to follow Will and Kyle, ignoring the sympathetic voices that called after her. She caught up with them at the edge of the gravel parking lot. Their faces were matched sets of frozen humiliation—lips thin, foreheads creased, eyes ominously dark. She ached for them.

She put one hand on Kyle's shoulder and with the other took Will's hand. "I'm sorry."

Neither of them answered. They walked back to Will's house in silence.

Once there Kyle quickly got ready for bed. Libby stood by while Will tucked him in for the night. His discarded costume lay in a heap on the floor, a poignant reminder of the childhood this little boy wasn't being permitted to have. She looked at Kyle, his young face stony with the effort to hide his feelings. Libby searched her heart for healing words, but everything seemed pitifully inadequate.

"Can we go back to Washington?" Kyle asked.

Libby felt her breath hitch. She wanted to say no, to explain why that wasn't the solution. But of course it wasn't her business.

"Is that what you want?" Will replied so softly Libby barely heard him.

Kyle nodded.

"If I can prove what happened that night..."

"You can't prove anything!" Kyle's high-pitched voice was tremulous. "You did it and you can't blame somebody else!"

Will turned off the bedside lamp and left the room, sliding past Libby in the dark. The room pulsed with tension. Libby's need to do something was stronger than her need to get away from all this pain. She knelt beside Kyle's bed and brushed the hair from his forehead with the tips of her fingers. He accepted her touch but didn't change his expression.

What did you say to an eight-year-old who only wanted a normal life?

She could think of no reassurance, no platitude, no promise that would soothe him. So she said the only thing she had to say. "I love you, Kyle. I love you very much."

She heard the sob he refused to give free rein. She waited, touching him, hoping he trusted her enough to turn to her. Instead, showing a restraint no boy his age should possess, he fought back the tears and turned his face to the wall.

"G'night, Libby."

"Good night, sweetheart."

She found Will on the narrow front porch gripping the banister, staring into the moonless night. She stood beside him, shoulder to shoulder. The platitudes that wouldn't have worked for Kyle wouldn't work for him, either. Nor could she fall back on the words she'd settled on for Kyle.

For a moment, though, it was tempting.

"Go home," he said gruffly, "before it gets any later."

"Tell me..." She stopped herself short of demanding he tell her he didn't do it. She realized that was what she wanted to hear. "Tell me the truth."

"About Mrs. Esterhaus?"

She nodded.

He turned to face her. The shadows were deep, so she couldn't see his eyes no matter how much she needed to.

"You were wrong," he said. "It wasn't me you saw."

His words hit home. He might have said them a dozen different ways, but she believed in her heart that he wouldn't have said that to her if it wasn't true.

"I wasn't there that night. I never hurt Mrs. Esterhaus."

She wanted to believe him, teetered on the edge of belief. She couldn't see his eyes, but surely she knew what she would see there if she could.

What she could see was his mouth, his lips rigid with wounded emotions. She touched them, the way she'd touched his son, to heal, to take away the pain.

He grasped her hand, his grip too hard. "Believe me, Libby. Please."

The words were the barest whisper, an anguished plea that gripped her heart as tightly as his fingers gripped hers.

"Yes."

He took her in his arms, roughly, desperately. He crushed her to him, taking her breath away, covering her lips with his in a kiss that was heedless and hungry. Answering hunger exploded within her. She opened to his kiss with abandon, tasting his need. She couldn't have said whose hands sought the other first. She felt his back, the sinewy back she'd watched as he worked; felt his hands on her breasts, her buttocks. She felt him hard against her, felt herself go soft and hot and damp with a kind of longing she'd never felt before.

If only they could love each other, if only they could be one, the darkness hovering over them would surely vanish.

He tugged at her sweater. She pressed her palm to his hardness, heard the groan in his chest.

Yes, this was the answer.

She felt his lips, the heat of his tongue against her breast. Sensations exploded in her, drove her to a place where conscious thought vanished.

But in another world the unconscious thoughts returned.

The cries from Mrs. Esterhaus's kitchen. The man in the leather jacket. Something tossed into the bushes. The leather jacket. So familiar.

She cried out, pushed him away. "No!"

He stepped back, instantly releasing her.

They were both breathing heavily. Libby's hands shook as she straightened her disheveled clothes. She stared at him, thinking he wasn't someone she knew. But the real stranger, she decided, was herself. Libby Jeffries was cautious and slow to trust, always in control.

So who was this woman breathing raggedly, flushed with passion, giving herself without a thought to the consequences? Giving herself to a man she'd almost allowed herself to believe, despite what she'd seen with her own eyes.

"I have to go."

She waited, wanting his absolution. *Of course, Libby. I understand.*

"Go, goddamn it. Go!"

She ran home, tormented by her hateful memories and her unmet needs.

CHAPTER THIRTEEN

LIBBY AWOKE in the middle of the night to the sounds of squirrels overhead, scrambling across the roof, maybe even scurrying around in the attic, hiding acorns for the winter.

"Go back to sleep," she grumbled at them, then pulled a pillow over her head and tried to take her own advice.

Tomorrow, she told herself as she drowsed back into slumber, she would call Will. He'd already repaired the obvious places where the squirrels were getting in, but they'd apparently found a new passage. She hated the idea of locking away their winter stash, but she didn't like the idea of having her sleep interrupted, either.

She almost fell asleep again, despite the sounds of the little creatures moving around overhead.

But at the moment when sleep almost swept her up, another sound jerked her back to wakefulness. This time it was a loud thump that even a heavyweight squirrel couldn't have caused. She sat straight up in bed, clutching the covers to her chest, where her heart thumped unpleasantly. She waited for another sound and finally heard it. Something scraped against the outer wall of the house, near the louvered attic vents.

Squirrels, she told herself. *You hear them all the time.*

Then she heard a clang, like a ladder being raised or lowered.

Terrified, on legs that had no strength, she willed herself out of bed. *Can't freeze this time. Got to do something.*

She stumbled to her bedroom window. Saw nothing but the expanse of lawn, the arbor, the flower beds.

Downstairs. Go downstairs.

She wasn't sure she could move. She clutched the windowsill, paralyzed by the similarities. Sounds in the dark. Sounds only she heard. She had to act. There was no one else.

She'd almost decided she'd imagined it all when she saw the figure dart across the backyard.

A cry escaped her lips. She covered her mouth with a trembling hand.

A man in dark clothes stashed the extension ladder against the side of the shed—where Will always stored it.

But no leather jacket, she thought, and recognized instantly that her thinking bordered on the hysterical.

She banged on the window, enraged and outraged that someone was doing this to her a second time. The man fled without a backward glance, vanishing between the hedges. Just the way someone had twenty years earlier.

LIKE MOST EVERYONE ELSE in Hope Springs, Will heard about the commotion at Mrs. Esterhaus's before he finished breakfast the next morning. His former sister-in-law phoned to ask where he'd been in the middle of the night.

"What the hell business of yours is that?" he growled.

"Plenty," Becky said, the contempt in her voice apparent even over the telephone. "My only sister's son lives with you, and I have every right to know if you're still breaking in on Alice Esterhaus."

"I never— Alice Esterhaus? What happened?"

"Don't play coy with me, Will. I—"

He hung up. Something had happened. Someone might have been hurt. That someone might have been Libby.

He hurried Kyle off to school, then sped the few blocks to the house on Old Oak Street. The sheriff's distinctive blue-and-yellow car was parked at the curb. Will dashed up the steps and through the front door without knocking.

"Libby!"

He looked into Mrs. E.'s room. She was alone, appeared unharmed. He called up the stairs. "Libby!"

Sheriff Al Tillman's head appeared at the top of the stairs. "What the hell are you doing here?"

"Where's Libby? Is Libby okay?"

Tillman scowled. "As if you cared, you son of a—"

Libby stuck her head around the bend at the top

of the stairs. Her face was paler than usual, her hair mussed. She clutched a baby blue robe tightly beneath her chin. "Oh, Will."

He took the stairs two at a time, but Al Tillman placed himself squarely and unyieldingly between him and Libby.

"Travers, you'd better get the hell out of here before you create even more trouble for yourself than you already have."

"What happened?"

Libby's chin trembled. "Someone—"

"Now, Libby," Tillman said, holding up a hand to halt her. "This is a criminal investigation. You're going to have to listen to what I say and keep quiet till we get everything pinned down." He pointed at Will and gestured down the stairs. "You get yourself into the parlor. I'll have a few questions for you right soon."

Will figured the only way he was likely to find out what was going on here was to submit to Al Tillman's questioning. He exchanged another glance with Libby, who was red-eyed and looked ready to collapse. If someone had hurt Libby, he wasn't sure what he might do. He backed down the stairs as the sheriff told her to pull herself together and calm down. Libby nodded. She looked as if she needed someone to hold her and comfort her, not admonish her.

Punching Al Tillman for his callousness wouldn't solve a thing, Will decided. So he went downstairs and paced in the parlor, waiting and wondering.

When Tillman came in a few minutes later, he wasted no time. For the second time that morning, Will heard the question, "Where were you last night?"

He wanted to respond exactly as he had to Becky, but knew he didn't dare. He'd tried the antagonistic approach with law enforcement twenty years ago and it hadn't furthered his cause one whit.

"Home. Sleeping."

"Alone?"

Will clenched his jaw. "You know anybody in this town eager to sleep with a man who batters old ladies, Tillman?"

"Watch yourself, Travers."

He took a deep breath. "Alone," he conceded.

"What about your boy?"

"He was sleeping, too."

"So he couldn't exactly verify your whereabouts."

"Leave him out of this, Tillman," he said, then caught the way the sheriff bristled in response to his demand. "Please, don't drag my son into this."

Tillman gave no indication he'd heard Will's words. "You're pretty familiar with this house. Is that fair to say, Travers?"

Will felt his throat closing up, felt the flow of air to his lungs constrict. He felt panic coming on. He wanted to run. He had to get out of here.

"Am I a suspect in something?" he asked through lips so dry he could scarcely speak.

At that moment Libby appeared in the doorway behind the sheriff.

The sheriff snapped back, "Does a bear live in the woods, Travers?"

A lawyer, he thought. He should call a lawyer. He'd thought he didn't need one before, and look where his arrogance had gotten him. Then he looked at Libby again. What would she think if he insisted on calling a lawyer?

"It wasn't Will," she said.

"Now, Libby, you don't need to be here for this," Tillman said. "Reckon I could convince you to put on a pot of coffee?"

She looked Will in the eye. All color, in fact all her liveliness, seemed to have washed out of her. She'd changed into one of her uniforms and pulled her hair back, but she still didn't look like herself. Right up to her eyes, the Libby he knew seemed to have vanished. In her hazel eyes lived only bewilderment. She'd spoken words of faith in him, but her eyes asked for reassurance.

If only he could reassure her. Comfort her. Promise her that whatever had happened here during the night, he wasn't responsible for it.

When she turned away, feelings of disappointment flashed through him. He shouldn't have to tell her that. If she felt anything like what he felt, he wouldn't need to declare his innocence. The hard edge of bitterness crept into his heart. Wishful thinking, that's what that was. And the vacant look in her wide eyes just proved where wishful thinking got a man.

"Now, sit down, Travers, and tell me everything you can about how you spent your night."

WILL WAS GOING to be late for work. He still had to stop by Hurd's Hardware for a new pair of work boots; he'd finally pitched his old pair in the trash when he left Blue Ridge Academy the day before. Most of what he'd intended to accomplish that day wouldn't get done. But he could at least replace the broken window in the classroom building and check the thermostat in the dormitory. That's about all he would have time for with what was left of the day.

It was also about all he had the concentration for, he thought as he wandered the aisles at Hurd's. His mind seemed to have emptied of everything except the past five hours.

Al Tillman hadn't been content with questioning Will in the parlor at Mrs. Esterhaus's. He'd put him in the official blue-and-yellow car with the town seal on the door and taken him to the municipal building. He'd put him in a small square room with a wooden table and two straight-backed chairs and asked him more questions. The same questions. Over and over again.

Al only let him go when Melvin Guthry came by with another attorney, a man named Davenport who was new to Hope Springs. It was only as he walked out of the municipal building, flanked by Guthry and Sean Davenport, that he learned what had happened during the night. Libby had awakened to noises coming from the attic, noises she first attributed to squirrels. But squirrels didn't climb down ladders. And squirrels didn't ransack boxes and trunks. The attic had been searched, thoroughly and methodically.

"Was anything taken?" Will had asked.

Melvin had given him a long hard look. Sean Davenport had said, "No way of knowing. Who knows what was up there? Not Miss Jeffries. And Mrs. Esterhaus..." He shrugged. "That speaks for itself."

They drove him to his truck, admonishing him not to talk to anyone else about the break-in without Sean Davenport being present.

"But I didn't do anything."

Melvin shook his head. "That's certainly a fine defense, all right. As I recall, it worked rather well the last time, didn't it?"

Will got out of the car. "But there'd be no reason for this."

Sean got out of the car and faced him over the hood. "Some folks have already remembered that you've been asking the school board to help you find some of Mrs. Esterhaus's old papers."

Will's heart sank all over again as he remembered that moment when he'd understood just what everyone in Hope Springs would undoubtedly be thinking today. He found the work boots, took a box from the shelf. Dejected, he sat on a low wooden bench to try them on. He attempted to shut it all out—the certainty of a new wave of doubt and suspicion, the vehemence in the sheriff's questioning, especially when Tillman discovered that Will had been the one to put down the new pine needles that prevented any shoe prints beneath the window.

The part he most wanted to shut out was the spiritless look in Libby's face. Libby. That was the worst of it.

With a jolt, Will realized he'd lost all track of time. He checked his watch. In two hours school would let out for the day. Kyle.

Oh, my God, Kyle.

To hell with broken windows and malfunctioning thermostats. To hell with new boots. He had to go after Kyle. He had to—

As he stood, he heard a gasp behind him. He looked around. An older woman he didn't recognize stood in the aisle, her face white, her lips quivering. A man stood at her shoulder, urging her to come with him, to back away.

Damn.

"You have no business in this town," the woman said, spitting the words out with undisguised venom. "My son had no business hiring you to be around those girls."

"Vera, don't do this," said the soft-spoken man at her side.

Vera Templeton. His boss's mother. One of the jurors who had set him free. Will's stomach churned unpleasantly. He shoved the shoe box back into its slot on the shelf. "Help yourself. You didn't convict me the first time, so maybe you're entitled to another shot.''

"Just leave us alone! You should be run out of town, terrorizing that poor woman all over again. Leave, or we'll find a way to run you off!''

"Vera, for God's sake!'' The man at her side looked at Will, clearly terrified of his reaction.

Will smiled, a smile as bitter as the woman's words. What was the point in even issuing a denial? He walked out on legs that trembled. He longed for Libby, for the comfort of her touch, for a gentle word to ease his hurt. But he owed it to her to stay away.

LIBBY KNEW HE WOULD COME. But she hadn't expected it to take three days.

She was finishing Mrs. E.'s physical therapy when she heard his truck out front, heard the crunch of his boots in the dead leaves along the side of the house, then the clang of the extension ladder. She was surprised that hearing the ladder didn't frighten her, didn't stir up nightmarish reminders of the break-in.

"But it's broad daylight,'' she explained to Mrs. E., who gave her a faint smile. "And I know it's Will.''

One hand on Mrs. E.'s knee, the other on the ball of her foot, she bent the leg slowly and gently. "I've told everybody it wasn't Will. But nobody believes me. You believe me, don't you, Mrs. E.?''

She took the unwavering smile as confirmation.

"If even you believe me, I don't know why nobody else does."

When she finished the therapy, she walked into the backyard. Will was on the ladder repairing the louvered attic vent where the break-in had occurred. She watched until he was done, watched as he backed down. He didn't seem surprised to see her.

"Thank you," she said.

He nodded curtly.

"I know you didn't do this."

"You're the only one."

"I've tried to tell them…"

"You shouldn't waste your breath."

"Don't shut me out, Will."

He stared at her. She imagined she could see a million things in his eyes he wanted to say to her but couldn't. She reached out to touch him, and he flinched away.

"Don't."

"You know how I feel, Will. I—"

"Don't!" He raised his voice.

His rejection didn't hurt her the way it might've once before. She thought she understood how he felt. She touched him, anyway, her fingers skimming the back of his hand. She felt the delicate ridge of veins, the down of dark hair. Her heart swelled.

He pulled away, but not so quickly that she didn't realize he'd wanted the touch as much as she did.

"It's going to blow over," she said.

"When, Libby? When's it going to blow over? In

twenty more years? When I've lost Kyle for good? When I'm too old to give a damn?''

He snatched the ladder away from the wall and marched toward the shed. She wanted to say more, but she realized she had no real hope to offer him. Maybe it wouldn't blow over. Maybe the ugliness of twenty years ago had such deep roots now that their lives would never be completely rid of it. It would always grow back, spreading, taking over, choking out anything good.

It wasn't like Libby to feel that way. But as she watched Will leave without another word, it was impossible not to give in to her feeling of hopelessness.

keeping at bay. Later, guilt had made her unable to
throw it away.

She didn't hear the Loockers on the attic floor
until it was too late. Paralyzed, she pointed until she
no longer held them. Instead, her fingers waved off
the heavy intrusion.

Her daughter-in-law was already behind her.

CHAPTER FOURTEEN

VERA TEMPLETON viewed her attic, fingers pressed
to her lips. She was having trouble thinking about
her behavior in the hardware store. Hurd's had been
filled with people. They'd gathered around, listening
to her rant, listening to her hate-filled words. If only
they knew...

Verbally attacking Will Travers had been hard.
What she had to do next would be hard, too. But it
had to be done. It was past time.

She hesitated. She didn't like to open the trunk.

She snapped the latches. She raised the lid. It
creaked a protest. Her heart thumped.

Why she'd kept it all these years was a mystery.
She should have destroyed it when she'd first laid
eyes on it, stuffed in the bottom of the trash basket
in her son's bedroom. But seeing it there, knowing
what it was and afraid to ask how it had gotten there,
she'd seemed to freeze. She'd snatched it up, shoved
it into the back of her closet for days while the ugly
event swirled through the town.

It was the key to everything, and only she knew
about it. Only she knew it had finally ended up in
her attic for twenty years. Hidden there for safe-

keeping at first. Later, guilt had made her unable to throw it away.

She didn't hear the footsteps on the attic stairs until it was too late. Paralyzed, she put her hand on the leather jacket and opened her mouth to ward off the person approaching.

Her daughter-in-law was already behind her.

"I called, but I guess you didn't hear," Nancy said, a little breathless from the climb. "I heard what happened at Hurd's and I was worried about you. So when I saw the door to the attic was open, I came on up. I—"

Her eyes landed on the leather jacket beneath Vera's hand. She reached for it, amusement in her eyes.

"What in the world is this?" She lifted the jacket by the shoulder seams and gaped at it. Vera was powerless to stop her, to speak, to do anything but stare in horror.

"You're not going to tell me Larry wore this, are you?" Nancy laughed heartily at the image. "Buttoned-down Larry in this scruffy-looking thing? I love it! Wait until I tell him I know his secret."

"No!" Vera snatched the jacket from her daughter-in-law and stuffed it back into the trunk. "No, don't do that. Please. I...I really don't want him knowing how sentimental I am. Please. Just our little secret?"

WILL USUALLY STAYED in the truck and honked when he picked up Kyle at Mrs. E.'s in the afternoon. Sean Davenport said it would be better if he didn't go up to the house, at least until this business of the break-in was settled.

Will thought it was better all the way around, anyway.

He gave his horn a beep and waited. His heart began to trip quickly, the way it did each afternoon as he sat here and wondered if Libby would walk out onto the porch with his son. Would he see her? Maybe she would walk down to the truck. Maybe she would speak to him.

Yeah. And maybe she'd suddenly remember that it was actually Fudgie Ruppenthal she saw leaving Mrs. E.'s that night.

Living in a fantasy world wasn't Will's way. He believed in facing hard reality. And hard reality was this: He lived under a cloud of doubt and suspicion. That cloud made his son hate him. That cloud made it impossible to muck up the life of a woman like Libby.

That was hard reality.

The front door opened. His heart kicked into high gear.

Kyle came out, head down. Libby was right behind him.

Will's attention was riveted. His insides turned somersaults.

She was talking to Kyle, smiling at him and snugging up the strap on his schoolbag. She looked so neat and pristine in her crisp white uniform, so untouched by anything ugly. The way Will wished his life could be. The way he couldn't afford to imagine it would be with her.

She stood on the porch and watched his son trudge out to the truck. She crossed her arms under her breasts. Will remembered the feel of those breasts against his chest, the way he could fill a hand with their soft perfection. He wasn't breathing well by the time Kyle opened the truck door and climbed into the cab.

"How was your day?" Will asked, but his gaze was still fixed on the front porch. And Libby's was still on the truck, even after Kyle disappeared into it.

"Okay," Kyle mumbled.

Will put the truck in gear. But he couldn't drive away. Couldn't even look away, not as long as she stood there in the twilight looking like an angel of mercy.

She stood there so long he imagined she was having trouble tearing herself away, too.

Hard reality, he reminded himself. He let out the clutch and pulled away from the curb with a frustrated squeal of his tires.

KYLE SAT CROSS-LEGGED on the bed beside Mrs. E. His computer was in Mrs. E.'s lap.

"All you have to do is push one button at a time," he said patiently, although it seemed to him sometimes that Mrs. E. didn't even try to understand. "Key, I mean. Push a key. They're not buttons. Anyway, if you push one key at a time, it'll spell out a whole word on the screen and I'll know what you're thinking about. Like this.''

He spelled out his name then, slowly, the way he had about a million times. Even the dumbest kids at school could work the computers there, and even though this one didn't do all the cool stuff the ones at school did, you could still spell and name the pictures and answer questions about geography and stuff like that.

"I know you want to," he said. "I see it in your eyes. Come on, Mrs. E. You're way smarter than me. If I can do it, so can you."

Still, she didn't do it. But her hand did sort of wobble around in the direction of the keys, so he did what he usually did. He picked up her skinny wrinkly hand and pointed her finger at the keys until he spelled out something for her.

This time he spelled out Libby's name. That made Mrs. E. smile, and he smiled back at her.

"I know," he said, quietly so Libby wouldn't hear if she was close by. "I like her a lot, too. She'd..." He hesitated, struggled with feelings of disloyalty. "She'd probably make a neat mom. For some kid who wanted a mom, I mean."

He shrugged and fiddled with the frayed toe of his sneaker. He wished he could tell Libby what his aunt had asked him, because he needed somebody to tell him what to do. It was too big to figure out all by himself, but there was nobody to ask. He had to figure out all by himself if he wanted to live with his aunt. She said he could if he wanted to, that all he'd have to do was tell a judge that his...that *he* was mean and hurt him sometimes. That wasn't true, but Aunt Becky said that would be okay. And Kyle wasn't sure, either, if he wanted to live with his aunt. What he'd really like was to live here with Libby and Mrs. E.

"But that's not gonna happen," Kyle said at last. "Libby being my mom, I mean. 'Cause of my...'cause of *him*. People say he hurt you."

He looked into her eyes and it seemed to him one more time that there was so much stuff Mrs. E. wanted to say. Sometimes he imagined that she wanted to tell him that somebody else hurt her, that all that junk had been a big mistake. Sometimes he thought how wonderful it would be if that happened, because then people would stop hating his...*him*. And Libby could marry him and they could all be a family.

Right. Like that's really gonna happen.

"I wish you could tell me," he whispered.

While he looked at her, it seemed to Kyle that Mrs. E.'s eyes got real sad and excited. She started waving her hand at the computer keyboard again.

"Wanna spell some more stuff?"

Then she did something really cool. She punched a key all by herself. And she laughed, sort of, when a letter appeared on the screen.

"Way cool!" Kyle said, forgetting all about his dilemma. "Way to go, Mrs. E.!"

LIBBY'S FINGERS trembled as she scrolled through the microfilm of twenty-year-old *Courier* articles.

"Are you really sure you want to be doing this?" Meg asked, her tone edgy.

Not sure at all, Libby thought. "It has to be done."

"A good hard game of tennis would do you a lot more good. That's my opinion."

Libby frowned at the screen. Meg grew quiet.

The *Courier* wasn't a busy place on Saturday afternoon, Libby had discovered. The Saturday edition was on the streets and almost everyone had gone home. There was no one in the press room, no one pasting up pages or writing stories or even selling ads. In fact, if the photographer hadn't been developing film from the Friday-night high-school football game, the place would have been locked up tight and Libby wouldn't even be sitting here second-guessing herself.

"I just keep thinking about what he said, that I was wrong," she said to her friend.

"What would you expect him to say?"

"What if I *was* wrong? It was so long ago. I was just a child. Kyle's age." That's what had begun to haunt her, realizing how unreliable a child Kyle's age could be, how young children perceived things so differently. Why, just this week Kyle had been full of notions about how Mrs. E. wanted to talk to him. She sighed.

She might have been able to put all doubts out of her mind if she hadn't taken on the task of looking through the attic for Mrs. E.'s old records, none of which she'd found. Or if she hadn't been forced to look at Will every day when he came by to pick up Kyle. Sure, Will stayed in his truck, didn't even roll down the window for a wave. But she saw him nevertheless. She saw the granite set of his jaw and the dark glare of his eyes. She saw the way he gripped the steering wheel with both hands, as if he had to hang on to something or lose control.

Or maybe she was just imagining he felt that way because she did.

Every afternoon when he came for Kyle, it was all Libby could do not to run down the front walk and fling herself at him. Beg him not to shut her out. Plead with him to make all this go away so she could get on with her life.

But that wasn't up to him, she always reminded herself. She was responsible for getting on with her own life. Will Travers wasn't going to save her. Even if Will Travers was completely innocent, he couldn't save her.

God help her, if Will Travers was completely innocent, nothing could save her.

And if he was guilty, she was equally lost. Because sometimes she just didn't care what he'd been capable of twenty years earlier. Today Will Travers wouldn't—couldn't—hurt anyone. She knew it. Beyond a doubt. But there seemed no way to convince anyone else of that. And as long as Will could see doubt and suspicion in the eyes of others in Hope Springs, nothing could save him.

Not even her love.

Libby's hand flew up to cover her mouth, even though the thought hadn't actually escaped her lips.

"What?" Meg asked, instantly aware of her reaction.

Libby dropped her hand. "Nothing. I... Nothing."

"This is making you nuts. You know that, don't you?"

Meg began to pace.

Love. It was bad enough that the thought had now been given voice in her private thoughts. She couldn't let on to Meg what she was thinking. She *couldn't* love Will Travers. She simply couldn't. But there was little point in denying it. Why else would she stand on her porch every afternoon hungry for a glimpse of him, aching for something that would reprieve them both?

She loved Will. Regardless. And the fact seemed doomed to break her heart.

She drew a deep breath, squeezing back the tears gathering in her eyes. She forced herself to continue turning the crank that advanced the microfilm. She was drawing closer to the dates. Her heart thumped sharply in her chest. She found the first story.

"Oh, golly."

Meg stopped behind her, looked over her shoulder. "You found it."

Reading the stories was like drowning in the past. Like being swept up and whirled back, landing in a time and place she had no desire to revisit. Every word, every photograph brought it all back so vividly. The way she'd felt sitting there in her bedroom, alone, unable to make a sound even as she longed to cry out for help. Watching, listening, knowing but helpless. The days leading up to the trial, the nightmares, the day of her testimony. The fear as she sat there, perched on a cushion on the witness stand, Will's eyes on her.

She understood what she had seen in those eyes better now than she had then. What she'd seen hadn't been a threat, but fear and anger at the injustice.

And as she read all of it, as she relived it, something struck her like a blow to the chest.

What she had seen that night, what she had identified for the sheriff hadn't been Will. What she had seen that night was a leather jacket.

Not one bit of her description of the fleeing assailant focused on the man himself. Not his size or shape or hair color or facial features. Not even his pants or his shoes. Only the jacket. The jacket she'd seen Will Travers wearing a dozen times.

The jacket he swore he'd left behind at Mrs. Esterhaus's the afternoon before the attack, a warm spring afternoon when jackets were easily forgotten.

Libby's heart began to race. Her skin began to prickle. Her breath came in shallow little spurts.

"Are you okay, Libby?"

The male voice jolted her. She cried out.

Walker Shearin had come into the library. He glanced at the microfilm screen and put a firm hand on her forearm. "Take it easy," he said.

"I told her this was making her nuts," Meg said. "She won't listen."

Libby gulped for air, put a hand to her chest. It didn't even seem to matter that she was making a fool of herself in front of the editor of the *Courier*. All that mattered was what seemed to be revealing itself to her in this old microfilm.

She could have made a mistake! She could have been wrong!

She looked at Walker, wondering what to say. He was looking at the screen, seeing the articles she was reading.

"Tell me what's the matter, Libby."

His gentle tone soothed her. Walker Shearin wasn't very old, midforties maybe, but he had a way about him that gave everybody confidence in him. Libby believed right now that if she told him what she feared, he would help her figure out what to do next.

She swallowed hard. "I just...I was reading and...it never—"

"Slow down."

"Right." She nodded. "You wrote all the stories when Mrs. Esterhaus was hurt."

"That's right. I was the only reporter old Hadley Wakefield had. Right out of college."

"Did you ever think...maybe I was wrong?"

Walker was silent for such a long time that Libby knew what his answer must be. She felt sick to the core of her being. She even heard a smothered groan from Meg.

"You were short on concrete details," he said at last.

"Except the jacket."

He nodded.

"I was wrong, wasn't I? I was wrong to say for sure that it was Will."

"I don't know that you were wrong. I've always wondered how eager the sheriff was to solve the case."

"What do you mean?"

"A little girl provides some sketchy information. The sheriff has a town that's terrified. He wants to lock somebody up and ease everybody's fears. He helps a scared little girl fill in the details."

She closed her eyes, felt her head begin to spin. "But that's so wrong."

"It didn't seem wrong. Everybody knew who wore a leather jacket. Everybody knew he was trouble. People even warned Mrs. Esterhaus about him. It all added up."

"But you never believed it."

"Who was I? A young kid out of journalism school thinking I ought to be a hero. Old Man Wakefield told me reporters weren't supposed to have opinions. Just write what you see and hear, he said."

Libby covered her face, overcome with the horror of what she'd done. "Oh, my God!"

Walker put his arm around her shoulders. "It wasn't your fault, Libby. You did the best you could."

"I ruined his life!"

"He was acquitted. He went free."

She looked into Walker Shearin's eyes and saw the truth he couldn't hide. He didn't believe what he'd said. Libby shook her head. "He's never been free. Never."

But he would be. She would see to it.

CHAPTER FIFTEEN

LIBBY SAT ON THE EDGE of the rocker and studied Mrs. Esterhaus's face, looking for answers she knew could never be had.

She'd known Mrs. E. for so long, had worked in this house and lived this life with her for so long that she sometimes failed to notice the changes in Mrs. E. Her face had grown thinner, her skin more fragile. The backs of her hands were a fine network of creases and veins. Her wispy hair was no longer iron gray, but as white as the cotton balls in the canister on her bedside table.

Libby took one of those hands in hers. She remembered the ornate wedding band it had once worn, a band that no longer fit her wasted finger.

"I messed up, Mrs. E.," she whispered. "I messed up real bad. I'm just grateful you haven't known about it all these years."

Mrs. E. looked at her, unblinking. Libby named what she saw in those watery blue eyes compassion, and that gave her courage to keep talking. She explained everything, from the night of the attack through the trial to Will's return. And then, with only the slightest hesitation, what she had realized earlier that afternoon.

By the time she finished, tears streamed down Libby's face. She wiped them on her sleeve, her other hand still clinging to Mrs. E.'s.

"So I ruined a man's life, Mrs. E. I'm guilty of precisely what I accused him of all those years ago. Oh, Mrs. E., what am I going to do?"

She looked up then and discovered that Mrs. E., too, was crying. A few tears trickled down her withered cheeks. It was probably wishful thinking, but she almost believed that Mrs. E. squeezed her fingers.

Their tears had run their course, but they still sat with hands entwined when Libby heard a knock on the front door an hour later. Mrs. E. was sleeping, so she got up quietly, patted the old woman's hand and put her own hands to her tearstained cheeks. She must look awful. She hoped it wasn't her father. He would want to know what was wrong, and she wasn't ready to talk to him.

Meg stood on the porch, twisting a pair of knit gloves in her hands. "Invite me in. I'm going to keep you company."

The idea of sharing a time like this was foreign to Libby, but it sounded, oh, so appealing right now. "Thanks."

Meg walked in. "You know, you are not the easiest person in the world to be friends with, Libby Jeffries. In fact, sometimes you're an honest-to-goodness trial."

The words were said with gentle affection, and Libby found tears returning to her eyes as she looked at her friend. "I know," she said shakily. "Oh, Meg, I'm such a mess."

Meg surprised her by taking her in her arms. "That's okay, sweetie. We all are. Have I ever told you the real reason my first marriage didn't last?"

They made coffee in the kitchen and talked about things that had nothing to do with Mrs. Esterhaus and Will Travers and an eight-year-old who'd been involved in a disastrous miscarriage of justice. They talked about Meg's fear of raising children, which she said had pushed her husband right out the door because he'd wanted a big family. They talked about Libby's runaway fiancé, whose mother told the women at the Busy Bee Church Auxiliary that he was losing his hair at an alarming rate. They talked about the seventh grader who made it to the national spelling bee the previous year and rumors that someone wanted to buy the old Bijou theater, standing empty on Ridge Lane for the past three years. It was pleasant, harmless gossip and should have been distracting. But none of it banished the one thing haunting Libby's thoughts.

"Lib, I was thinking," Meg said as she finished her second cup of coffee. "If you had something you needed to do tonight, I could stay for a while. Keep an eye on Mrs. Esterhaus."

Libby's refusal was almost automatic. She rarely left the house at night. Then she realized what her friend was offering: a chance to start correcting her mistake.

A chance to tell Will Travers what she had done to him.

WILL WAS ALONE.

He hadn't yet turned on the lights. The gloom that settled over the house as the sun set suited him, suited his mood. Suited his life. He loathed himself when he climbed into this pit of self-pity, but tonight he didn't have what it took to climb out.

Kyle was gone. Just for the night, it was true. But the uneasiness in Will's gut told him his son's temporary absence might not remain temporary for long. His former sister-in-law had dropped her bombshell on Will when Kyle was taking his backpack out to her car for a sleepover.

"I saw an attorney down in Roanoke, Will," Becky said, both compassion and conviction shining in her eyes. "He said I have a good shot at custody."

"You can't do that." Will took a step in her direction.

She didn't flinch. "Oh, yes, I can. Especially if Kyle tells a judge he's afraid of you."

He'd wanted to roar at her, to snatch his son from her car and run her off with threats and rage. Which he'd realized, not a moment too soon, would play perfectly into her hand. He'd restrained himself. But not easily. And not without the residue that comes with stuffing such powerful emotions. Those feelings didn't just vanish because he refused to let them out; they stayed inside him, eating at him, poisoning him, dragging him into the darkest places of his soul.

At least they were familiar places. He'd gone there often these past twenty years.

He wished, as he sat in the dark living room, that he could commit the kind of violence everyone believed him capable of. He would do whatever he had to do to keep that woman from stealing his child.

Except that living with Becky might be best for Kyle.

That thought was what really made his insides wither and die.

He heard footsteps on the porch. He ignored the knock, he had no desire to see anyone tonight. When he heard the door creak open, he didn't even turn to see who it was. Then he caught a scent—the baby powder she used to keep Mrs. E.'s skin from becoming irritated. Not romantic, he supposed, but enough to squeeze the breath out of his chest.

She walked around to his chair and knelt before him. In the darkness her fair hair and skin shone. He wanted to bury himself in her, to find the soft comfort of her and let that softness absorb all his pain. But he couldn't. Libby tried too hard to save everyone as it was. She might be an angel, but she wasn't *his* angel. Mrs. E.'s, maybe. Even Kyle's. But not his.

"I'm sorry." Her voice trembled when she spoke, echoing with tears begging to be shed.

"You've got nothing to be sorry for."

She nodded. "Oh, yes. I've done something I can never make up to you."

He ached to touch her. She looked so anguished he forgot his own despair. "That's not possible."

"I was wrong." Her face contorted as she fought her tears. "All those years ago. I thought I saw you, but I didn't. All I saw…" A sob broke loose. He put his hand on the back of her head, his heart beginning to race. "I saw the jacket. That's all. And I thought… Oh, God, Will, I thought that meant it was you. Had to be you. But it wasn't. I can see that now. Oh, God, Will. I'm sorry. I'm sorry. I'm sorry."

She kept murmuring the words over and over. He tried to shush her, tried to take in what she was telling him. Her head dropped to his knees; her shoulders heaved with her sobs. And it sank in.

She knew the truth.

His eyes filled. *My God, she believes me.* He couldn't choke back the tears. He cupped her face in his hands and looked into her eyes. For the first time in twenty years, he looked into the eyes of a woman who didn't harbor a single doubt.

He took her into his arms, pressed his tear-streaked face to hers. He was free.

DINNER AT LARRY Templeton's house started no differently than most Saturday-night dinners. Nancy liked a little elegance on Saturday nights. So they ate in the dining room, with candles and their best china. The aroma of beef Wellington filled the house. It tasted as good as it smelled. The children had eaten early and were already upstairs in their game room, attached to the TV or the computer.

Nancy had a twinkle in her eye as she raised her wineglass. "I'd like to propose a toast," she said.

He wondered at the teasing grin. He raised his glass and touched the rim of hers, questioning her with his eyes.

"Here's to the young hoodlum I never knew I married," she said, clinking his glass lightly and taking a sip of Beaujolais.

"I beg your pardon?"

She laughed. "Your secret is out. But if you're very very good I promise not to let the children in on it."

Larry felt a jolt until he realized she would hardly be laughing if his secret were really out. "What on earth are you talking about, Nancy?" He strove to keep his tone light.

"I was at your mother's this week. I saw that leather jacket you wore in high school."

The vaguely unpleasant jolt instantly escalated to panic. "What?"

"Now, don't say anything to Vera. She doesn't want you to know how sentimental she is. She's got it hidden in a trunk up in the attic. Larry, I had no idea you were the leather-jacket type in high school."

She chattered on, sipping her wine, eating her dinner. He couldn't concentrate on anything she said.

His secret was indeed out. Had been out all these years.

His own mother knew the truth.

He forced himself to eat. To stay calm. He had to stay calm.

That was the mistake he'd made in the first place. He hadn't stayed calm. When he'd found out that Alice Esterhaus intended to blow the whistle on him, he'd been terrified. His entire future had been at stake. After twelve years of perfect grades, of being a student leader, of constructing the perfect future for himself, she had intended to bring him down. All because of one foolish mistake. He'd taken his college entrance exams late in his sophomore year. It had been a mistake to take them so early, but he'd been young and arrogant and he hadn't listened when Mrs. E. told him to wait until he'd completed trig in his junior year. He'd done badly, but there was time to make them up.

But as the time for retesting approached, he'd panicked. What if he did badly again? What if the best he could do wouldn't win him a scholarship? Would only get him into one of the ordinary state colleges? Everything he'd planned for his future would have been shot.

He'd bought the answers. It hadn't seemed like such a horrible thing. He had the brains to ace the silly test, anyway. This just took the pressure off.

Then Mrs. E. found out. Just when the scholarship offers were pouring in. She said she was going to expose him. He'd begged her, that night, to reconsider. She was adamant. If she let him go, he would take a scholarship someone else deserved. Someone like Will Travers.

Being compared to someone like that trouble-maker Travers had made him see red.

And now it was all coming back to haunt him. If he'd thought he had a lot to lose twenty years ago, just think how much he had to lose now. What if Nancy heard people talking about Will Travers and his famous leather jacket? What if she put two and two together? And his mother. What if she lost her nerve? Or found her conscience?

His stomach churned. His own mother could ruin his life. She'd already let a dangerous bit of infor-mation fall into Nancy's hands. He hoped he wasn't too late to contain the situation.

LIBBY WAS CURLED against Will's side, her feet pulled up beneath her on the couch, his arms tightly around her. He hadn't been willing to let her go since he'd taken her into his arms an hour ago, even though she could barely bring herself to look him in the eye. How could she allow herself the comfort of his closeness—his warmth, his strength, the familiar earthy scent of him that said she was in safe hands?

"I'm as bad as whoever really hurt Mrs. Ester-haus," she said softly. "I ruined your life."

He put a finger under her chin and forced her to look at him. "Libby, don't do this to yourself."

His gaze was so tender it brought tears to her eyes again. He kept saying it didn't matter. That he didn't blame her. And she certainly saw no accusation in his dark eyes, which held no more guarded anger.

Will might not blame her, but she blamed herself. "Look at all the damage I've caused. To you and your mother and your brother. And Kyle. He'll never want to see me again when he finds out what I did."

"It won't be like that."

"You don't know that."

He brushed away the tears clinging to her eyelashes. His thumb was rough yet tender. How could he be tender with her? Where had all his pent-up anger gone?

"You should be yelling at me. Calling me every bad name you can think of."

He chuckled. *Chuckled.* Will Travers never chuckled. "You're the woman who saved my life."

He touched the side of her face when he said it, and Libby wasn't sure which unhinged her more, the touch or his claim that she'd saved his life.

"Will, you're crazy. I'm the one who sent the police after you."

He brushed the corner of each eye with a kiss. "But when you couldn't testify against me, that bought me my freedom. Don't you see that?"

"Oh, Will, no." But his closeness and the sweetness of his caress were making it impossible to concentrate on her guilt. Soft and slow, the sensations seeped through her, warming her flesh and filling her with heat.

But now that she was free to fully desire Will

Travers, how could he ever bring himself to want her?

He stopped kissing her face and gave her a long, determined look. "If you had testified, I would have spent these past twenty years in prison. There would be no Kyle. There would have been no reason for anyone to ask questions. I would have lived and died a guilty man. That scared little girl saved me from that."

She saw in his eyes that he meant it.

"You weren't very grateful to me for that when you first came back to Hope Springs," she pointed out.

"I didn't know how soft your skin was then."

Her heart leaped. "Oh, Will..."

He brushed his lips over her cheek. She sought blindly for some distraction, something to save her from what she wanted and feared.

"Will, if you didn't do it, somebody in this town did."

He reached the corner of her lips with his. They were damp, his breath hot. And his fingers were making their way up the back of her neck, tangling in her hair and molding to her head.

"Listen, Will. We have to talk about this. Somebody knows something and—"

"Not now, Libby," he murmured before his lips covered hers.

The urgency of finding out who did attack Mrs. Esterhaus vanished in the rush of sensations as Will kissed her, ran his lips over her neck, cradled her body in his arms, worshiped her with his hands. He touched her like a man in awe of the treasure he had discovered. Her flesh quivered beneath his touch.

"I love you, Libby," he whispered.

"I love you, Will."

He lifted her and carried her into the bedroom, placed her gently on the bed and undressed her. Libby felt shy and eager—shy when the moonlight shone on her body, eager when it revealed the planes and hollows of his. She looked into his eyes and saw an awe that reflected what was in her own heart.

"Is this really happening?" she whispered.

"I never believed in miracles," he said hoarsely, lowering himself onto the bed beside her, "until now."

She wanted to reply, but the only sounds she could find as he fit his body to hers were little moans and sighs. They made love slowly and tenderly, like people allowing themselves to feel for the first time in years.

CHAPTER SIXTEEN

LIBBY WAS EMBARRASSED when she arrived home just before daybreak to discover Meg asleep on the sofa in the living room.

She touched the back of one hand to her cheek and felt the heat. She couldn't believe she had so completely forgotten her responsibilities, that lying in Will's arms had driven everything else out of her head.

But last night was like nothing that had ever happened to her before. Will's touch drew more than passion from her. It awakened a deep and abiding need to be the beginning of something good in the life of this man who had known so little good. And to let him open the door to goodness in her life. She believed with all her heart that each could give the other the wholeness, the healing, the fullness of emotions that had been missing so long.

She loved Will Travers. And he loved her. It was nothing short of a miracle.

But miracles sometimes didn't look that way to others, she thought as she stared at her sleeping friend. She started to wake her, then decided it might be wiser to let her sleep a few minutes longer.

If she could shower first, make herself look a little

less like a woman who just spent the entire night drowning herself in desire, maybe Meg would assume she'd been home all along.

Maybe she could save face.

It was a decision she would regret.

The pounding on the front door began when she was halfway down the stairs after showering and putting on a fresh uniform. Meg stumbled out of the living room about the same time Libby reached the front door. She looked like a woman who had slept on the couch.

But at least I don't look like a woman who slept in the arms of her lover.

"What...happened?" Meg mumbled, the brief question broken by a yawn.

"I... You were sleeping when I got home," Libby said, rationalizing that it was true, even if the implication was false. "I hated to wake you, so..."

Meg began to look a lot less sleepy as she considered her friend's excuse. But before either of them could say more, the pounding on the front door resumed. Libby peeked through the curtain, wondering if it was Will, expecting it would be and already agonizing over Meg's reaction to his appearance.

It wasn't Will. It was her father, white-faced and red-eyed. Sheriff Al Tillman stood at Noah Jeffries's shoulder, looking grim and official.

Libby felt her heart squeeze unpleasantly. She opened the door. "Dad, what's wrong?"

Noah grabbed her in a fierce hug. "Thank God you're all right."

"Well, of course I am. Why wouldn't I be?" she asked, guiltily wondering if he'd somehow figured out that she hadn't been home all night. Oh, dear, this was already too complicated.

Sheriff Tillman muscled his way past them. "Meg? This is a surprise."

Libby took a deep breath. She glanced at Meg, who already looked her usual unruffled self.

"I stayed on the sofa last night," Meg said. "I saw Libby yesterday and she mentioned she's been a little jittery since the break-in. I came by to check on her last night on my way home and...she was more uneasy than I realized. So I stayed to set her mind at ease. She seemed to need one good night's sleep."

"That right, Libby?" the sheriff asked.

It didn't occur to Libby to ask why it was any of Al Tillman's business in the first place. She was too busy being grateful that Meg was on her toes only minutes out of a sound sleep. "That's right, Sheriff."

"Well, might be that's a real lucky thing," Tillman said. "Either of you hear anything last night? Anything unusual?"

Libby felt a different sort of uneasiness. Something was wrong; something had happened. "Dad, what *is* this?"

Noah opened his mouth but couldn't seem to find the words. Instead, he put his arms around her again and held on for dear life. She felt the shudder in his chest. Startled and afraid, Libby clutched him. Over her father's shoulder, she saw Al Tillman exchange a glance with Meg and shake his head morosely.

"What's going on, Sheriff?" Meg said.

The sheriff shook his head again. "It's Vera Templeton. Somebody hurt her last night. Real bad."

Libby felt her father's sob and tightened her arms around him.

"How bad?" Meg asked.

Libby knew the answer before the sheriff spoke, as a sudden hard swelling of horror filled her insides.

"She didn't make it."

"Oh, my God," Libby breathed. Her knees grew weak. Meg's hand was on her elbow in an instant. Meg led Libby and her father into the living room, cleared away the afghan she'd used for a cover and eased them onto the sofa.

Libby could barely follow the conversation as Sheriff Tillman filled them in on the details. Vera Templeton's body had been discovered early this morning when a next-door neighbor came by to borrow coffee. No one answered her knock and she became worried. Vera was always up early, but her car was in the driveway, so she couldn't have been out and about. A deputy came to make sure nothing was wrong with Vera and discovered her bludgeoned body in the living room.

"Happened sometime during the night." The sheriff pursed his lips. "When I went out to the scene, it was just like before."

Libby snapped to instant attention. "Before when?"

Noah took her hand in his. "I should never have let her near him."

"Who?" Libby's stomach rolled.

"Vera made no secret of how she felt," the sheriff said. "Noah said half the town saw her at Hurd's just a few days ago telling Will Travers he ought to be run out of town. Looks like Vera's outspokenness could've gotten her killed."

"You mean…" Libby could barely take it in. "You think *Will* did this?"

"Don't know many other folks in town with a history of violence."

"But it couldn't have been," she said.

"You're not to worry about that, Libby," the sheriff said, rising. "We'll get whatever evidence we need. We'll nail him this time. Travers isn't going to hurt anybody else."

"It wasn't Will!" Frantic, she followed the sheriff to the front door. "It couldn't have been. I was with him!"

Tillman glanced at Noah and Meg. "Now, Libby, what are you getting at?"

"I was with him. All night. It couldn't have been Will."

She heard her father gasp, but it didn't matter. Nothing mattered but making sure no one leveled this new accusation at Will. It would kill him. It would destroy Kyle, too. Her only relief came from knowing that this time she held the power to clear his name, instead of cast suspicion on it.

"Excuse me, but don't I recollect that you just

told me Meg stayed overnight because you were a mite skittish?'' Tillman looked and sounded skeptical and irritated with this development. "Now you're telling me you and Travers were together. Mind if I ask which it was?''

"I was with Will. I told you.''

"In other words, you're changing your story.''

"I'm telling the truth!''

If anything, Tillman looked grimmer than he had when he first walked through the front door. Noah was even whiter. And poor Meg looked as if she genuinely wanted to cover her head with the afghan.

"You have to believe me,'' Libby said, looking desperately from one to the other. "Will couldn't have hurt Vera. We spent the whole night together.''

Al Tillman leveled a finger at her. "You may not realize what a world of trouble you can get into providing false evidence, Libby Jeffries. I've got a murder to investigate, and I suggest you think twice about your story before we have our official talk.''

WILL HEARD THE BELLS calling people to worship from the tiny church on the corner of Dogwood and Tarkington. He hadn't been to church since he was thirteen or fourteen. That was when his mother had been able to force him to go with nothing more than a determined look and the unspoken threat of consequences.

This morning he could almost convince himself that a kind and loving God was looking out for him, after all. How else to explain a woman like Libby loving him, touching him with all that emotion in her eyes and lips and fingertips? How else to explain that a man like him could feel new and fresh and filled with hope for the first time in twenty years?

The idea of walking into church in this town made him smile. That would set tongues wagging. Almost made the idea of sitting through a sermon worthwhile.

The vague notion of walking into church with Libby on his arm was beginning to take definite shape when a vehicle crunched over the gravel in his driveway. He peered out the bedroom window, knowing it was wishful thinking but still hoping Libby had come back. She didn't even have a car. And she had Mrs. E. to tend to. Still…

The sight of one of the sheriff's cruisers gave him a nasty start.

He froze, his hand on the blinds. One of the deputies got out of the cruiser and looked around cautiously. A hand rested lightly on the gun holstered on his hip. He peered into the bed of Will's truck, and that was when Will saw the deputy tense and curl his hand firmly around the butt of his gun.

The shocked look on the deputy's face galvanized Will. He jumped out of bed, pulled on his jeans, dragged a sweatshirt over his head and shoved his bare feet into sneakers. Without bothering to zip or tie, he headed for the driveway.

The deputy was on his car radio, eyeing his surroundings with even more caution, his hand still resting on his gun.

When Will appeared on the front porch, he saw the young law enforcement officer's fingers release the safety on his firearm. He didn't pull it, but he was prepared. And he didn't take his eyes off Will.

Will stepped off the porch in the direction of the deputy, who was signing off the radio and tossing it back into the cruiser. "What's going on?"

"Will Travers?"

"That's right."

"Mind if I look around?"

"Yeah, as a matter of fact, I do."

"Okay. Mind answering a few questions?"

Will felt his irritation rising. "Am I going to be the first person you guys come to every time there's a two-bit crime in this town?"

"Where were you last night, Mr. Travers? We can talk now or we can go down to the station."

"Does that mean I'm under arrest?"

"You're not answering. Does that mean you've got something to hide?"

Smart-ass punk. Thinks he's tough. Learned his technique from TV cop shows. "I was here last night."

"Alone?"

Will didn't hesitate. There was no question of dragging Libby into yet another mess. No question of giving the people of Hope Springs their hot gossip of the week. Libby Jeffries spending the night with infamous would-be murderer Will Travers. They could chew that one over for weeks. Months, maybe.

"Yes, alone. My son spent the night with his cousins."

"Did you leave the house anytime between nine last night and six this morning?"

"No."

"You're sure?"

"Positive."

"But nobody can vouch for you on that?"

"Nobody."

That was when he heard the sirens approaching. His heart began to thump and cold sweat beaded his upper lip.

"What's going on here, Officer?"

Two more squad cars careered onto Birch Street, fishtailing as they almost missed the sharp turn off Tarkington. They screeched to a halt in front of Will's house. Will noticed, from the corner of his eye, that his next-door neighbors had come out onto their front porch to watch.

Sheriff Al Tillman stepped out of the first car, followed by another deputy. Two other deputies jumped out of the second car. Will couldn't believe Hope Springs had that many deputies. He stared at Tillman, unable to sort through what was happening. He remembered that he'd felt this way before, as if what was happening must be happening to someone else. Not him. Not Will Travers.

Tillman conferred briefly with the first deputy, glancing at Will as he no doubt listened to the deputy recount everything Will had said. Will realized he was surrounded. He wanted to bolt. He had a clear vision of himself lying facedown on the cold ground, a bullet hole in his back. He tensed against the shaking starting deep inside and working its way to the surface.

Tillman approached him, stood beside the truck. He glanced into the bed, as the deputy had earlier. "You spend a lot of nights alone, don't you, Travers? That's a real shame."

"What's your game, Tillman?" He didn't feel tough; he doubted if he even sounded it.

"Appears we've had a murder right here in our fair town."

The words seemed to puncture Will's lungs. He couldn't grab hold of enough air.

"Somebody just bashed that poor lady's head right in. Wonder who'd do that." The sheriff took off his hat and ran his thumb and forefinger around the brim. "Mind if I take a look at this shovel, Travers?"

"What lady?" he croaked. "What shovel?"

"Why, the one here in the back of your truck."

The memory of the deputy glancing into the back of his truck and his shocked reaction replayed in Will's head. A nightmare. That's what this was. "I've got no shovel in my truck."

Tillman looked into the truck bed again, nodded and replaced his hat. "Yeah, I believe that's a shovel. Don't you reckon that's a shovel, fellas?"

A couple of the deputies nodded without even looking.

"You want to tell me about it, Travers?"

Will took two unsteady steps closer to the sheriff, close enough to gaze into the back of his truck. A shovel did indeed lie there. The shovel he used at the academy, maybe, judging from its weathered blue handle. Along with his old work boots, the ones he'd discarded days before. The sight dealt him another blow.

Both the shovel and the boots were splotched with blood.

LIBBY MADE A LIST of everything she was supposed to do for Mrs. Esterhaus and when. She didn't trust herself to remember a thing. She'd gone blank inside, her heart frozen, her mind empty. She couldn't even operate on automatic pilot as the day ticked to an agonizing close.

She had to see Will.

Where was he? Why hadn't he come? They couldn't have arrested him, could they? She called his house every half hour, but there was never an answer. She would have called for a replacement nurse and gone to him, but her father hung at her side, looking as hollowed out as Libby felt. Much of the time he sat in the living room, hands clasped between his knees, his white face now gray. When Libby was busy with her work, he followed her, watching her with bewildered eyes.

What Libby dreaded the most was his conversation, which started with anguish and disbelief over Vera's death and progressed to greater anguish and disbelief over his daughter's defense of Will Travers.

"Why'd you do it, Libby? Say something like that?"

She pursed her lips tightly. "It's the truth."

"Don't say that, Libby. You wouldn't... I know you better than that."

"He never hurt anybody, Dad. Not Mrs. Esterhaus. Not Vera."

The words seemed to cause Noah physical pain. "Don't, Libby. Don't do this. You've got to see— he's done something to you. Turned your head somehow. He's...he's dangerous, honey. Think about it."

Libby tried to explain to him about her painful realization that she'd identified him all those years ago based on one detail—a leather jacket. But he wouldn't hear it. He grew too agitated. She had to let it go. When he talked about Vera, she tried to comfort him. But when he talked about Will, she closed out his words, took herself somewhere else.

News about the murder spread quickly through town. After church let out, people dropped by all afternoon to commiserate with Libby and her father and to dissipate their own fear by sharing it. Libby told everyone who came that Will Travers had nothing to do with the murder, and she told them why she was so certain of it. Her declarations were met with horror and doubt and sometimes ill-disguised disgust.

Only Meg believed her story. Meg sat with her in

the kitchen, drinking one of the hundreds of cups of coffee consumed in the house that day, and stared at her friend.

"You really know how to jam yourself up, don't you?"

"I love him, Meg." She saw compassion that bordered on pity in her friend's eyes. "He loves me. Trust me, I know what kind of man he is."

"Hon, I sure hope so."

She tried to see him, but the sheriff wouldn't allow it.

"So the two of you can get your stories straight? I don't think so, Libby. No disrespect intended, but if you aren't careful, I'll have to consider you an accessory after the fact."

As the day wore on, Libby's defense of Will was counteracted with news of progress in the investigation. She heard about the shovel from the maintenance shed at the Blue Ridge Academy for Girls. A shovel covered with blood and fingerprints. Vera Templeton's blood and Will Travers's fingerprints. Nobody seemed to need to wait for lab results to confirm the rumors; all of it was passed on as fact. She heard about footprints found in the soft earth outside Vera's home, prints that matched the pattern in the bottom of Will's old work boots and earth that matched the dirt in the floorboard of Will's truck.

And she heard that Will Travers continued to deny that he and Libby had been together that night.

"Anyone could have done this," Libby said with

growing desperation when Larry Templeton brought the latest news of both the investigation and funeral arrangements for his mother. "Anybody could have planted evidence against Will."

Larry looked at both her and her father with contempt. "My mother is dead because she knew that man for what he was. And you're defending him. I'm going to see Will Travers in hell for what he's done." He glanced at Noah, then back at Libby. "And if you get in the way, I'll see you with him."

Libby understood Larry's venom, but it still shocked her to be the object of it. She felt for the first time some inkling of what Will had been subjected to all those years ago, and again when he returned.

What she didn't tell Larry Templeton was that she was ready to follow Will Travers into hell if need be. If it meant facing down the entire town, she would stand by him. If only she could get to him to make sure he knew that.

WILL SAT IN HIS HOUSE and thought about running. He couldn't bear the thought of never seeing Libby again. He couldn't bear the thought of leaving his son behind.

But as agonizing as those prospects were, the idea of going through another trial was enough to send him right over the edge.

The only thing that kept him rooted to the chair in his living room was the certainty that he might run but he could never hide. They would track him down and bring him back. And the very act of running would be the only admission of guilt most people in this town would ever need.

Besides, the house was under surveillance. Tillman had no intention of letting Will out of his sight while they gathered the evidence they needed for an arrest.

The phone kept ringing, but he didn't answer it. He was too afraid of hearing Libby's voice if he picked it up. She would try to talk him into using her as his alibi, and he knew that was pointless. He knew by now that Libby had told the sheriff they'd been together last night. And he also knew that Tillman wasn't buying it.

"You already told me yourself that you were alone last night," Tillman said. "And she'd already told me she was home all night, too. It was only after she found out what was going on that she came out with that story. Wonder why she did that, Travers."

Will hadn't replied. There was no reason to reply. Nobody believed Libby, and that was just as well.

He heard a vehicle in the drive again and his stomach lurched. They must be coming after him. He felt cold to the very marrow. He would have given everything he owned and more to hold Libby Jeffries one more time before this nightmare cranked up to full speed.

Drawing a deep breath, he stood and walked to the door. He would meet them at least with his dignity intact. He had that much and they couldn't rob him of it without his cooperation. He opened the door and was met with the sight of his son running up the gravel drive. Will's heart sank.

Kyle stopped on the steps, his eyes wild as he stared at his father, his chest heaving.

"They said...you were...gonna...that you..."

Will knelt to bring himself to the boy's level, but he didn't move to take Kyle into his arms, even though it was what he really wanted.

"I didn't do anything, Kyle," he said, mustering as much calm as he could.

"But they think you did."

Will nodded.

"Like before?"

"Like before."

"Are they? Gonna arrest you?"

"I don't know, son."

As soon as he had the words out, the answer appeared in the form of a blue-and-yellow cruiser pulling into his driveway behind Kyle's aunt, who still stood stiffly beside her open car door. Al Tillman got out and approached the house. Panic made insidious inroads into Will's heart.

"Kyle, you're not to worry," he said. "No matter what. Promise me?"

Kyle looked over his shoulder and saw the sheriff, too. When the sheriff was just feet away, Kyle threw himself at Will and grabbed him around his neck.

"No!" he wailed, a sound that broke Will's heart. "No, no, no!"

Tillman stood on the bottom step, waiting.

Will squeezed his son, grateful for this one moment with his son and angry that this was happening to a little boy who had already been hurt too much. He whispered against Kyle's hair and squeezed his eyes shut to hold back the tears. "I've gotta go now, son. You're gonna be okay. Becky's gonna take care of you. Libby's gonna take care of you. And I'll come back myself as soon as I can, okay?"

Kyle looked up at him, tears streaming down his flushed cheeks. "Promise?"

Will didn't like lying to his son. But he liked the alternative even less. "I promise I didn't do anything. And I promise I'll do the very best I can to come back soon. Okay?"

Kyle studied him for a moment and finally grew calm. "Okay," he said softly.

They hugged once more, then Will pointed Kyle in the direction of his aunt, who had also approached the porch. Will walked over to Sheriff Tillman, who took out a pair of handcuffs. Will stared at them, then gave the sheriff a pleading look.

"After the boy's gone?" he said.

Tillman grabbed him by the shoulder and jerked him around. Will felt cold metal close over his wrists. He sought out Kyle and gave him what he hoped was an encouraging smile.

"You should've thought about the boy before," Tillman said, shoving him in the direction of his cruiser.

The last thing Will heard as the cruiser backed

out of the driveway was Kyle. He turned and saw the boy running toward the sheriff's car.

"I'll get you out, Daddy! I'll find out who did it, Daddy!"

Will hadn't known a heart could break so many times, so many ways. For months he'd wanted nothing more than to hear his son call him Daddy. This wasn't the way he'd dreamed it would happen.

Two Sisters Story   2073

Put on the driveway was Kate. He turned and saw
the boy running toward the sheriff's car.

"I'll get you out, Dad. I'll find out who did it, a

Dad ...

Will to ... away ... the ... er came
slowly to him ... here ... the gunnin' fela
one more ... he can call the Dads. The
... le ...

CHAPTER SEVENTEEN

LIBBY STEPPED through the door, holding her breath,
unsure of what she would see or how it would make
her feel.

The Hope Springs Municipal Building housed
only two cells in its tiny jail. They sat side by side,
separated from the sheriff's offices and the emergency dispatch center by a green metal door with an
eye-level window. Libby didn't allow herself to look
very closely at the cells, with their narrow beds and
lack of privacy.

She only allowed herself to see Will.

He was the only person in either cell. He lay on
a cot, hands behind his head, staring at the ceiling.
He gave no indication that he'd heard anyone enter
the area. Al Tillman gave Libby a disgruntled look,
obviously still peeved that Sean Davenport had
wrangled the court's permission for her to visit. The
sheriff backed out, leaving the door open.

"Will?"

She whispered his name. She saw him flinch, although he didn't move right away.

"I'm sorry," she said. "I told them they were
wrong. Told them and told them. But they won't
listen."

He didn't look at her. But she could see how gray his face was, as if he'd already been here for months, instead of just overnight. He needed to shave. He needed fresh clothes.

He needed her, she thought, her throat closing.

"Go home, Libby."

She steeled herself. She'd known this wouldn't be easy. He probably didn't believe anyone in this town would stand by him a second time.

She intended to convince him otherwise.

"I brought Kyle home with me, Will. I hope you don't mind." Still no response. "Becky wasn't crazy about the idea, but when he said he wanted to stay with me, she gave in."

She waited for a reaction. His profile remained stony, unyielding. She blew out an unsteady breath, wishing for some sign of the man who had touched her so tenderly.

She needed to talk about that, too, about the night they'd made love. She didn't want to bring it up in here. She didn't want to use the memory of their lovemaking to bring him around, to break down his resistance. She wanted him to come around solely because of what was in his heart.

But she was desperate. She couldn't take being shut out. She had to reconnect with him.

The memories of his touch, their joining, the level of intimacy they'd shared were so strong in her that she couldn't think of that night without her emotions rushing to the surface. Surely Will felt the same.

"Talk to me, Will. We…we made love. It was…

it was something special to me. To us. I know it was. You can't shut me out after that.''

Still nothing. No sign he'd even heard her.

''Will, please. Remember how it was?''

She felt herself flying apart at his refusal to acknowledge her. She grew desperate.

''When you were inside me, Will, it was like stripping away our skin,'' she whispered. ''All that was left was our hearts, touching.''

She held her breath, waiting. He couldn't hear her words without remembering, reacting. She just knew it. She'd seen it in his eyes.

''I know you remember,'' she whispered, tears tinging her voice.

But he didn't move. He lay there like a dead man.

His silence in the face of her emotion-laden words tore through her, the sting of his rejection sharper even than the pain she'd felt when she learned they'd arrested him.

''Don't make me feel used, Will. Don't try to make me believe it meant nothing.''

She waited, but it was futile. He said nothing. Did nothing. Each second that ticked by was another knife blade to her heart. Tears began to trickle from her closed eyes. She opened her mouth to make one more appeal, but there was nothing more to say.

She left, knowing she couldn't bear to come back.

WILL HELD HIMSELF stiff as granite until he heard the door close behind her. He bit the insides of his mouth to hold back the words he wanted to say, the sob that threatened to break loose.

He would die if she left.

She would die if she stayed. Not right away. But sometime, sooner or later.

When he heard the hollow thunk of the metal door closing, heard the clang of the outer lock that separated him from her, he turned toward the wall, huddled in a tight ball and heaved deep silent sobs into his pillow.

He was adrift in hell, but he wouldn't take her with him.

KYLE SAT CROSS-LEGGED on Mrs. E.'s bed and stared at the screen of his toy computer.

S-A-D

He nodded morosely at her message. "Yeah. I'm pretty sad."

He scrunched up his mouth. He was close to tears, but he didn't want her to see them. He could tell that when he got upset, so did Mrs. E.

"But I'm mad, too."

He spent most of his days like this, playing and talking to Mrs. E., or sitting in the kitchen doing his lessons while Libby cooked. He wasn't going to school right now. Libby and his aunt had worked something out and he was doing his lessons at home for a while. Until all this blew over, Libby said.

Kyle didn't suppose it was going to blow over soon, but he didn't have the heart to tell Libby that.

He didn't have the heart to talk to her about most of what he was feeling now. Seeing his father hauled away in handcuffs had done something to him, had knocked something out of whack inside him. He felt confused and afraid and hurt, worse than he'd ever felt. And the only thing he had to hang on to was the stuff Libby had told him.

"Your father didn't do this," she'd said, holding him close to her on the couch in Mrs. E.'s living room. "I was with him when Mrs. Templeton was attacked. He couldn't have done it. I want you to believe me."

"I do."

And he did. What he couldn't understand was why nobody else believed her. Libby had a harder time explaining that. Nothing she said made much sense to him, although he listened carefully and tried to take it in.

"If they're wrong this time," he'd said, "maybe they were wrong before, too."

Libby had taken him by the shoulders then and looked him squarely in the eyes. "They were wrong. I was wrong. Your father never hurt anybody. It was all a big mistake. And we're going to get it straightened out. All of it."

He wanted to believe that, too. Really he did. Because he wanted another chance with his dad. He wanted to make up for all the times he'd been so mean and believed lies about his own father.

But as he sat here on Mrs. E.'s bed and watched her press one key after another with those shaking, bony fingers, he wondered if he would ever have the chance to set things right with his dad. Most of the time it didn't seem that way. Most of the time it seemed hopeless.

WILL'S ATTORNEY, Sean Davenport, sat across from him on the empty cot in the cell. He didn't look like an attorney, the way Melvin Guthry always had with his suspenders and his bow ties. Davenport wore khakis and a sweater. He'd tossed a windbreaker bearing a golf-club logo on the foot of the cot. Will had wondered at first if Davenport would go over very well in court, but Melvin had assured him that the town's new attorney had come from one of the best firms in Richmond. He could make hash out of most of the attorneys Melvin had run across.

But the way Sean Davenport was making things sound, the one who was going to be made hash of was Will.

"I have to tell you, things are stacked against you," Davenport said. "They have motive, they have the murder weapon, they have fingerprints and a match with the impression on your boots. Plus, and I hate to say this, but the sentiment in town is pretty much against you."

Compassion was evident in Davenport's face. "I'm sorry we couldn't get bail."

"It's okay," Will said. "I don't expect a miracle."

He'd had his miracle, he figured. Libby, then Kyle, both of them loving him and believing in him. His life was fresh out of miracles.

"Our best bet is a change of venue. Then, with Libby's testimony and—"

"I don't want her dragged into this."

Davenport shook his head. "She's already dragged into it."

Will remembered watching a terrified little girl sitting on the witness stand twenty years earlier. "I won't have it."

Davenport stood, his hands stuffed loosely into his pants pockets. "I'm going to do the best I can for you. You need to leave things like that up to me."

Will wanted to argue, but he didn't figure he had a lot of bargaining power right now. He also wanted to see his son, but not under these circumstances. Having his son see him in handcuffs had been hard enough; to see him through iron bars—he just wasn't able to do that.

He wondered if he would ever put his arms around his son again, or if that one time on his porch would be the last.

He wondered, too, if he would ever put his arms around Libby again. He could almost feel the silken texture of her skin, see the way the moonlight through his window had fallen on her. He could almost smell and taste her. Almost.

Sometimes the frustration was so great he didn't think he could live with it. He dreamed, sometimes, about breaking out. Running. In his dreams Kyle and Libby were always waiting for him at the end of his escape.

But in the cold light of day, he knew that would never happen. If he ran, he would be running from the only chance he'd ever have—no matter how slim that was—of one day being with the two people he loved.

Kyle and Libby. At least they were together. At least they believed in him. He tried to convince himself that was all that mattered.

But when darkness fell each day, it wasn't enough to ward off his despair.

LIBBY FELT THE LOVE from everyone in Hope Springs, even when she knew that few of them believed her. Being wrapped in their caring warmth gave her hope and strength for the days that stretched out before her. Days when Will's rejection tore at her heart, threatening to destroy the very things their lovemaking had restored to her—her belief in herself, in love, in hope.

She wouldn't give up again, wouldn't let herself die inside all over again. Not when she'd just remembered how to open her heart. She simply couldn't.

But sometimes she didn't know how to hold on another minute. Times like that, someone from Hope Springs always seemed to appear to shore her up.

When she shopped for the Thanksgiving dinner that she had no appetite for, Faith O'Dare Davenport stopped her in the grocery store to express her support.

"Hang in there," Faith said, kindness in her eyes. "Sean tells me that, with a change in venue and your testimony, things will look up for Will."

Luisita Mendoza gave her a silent hug on the sidewalk one day. Ester Hurd brought over one of her famous tunnel of fudge cakes, and although Libby knew from the look in her eyes that she didn't believe in Will Travers, Ester pressed Libby's hand and said, "Take care of yourself, Libby. You're strong and you've got a lot of people on your side."

Ida Monroe from Sweet Ida's Tea Room waved her down and crossed the street, imperiously stopping traffic in both directions, to give her encouragement. "We all love you, Libby. No matter what else happens, don't forget that."

Moments like that brought tears to Libby's eyes. She knew they all meant it. They might believe she'd lost her mind in defending Will Travers, but it didn't matter to them. They cared about her. They were like family. She could always count on them.

And she knew, deep in her heart, that one day they would see the truth about Will.

The outpouring of support almost made it possible for her to ignore her own father's reaction.

"It's like you're killing Vera all over again every time you stand up for that man," Noah said, his eyes hollow, his face sagging with grief.

Libby couldn't reply. She just hugged him and held the truth close to her heart.

The best thing to happen in the week following Will's arrest was on Thanksgiving Day. She was filling the table with the small turkey she'd bought, the corn-bread dressing, the sweet-potato soufflé— far more food than she, Mrs. Esterhaus, her mourning father and the listless Kyle could eat—when a knock came on the front door.

The man standing there startled her; he reminded her so much of Will, even with his beard and wire-rimmed glasses. She clutched the edge of the apron she'd been using to dry her hands and stared at him.

"I'm Paul."

"Paul. Will's brother."

"Kyle's uncle," he said, and seemed to be correcting her.

"Of course. Please, come in."

He hesitated. "No, I—"

"We're about to have Thanksgiving dinner. It would be nice if you could join us."

He was shaking his head when Kyle sidled up to Libby and leaned against her. "Who's that?"

"This is your uncle Paul," Libby said when it was clear that the boy's appearance had rendered Paul Travers momentarily speechless. "Your dad's brother."

"I saw you fight with my dad before," Kyle said, a hint of belligerence in his stance that was so like Will. "How come nobody told me you were my uncle?"

Libby watched the emotions war on Paul's face

as he looked at the boy. Finally he hunkered down to bring himself to Kyle's level.

"I've been kind of a hermit," Paul said.

"Yeah? Like Paul Bunyan? He had a beard, too."

Paul grinned weakly. "Yeah, something like that."

"Cool." Kyle studied him. "And 'cause you and Dad don't like each other? The way Aunt Becky doesn't like him?"

Paul drew a long breath and glanced toward the door. "Yeah. I guess that's part of it."

Kyle nodded. "So, are you staying for dinner?"

"Well…"

"I could use some help carving the turkey," Libby said.

Paul looked up at Libby, then back at the little boy.

"You could tell me about when you were kids, huh?" Kyle said.

Paul drew another long breath. "Yeah, I suppose I could."

KYLE KNEW NOW what he had to do. He'd been thinking about it all day. All night, too. He started downtown after breakfast. He wasn't sure where to find the newspaper office, but he would go up and down the street until he did.

He knew that nobody believed Libby, so there was no point in telling her. He figured nobody would believe him, either. But he had to try. And maybe, if he told it to the newspaper, instead of to the sheriff, somebody would listen to him.

A bright orange newspaper box stood in front of a building that said Hope Springs Courier in big letters over the door. His heart began to thump as he approached. He wanted this to work. It had to work. He pushed on the heavy front door and walked inside. The place was noisy and smelled funny, and the counter was higher than his head. He began to feel like a little kid. He wanted to turn and run.

So he reminded himself of the morning they came and took his dad away in handcuffs.

He walked behind the counter when nobody saw him or asked him what he wanted, probably because he wasn't tall enough. He looked around the big open room and saw a man with silvery hair and a white shirt with the sleeves rolled up. He was pushing keys on a computer. Swallowing hard, Kyle walked right up to him.

"I need to see the boss of the paper."

The man stopped typing and looked at Kyle. He smiled a little, and Kyle didn't feel quite as scared.

"I'm the editor," the man said, offering his hand just as if Kyle had been a grown-up. "Walker Shearin. What can I do for you?"

Kyle shook his hand. "I'm Kyle Travers. And I think you ought to do a story about who really hurt Mrs. Esterhaus."

"Do you now? And how am I going to find out who that person is?"

"You could interview Mrs. Esterhaus. She already told me about it, and she said she'd tell you, too."

CHAPTER EIGHTEEN

AFTER THANKSGIVING, Libby worked up the courage to visit Will again. She brought him magazines and news of Kyle and her own love and hope.

He rejected all of it.

And no matter how often she told herself that it shouldn't hurt, that it was just his way of sparing her, it cut her to the quick each time she stood outside his cell and met the stone wall of his apparent indifference.

"Don't keep doing this, Will," she pleaded softly.

He didn't move. He was lying on his cot, facing the far wall. All she could see was the top of his head, where the sunlight was already fading from his hair.

"Every time you do this," she said with a catch in her voice, "it makes it a little harder to believe that what happened between us meant something. That it wasn't just...sex."

She almost turned to go, but she forced herself to keep trying. "Kyle said to tell you he loves you."

At last he reacted. He sat up. She saw him swallow hard.

She clutched the bars. "*I* love you."

He covered his face. "Don't, Libby. Don't make it harder."

The sound of his voice flooded her with hope. At least he was speaking to her again.

"Loving each other won't make it harder," she said, her voice thick with emotion. "That's the only thing that'll get us through this."

"Nothing's going to get us through this."

"Come over here, Will."

She could almost feel the struggle within him, but he finally glanced in her direction.

"Let me touch you."

"They can hear you," he said.

"I don't care. Let them hear."

He stood and came toward the bars. "You'll make things harder on yourself."

"Don't shut me out, Will. *That* will make it harder on me."

She reached for him. He held back, although she was certain she saw her own yearning reflected in his eyes.

"This town will turn on you, Libby."

She had to have this one thing, a single touch. She strained her fingers in his direction.

"Some might. Not the people who matter. And there are more of them, more good people, than there are the other kind."

She waited, her heart pounding.

"They think I'm a killer."

"I know you're not. I'm going to make them believe me."

His eyes grew damp. He looked down. She kept reaching for him, kept her fingers outstretched for him. The ache to touch him grew almost more than she could bear.

"I won't see you hurt," he said, his voice a hoarse whisper.

"There's only one way you can save me from more hurt. Let me love you."

He put his hand out haltingly. The tips of their fingers touched. They were in this together. And that was enough.

LIBBY'S ELATION over reaching Will lasted until she turned the corner onto Old Oak Street.

The front of Mrs. E.'s house looked like a crime scene all over again when Libby approached. She spotted the swarm of blue-and-yellow sheriff's department cars and the uniformed man standing guard on the front porch, and the lightness she'd carried in her heart since leaving the town jail died.

She ran to the porch. "What happened? Are they hurt?"

The deputy looked at her as if uncertain what to do. "No, ma'am."

"Then what?"

"Maybe you ought to go on inside."

She dashed through the door, fear putting her pulse into overdrive. She looked into the living room. Empty. She kept going down the hall until she heard the voices coming from Mrs. Esterhaus's room.

"Mrs. E.!"

The bed was surrounded. Sheriff Al Tillman and two of his deputies. The county attorney, a rumpled-looking man Libby barely knew. Walker Shearin, a deep frown on his usually easygoing face.

And in the bed, Mrs. E., propped up with Kyle at her side.

They both looked fine. Unharmed. She stifled a sob of relief. "What is it? What's wrong?"

Kyle looked up, his face flushed with excitement. "Come on, Libby! Come and see!"

Looking from the sheriff to the editor and back to Kyle, Libby approached the bed warily.

"Ask her again," Kyle said.

Al Tillman cleared his throat and nodded toward the county attorney.

"All right, Mrs. Esterhaus, could you tell us one more time—do you remember the night you were injured?"

Libby opened her mouth to protest. But before she could get a word out, she saw Mrs. Esterhaus move her hand over the keyboard of Kyle's computer, which rested in her lap. Libby watched, mouth agape, as letters appeared on the tiny screen.

Y-E-S

"And who was the person who attacked you that night, Mrs. Esterhaus?"

Libby put her hand to her mouth.

L-A-R-R-Y T-E-M-P

The old woman stopped for a moment, leaned her head back against the headboard.

"She's tired," Kyle said. "She already spelled it for you five times. Isn't that enough?"

The men surrounding the bed exchanged glances. The attorney nodded. "For the moment. We'll bring one of the office computers out here, hook it up with a printer so we can get a written statement. Maybe videotape the whole thing, too. That should hold up in court as long as we have witnesses."

"What...what's happening?" Libby asked, dropping into a chair by Mrs. E.'s bed as two of the men left, taking Kyle's computer with them.

Walker Shearin stuck his notepad into his jacket pocket. "Young Kyle here cracked the case. Larry Templeton attacked Mrs. Esterhaus all those years ago. And if I had to guess, he found it necessary to silence his mother a week ago, too."

At that, Kyle threw himself into Libby's lap and wrapped his arms around her neck. She felt his soft cheek against hers. It was damp with tears.

"They have to let him go, Libby! They have to let him go!"

Libby felt the hurt melt from her heart. She could only pray that Will's bitterness healed as easily. If it didn't, she was lost. And so was Kyle.

PAUL TRAVERS didn't notice the flurry of activity in the municipal building when he came in to visit his brother. All he could think about was the next few minutes, when he would do something he should have done a long time ago.

Will was eating lunch from a plastic tray when they let Paul into the cell area. He didn't look up, didn't seem to notice that someone had entered. Paul stood beside the cell and stared at his brother through the bars. Will looked older than he'd looked just weeks earlier, older and more defeated.

Little wonder.

Paul had a moment of worry that he was making a mistake. But something had happened in his heart and he couldn't turn back now.

"Will? It's me. Paul."

Will glanced at him, slowly replaced the spoon on his tray. "Paul?"

Paul nodded. "I went to see Kyle."

"You did?"

"I thought he…maybe he'd need somebody. His uncle."

"That was…good of you. Considering."

"He's a fine boy."

Will nodded.

"He believes in you, Will."

Will looked hopeful.

"You were all he wanted to talk about. What we did when we were kids. That kind of thing."

The conversation had been agony, especially at first. Remembering all the things he'd determinedly banished from his memory. Going back in his mind to a time when his big brother had been his hero.

He'd been willing to do it for the sake of a little boy who still needed a hero.

Listening to himself, Paul had realized he still needed a hero, too.

And in the days since, Paul had found himself listening to other things. To his heart. To people in town whose opinions he respected. To Libby Jeffries. Her story had stunned and pained him.

He looked at his brother. "I believe in you, too, Will."

Will stared at him, shock in his eyes.

"I'm sorry I didn't all those years. I...I hope you can forgive me."

Will walked over to the edge of the cell, close enough that Paul could have touched his brother if he'd had the guts.

"But all the evidence... You can't... Why? Why now?"

"I know it's late," Paul said. "All I know is, I remembered everything I knew about you. And that seemed like better evidence than anything they've got. I want to stand by you this time, Will. I just hope it's not too late."

The brothers embraced through the cold iron bars.

WILL COULDN'T TAKE IN what Sean Davenport was telling him.

"You're a free man, Will," the attorney said, holding open the door of the cell. "Thanks to your son and Alice Esterhaus."

Will shook his head and hesitated to walk through the cell door. "I don't understand."

"They're going to be bringing in Larry Templeton in about five minutes, Will. I think it'll be better if you're already gone."

Davenport explained everything again as he led Will down the back hall of the municipal building to the courtroom where he'd been indicted days earlier. Where the gavel had banged on the bench and in his head when bail was denied, just as it had been twenty years earlier.

Larry Templeton, the ideal student and the spotless citizen, had attacked Alice Esterhaus when she discovered he'd cheated on his college entrance exams. She could have ruined his chances for a scholarship, and so he hadn't let that happen. The only one who knew the truth, apparently, was Vera Templeton, who had somehow discovered the infamous leather jacket Will had left at Mrs. E.'s when he'd visited the afternoon before the attack. Larry took it, hoping that if anyone saw him leaving they would identify him as Will.

Vera Templeton had been the one holdout juror who had convinced the rest to reverse their votes and set Will free, a decision that had stunned the town.

"Now it's obvious why she did that," Davenport said. "But it came back to haunt her when Larry found out a few weeks ago. He didn't trust her to keep his secret any longer. And since he had access to your work tools and even your old boots, it was an easy matter to cast the blame on you one more time.''

Will barely heard the brief proceeding that set him free. He was awhirl in emotions. He didn't trust what was happening enough to give in to the relief and happiness that threatened to overtake him. After all these years, could it be so simple? Could he really be free? Would the people of Hope Springs give up their mistrust of him and let him get on with his life?

Or would it still be best if he and his son simply left and started over somewhere else?

And Libby? After what he'd done to her, he couldn't expect her to change her whole life for a man who was just starting over.

He was free, but he wasn't. Not yet. He wasn't sure what it would take to make himself believe that, feel it in his heart. It would take time, for one thing. Maybe a lot of time.

He gathered his belongings, half listened as Al Tillman offered his apologies and his congratulations. He walked toward the front door. Sunshine was streaming through the glass. He hesitated. Felt Sean Davenport's hand on his shoulder.

''It's okay, Will. You're a free man. Nobody's going to take it back.''

Will nodded.

He wondered what it would be like to walk the streets of Hope Springs and really feel like a free man. He wondered if that was even possible.

He pushed the door open. What he saw on the

other side of the door made him freeze all over again.

The people of Hope Springs lined the street in front of the municipal building. His heart leaped to his throat. Of course. You couldn't arrest a respected man like Larry Templeton and let a man like Will Travers go without stirring up a lot of fury.

He swallowed hard and took a step out of the building. He would walk right past them. Ignore them. Keep his eyes straight ahead. Get his son and keep right on walking.

When he exited the building, the person nearest the front stepped forward. It was Fudgie Ruppenthal, his white barber's apron still in place.

"Mighty pleased for you, Will," Fudgie said. "Welcome home."

Will wanted to thank him, but his throat was clogged. All he could do was shake the hand Fudgie offered and nod.

"After all this time, it's a miracle, son," said Ida Monroe, who then wrapped him in a hug that smelled of camomile and cinnamon, like her Tea Room.

And in sharp contrast, there was Clem Weeks, smelling of antifreeze and brake fluid. She gave him a quick, awkward hug and whispered, "You don't know how good it feels to see somebody finally free of the past."

Then there was Bertie Newsome and Hezzie Stuart and Cookie Langtry. They all spoke words of encouragement. They shook his hand or gave him a pat on the shoulder. One by one, the people of Hope Springs asked his forgiveness for misjudging him.

"Guess we've all learned a lesson," said Lavinia Holt. "I know I have."

His fingers began to cramp from all the handshakes. And the tears were harder to hold back with each word of support from the people who seemed so eager to humble themselves.

Waiting at the end of the line were the two people Will most wanted to see.

First was Kyle, who ran at Will with such force Will could barely keep his feet. He swept his son into his arms and squeezed, inhaling the scent of little boy, feeling the soft cheek against his neck.

"I love you, Dad."

Will gave up trying to hold back his tears. "I love you, too, son."

Right behind Kyle stood Libby. Will shifted Kyle to his hip, even though the boy was really too big to carry; he wasn't yet ready to relinquish his son. He took another step toward Libby. She wasn't smiling. She didn't look sure of herself. Did she even look sure of him? he wondered.

But before his doubts had a chance to take hold, she took his free hand in hers. "Let's go home, Will."

He looked deeply into her eyes and saw all the dreams he harbored in his heart—dreams of family and nights wrapped in the security of unshakable love. He saw no fear or reservations and felt none in himself.

For the first time in twenty years, they were free to love.

The three of them walked down Ridge Lane together, with the happy and excited murmur of their community behind them.

ALICE ESTERHAUS had certainly never expected to see a wedding right here in her own bedroom.

She'd seen plenty from this room over the years. The change of seasons, which remained a joy to her as the birds and the leaves and the butterflies came and went and came again. The way Libby had matured over the years. The return of life to this house when young Kyle Travers had burst in and shaken them all up.

And now a wedding.

The bride looked shy and emotional. The groom looked as if he might jump right out of his skin if the Reverend Haigler spoke too loudly. Will had always been that way. Jumpy. Afraid the world was going to deal him another blow. And it had, starting when his father died and getting worse from there. The brother of the groom looked acutely uncomfortable. And young Kyle could barely keep his feet still.

Alice Esterhaus couldn't do much but be grateful that she'd finally been given a way to free all these people from the past.

It had freed her, too. She could live in this room now and find joy in the passing of the seasons and the lives of the family that would now live here with her. Mrs. E. smiled.

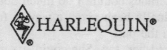

**SEXY, POWERFUL MEN NEED
EXTRAORDINARY WOMEN WHEN THEY'RE**

Destined for Love

Take a walk on the wild side this October
when three bestselling authors weave wondrous stories
about heroines who use their extraspecial abilities to
achieve the magic and wonder of love!

HATFIELD AND McCOY
by HEATHER GRAHAM POZZESSERE

LIGHTNING STRIKES
by KATHLEEN KORBEL

MYSTERY LOVER
by ANNETTE BROADRICK

Available October 1998
wherever Harlequin and Silhouette books are sold.

HARLEQUIN®
Makes any time special™

Silhouette®

Look us up on-line at: http://www.romance.net

PSBR1098

HARLEQUIN SUPERROMANCE®

BUFFALO GAL

by Lisa McAllister

**Welcome to White Thunder Ranch
in North Dakota!**

Andrea Moore learns on her wedding day that she's won a
buffalo ranch. In less than twenty-four hours, Andrea's
life changes completely. It goes from predictable to surprising...and exciting. Especially when she meets White
Thunder's foreman, Mike Winterhawk—who's determined to protect his business from a city woman who
knows squat about ranching!

**Watch for *Buffalo Gal* in November 1998.
Available wherever Harlequin books are sold.**

HARLEQUIN®
Makes any time special ™

HARLEQUIN SUPERROMANCE®

FINDERS, KEEPERS

Is a detective agency that specializes in finding lost loves, friends, family, etc...

If Noah had been adventurous enough to discover the world and himself, he could be adventurous enough to visit an agency that specialized in finding lost lovers. But meeting Maggie Tyrell, proprietor, was an adventure in itself. However, Maggie wouldn't be deterred from the task at hand—even if Noah wanted her to call off the search. *Even if it meant her heart would break...*

Found: One Wife
Harlequin Superromance (#809)
October 1998

by Judith Arnold

Available wherever Harlequin books are sold.

HARLEQUIN®

COMING NEXT MONTH

#810 BUFFALO GAL • Lisa McAllister
Home on the Ranch

When Dr. Andrea Moore awakes on her wedding day, the last thing she expects is to end up—still single—stranded with a rock band on her new buffalo ranch in North Dakota. True, she is a vet, but a *buffalo* vet? More surprising still is her attraction to the foreman, Mike Winterhawk. He wants her ranch, and she seems to want...*him!*

#811 BEFORE THANKSGIVING COMES • Marisa Carroll
Family Man

Widower Jake Walthers is a hardworking man who's busy taking care of his three young children. He doesn't have time for anything else—certainly not love. Then an accident leaves him in need of help, and his neighbor Allison Martin is the only one he can turn to. He doesn't mean to fall for Allison—she's too "big city" for his liking—but when he does, he learns she has her own reasons for not getting involved....

#812 IT HAPPENED IN TEXAS • Darlene Graham
Guaranteed Page-Turner

Every morning since her husband's death, Marie Manning wakes up and reassures herself that her children are fine and her home is secure. But her world goes from safe to scary when a neighbor makes a grisly discovery on Marie's ranch. It doesn't help that Sheriff Jim Whittington thinks Marie knows more than she's telling. And it *certainly* doesn't help that her heart beats a little faster every time the sheriff comes over.

#813 JULIA • Shannon Waverly
Circle of Friends

They'd been friends growing up, living on the small East Coast island called Harmony. Now one of them is dead, and Julia Lewis goes home for the first time in seven years. To a funeral... But coming home is also a chance to reconnect with her circle of old friends—and to meet a new man, Ben Grant. A man who causes complications in Harmony's world...and in Julia's.